Minishrinks

Leslie Wooddavis

Minishrinks

By Leslie Wooddavis

Dedication

To Goldie –

Real, imaginary or invisible, – thank you for my life…

Lwd

Table of Contents

Prologue

SECURITY FILE # 61922
TO: D.B. Hastings, FS HQTRS

On February 15 of this year, Ambassador Charles Anson DENNING removed a .38 combat masterpiece revolver from the gun cabinet of his home in San Diego. He loaded six shells (see attached fingerprint report) and fired five rounds into his big screen television set. Upon successfully destroying his television, the Ambassador then turned the revolver onto himself, firing the final round into his chest. (Paraffin examination and medical report attached).

Ambassador DENNING was found by his personal aide, Raymond HAYES, who had arrived at the Denning home to escort the Ambassador to an informal diplomatic dinner welcoming President ARTURO of the newly formed South American Block.

It is to be specifically and officially noted and documented that HAYES did not adhere to normal security restrictions, but instead called local authorities and paramedics to the scene. By the time this office was notified, the scene had been contaminated by local police, rescue squads and the local media.

The cover story of a burglary attempt put out by HAYES, has been approved and confirmed by this office.

This is the second violent emotional outburst by Ambassador DENNING in less than two years. The first incident was in January of last year, when his son was kidnapped and killed by an unknown terrorist group in South America. In that incident, Ambassador DENNING vented his frustration on the embassy pistol range, spending seven hours and more than nineteen hundred rounds of ammunition before he collapsed in exhaustion. Routine psych tests conducted by PSR showed DENNING, at that time, to be mentally sound, albeit emotionally "fragile" concerning his son's death.

Despite warnings of degenerate emotional instability, Ambassador DENNING was encouraged by the State Department to return to South America and continue his efforts with President ARTURO. (See attached report, psych exam, #210, 1/3)

Until further notice, Ambassador DENNING will be residing at the Psychiatric Surgical Rehab Center in La Jolla, California, under the direct observation of Dr. Matthew JEFFERS, Chief of Psychiatry. Dr. JEFFERS has requested that Ambassador DENNING be removed from all political duties until further notice.

As a standard security measure, any and all questions regarding Ambassador DENNING or his treatment, will be channeled through L.R. SIMMONS, Head of Security, PSR Institute, FS0215, La Jolla, CA.

SECURITY FILE #61939, PSR FILED #212, 5/18
TO: D.B. HASTINGS, FS HQTRS

After merely sixty-one days of medical and psychological treatment, this office has been informed that the State Department has arbitrarily determined that Ambassador DENNING will be physically and mentally sound by June twenty. This prognosis has come as a complete surprise to Dr. Denise PARKER, the Ambassador's medical physician and to Drs. Neil DAVIDSON and Matthew JEFFERS, his psychiatric counselors. This office can only assume that the State Department has begun to dabble in black magic, for the prominent physicians at PSR do not, UNDER ANY CIRCUMSTANCES, concur. Please advise.

TO: L.R. SIMMONS, FS 0215, PSR, La Jolla, 5/19
FR: D.B. HASTINGS, FSHQTRS

Crystal balls, black magic or whatever, the State Department respectfully requests that you tell Dr. JEFFERS to get his act in gear, DENNING will go back to work on 20 June, hopefully sooner, with or without the omnipotent approval of the staff at PSR. Raymond HAYES, DENNING'S personal aide, has informed the powers that be that DENNING is the only one who can handle the delicate diplomatic problems necessary when dealing with President ARTURO, who will be arriving in this country on 25 June.

TO: D.B. HASTINGS, FS HQTRS
FR: L.R. SIMMONS, FS 0215, PSR

I have carefully explained the situation to Dr. JEFFERS and I have further explained to him that telling the State Department to "fuck off and die" is against the general policy of this office. Dr. JEFFERS has conceded that he might be able to have DENNING walk and talk by the twentieth, but that he was more liable to blow up like a time bomb, not further diplomatic relations with the Latin block, or President ARTURO. I respectfully request that your office get the schmucks at the State Department to lay off DENNING, JEFFERS firmly repeats that the Ambassador will not be fit to resume his duties by 20 June, if ever.

TO: L.R. SIMMONS, FS 0215, PSR
FR: D.B. HASTINGS, FS HQTRS

I suggest you read your scout manual again, Lloyd, this office doesn't tell the State Department jack shit, they tell US.

Chapter 1

Prospero: Approach, my Ariel, come...

Dr. Kristen Michaels sat on the edge of a desk on the platform of the lecture hall. She wore brown wool slacks and a matching turtleneck sweater, her light brown hair was caught up at the sides in gold barrettes that flashed with light when she turned her head. Twenty-five students were filing noisily into the hall, notebooks were taken out, pencils were poised and ready, some of the more industrious students pulled out recorders and checked the charge, hoping to sleep through the lecture and still catch every word.

The final sounds of voices being cleared died down, Kristen repositioned herself in the center of the desk, crossing her legs Indian fashion.

"Hi!" she announced clearly. The lecture hall was well designed, her voice carried easily without additional amplification.

There were a few scattered responses and several nervous laughs.

Kristen sighed audibly and shook her head. "Hey, folks, I'm the one sitting up here all alone, your position is much more secure, therefore your response should be much stronger. As a child psychologist, you will be required to sing silly songs at the top of your voice, make funny faces and pretend to be cowboys or Indians. Loosen up! Shall we try it again?" She looked encouragingly at the audience. "Hi!"

"Hi!" the group responded with more volume.

"Thanks," she grinned at them, then picked up the eyeglasses next to her on the desk and put them on. The thick glasses became a new focal point, effectively dominating her tiny face, making her pale blue eyes look huge.

Kristen smiled again, showing deep dimples. "Believe it or not, this is the right classroom for Child Psychology two, you have not wandered into the wrong building. This is the only time we will meet here on a Tuesday. After today, we will meet here every Thursday and will be splitting into three rotating groups on Tuesdays, meeting at the pediatric ward at Claren General, the Crisis House, or the military daycare center. Your schedule will be posted. If you want to work at the military daycare center, you must have a valid 'secret' clearance or better.

"Let me introduce myself. I am Dr. Kristen Michaels. I am a practicing Child Psychologist here in Claren, I am thirty-six years old, I am not married, I have no children. I am five feet two inches tall, I weigh one hundred and five pounds in the winter, ninety-nine in the summer and I wear these huge glasses, not for comic effect, but because I am terminally nearsighted. Those are my physical and social statistics, my psychological abnormalities are a bit harder to grasp."

A few more people cleared their throats, the room became silent. The door to the lecture hall opened, a tall young man entered self-consciously, Kristen waited until he had shaken the snow off his outer coat and found an empty seat.

"Okay. Since this is not an open class and to get here you had to have taken basic psychology, child psychology one, plus several other entry level courses, I am going to assume that you all have a working knowledge of the basics. Let's start with an easy one. Who is the best physician of the mind?" She looked around the room. "Anyone?"

There were a few quiet responses.

"We don't get points for polite timidity here," Kristen advised them. "Consider this an interactive workroom."

"The patient himself," came a clear response.

Kristen looked in the direction of the voice. "As I mentioned, I am terminally nearsighted. Would you stand up please, give your name and repeat the answer? Who is the best physician of the mind?"

The young man who had entered late, stood up. "The patient is the best physician," he repeated, then flushed to the roots of his hair.

"Good answer," Kristen told him, giving him an encouraging smile. "What's your name?"

"Patrick McClary."

"Tell me, Mr. McClary, since the patient is the best physician of the mind, as a psychologist, what is *your* function?"

His face flushed more violently, but he answered without hesitation. "To allow my patients to look within themselves for answers, to trust their own instincts, to encourage them to learn from their own experiences and prejudices."

"A perfect, textbook answer," Kristen nodded. "How are you going to do that, Mr. McClary, how do you teach someone you have never met, about themselves?"

"By listening to them," Patrick McClary answered instantly.

"Thank you, Mr. McClary, you may resume your seat, I won't embarrass you further." She waited until he had sat, then looked around at the rest of the class. "I like textbook answers, they are in textbooks for very good reasons." She took a sip of water from the glass next to her on the desk. "You are here to become paid listeners, paid guides into the inner self. You are not here to become physicians, you are not 'healers'. The only physician of the mind is the patient himself. Left alone, the majority of the

10

populace will find their own solutions to life's difficult problems, their own cure for mental illness. This they will do, simply by talking to themselves, answering their own questions. Hence, our standard question to every patient is, 'I don't know, what do you think?' It's cliché, but it is the only valid question we ever ask."

She gave a cheerful smile. "Psychology is a great scam, if you think about it. We sit by looking pompous and all knowing, then quietly pay off our huge mortgages by virtue of a plaque on the wall that gives us a fancy title."

"Isn't that a little cynical?" came a female voice in the audience.

Kristen looked toward the voice. "This is our first class this semester, let's make a rule, now. Please stand when making a comment or suggestion."

A blond woman about thirty stood. "Sorry, Doctor. My name is Joanna Sullivan, third year psych."

"What was your question again?"

"I said, isn't that a little cynical?"

Kristen seemed to consider it. "Hmm. I don't know, what do you think?"

There was a mild giggle from the back of the room.

"I think it's cynical," Joanna answered, a little less sure of herself. "There is a lot more to therapy than simply looking on."

"Do you really think so?" Kristen studied her for a moment, nodded and said, "Okay, Doctor. I am your patient. You have started the session by asking me to tell you something about myself. I tell you that I am nothing special, a teacher, that I have lived a normal life, except for one short year when I was sent to live with my Aunt and her husband."

"Okay."

"Draw me out, Doctor. Get the ball rolling."

Joanna Sullivan frowned lightly. "Oh." She thought about the question. "Why do you say you're nothing special?"

"I dunno. Just 'cause," Kristen shrugged.

Joanna frowned again, thinking about it. "How old were you when you lived with your aunt and uncle?"

"I didn't say he was my uncle!" Kristen answered in a shrill voice. "He wasn't my *real* uncle, he was just married to my aunt!" she covered her mouth with her hand. "Oh, my gosh! I'm sorry. I don't know why I yelled! Why did I do that, Doctor?"

"Ah..." Joanna looked worried.

Kristen held out a hand. "Fourth year students?" she gestured for a response.

"I DON'T KNOW, WHAT DO YOU THINK?" came the answer from several students at once.

Joanna laughed nervously and started to sit down.

Kristen stopped her. "Don't leave me, Doctor, our session isn't over. What's your next step?"

"Obviously to find out why you hate your uncle, see if he abused you in any way..."

Kristen shook her head. "Don't speculate, Doctor. You are assuming something that may not have occurred. What is your next logical step?" She held up a hand in anticipation of an answer from another student. "Mr. McClary gave you the answer a few moments ago."

Joanna looked at Kristen for a moment. "My next logical step is to listen to you."

"Okay, I start talking, maybe only rambling, what are you going to do?"

"Continue to listen," Joanna grinned. "I'm going to sit there, looking pompous and all knowing," she answered.

Kristen smiled. "Thank you, Doctor, I feel much better now. If I've embarrassed you, I apologize. Consider it dues paid, I'll pick on everyone here before the semester is over."

Joanna resumed her seat.

"Write this down, it's probably the most important rule you will ever learn, if you haven't already." Kristen waited while notebooks were opened and papers rustled. "Do not assume. Do not speculate. Speculation and assumption is the killer. As a psychologist, you can create memories that are not real and extremely damaging."

A young man stood. "Dr. Michaels. The patient you were pretending to be... if she wasn't abused by her uncle, if she didn't hate him, why was she so upset?"

"I wasn't pretending," Kristen smiled, "I was acting out a situation from my own personal history. When Dr. Sullivan *listened*, she found out that my aunt's husband was not a bad man. He simply took the place of a favorite Uncle who had died under extremely tragic circumstances. If she had listened even longer, she might have found out why my real Uncle's death was so tragic to me. Once that plateau is reached, some real psychological issues might be revealed. The more you're willing to listen without judgment or interruption, the more I'm willing to tell you."

"Thank you."

"You're welcome. Believe it or not, that's the first time anyone has asked me that and I've been teaching this course for eight years."

There was a slight murmur in the room.

"Okay, again. Who is the best physician of the mind?"

"The patient," came the response from everyone in the class.

"Even if that patient is only four years old?" Kristen asked.

"Yes," the response was mild, uncertain.

"Yes," Kristen agreed firmly. "That's a tough one to admit, isn't it? Four years old, five, six... fifty, the age does not matter. Child or adult, the patient still knows more about himself than you will ever know, no matter how much you spend on your education. Bedwetting can be caused by something as simple as a child seeing a spider on the floor and not wanting to get up to go to the bathroom. It can be something as serious as fear of getting up because the last time they did, an abusive parent violently spanked or molested them. The child knows the answer to that question, *you do not.* If you speculate, and, if you are wrong, you will either overlook a very real monster, or you will create a new one. The possibilities should boggle your mind. You can't treat a condition you don't understand."

Kristen looked at her watch. "That finishes the basic overview of our superfluous title of 'child psychologist', as opposed to 'adult psychologist'. The principles are the same, only the techniques might be different. We are going to take a fifteen-minute break, to work out the registration kinks, be prepared to take notes when you return. For those of you who wish to crash and have the necessary pre-classes, I'll see you up here, or you can talk to my secretary. We are already overbooked, but I will try to make room for any students who are working toward their doctorates in Child Psychology."

Books, papers and recorders were packed away, people started moving, a few toward the center of the lecture hall. A tall brunette woman made her way toward Patrick McClary, tapping him on the shoulder.

"Good answers," she smiled at him. "Hi. I'm Heidi Schaeffer. Are you a psych major?"

The girl was attractive, Patrick looked interested. "Pediatrics. You?"

"Fourth year child psych. Are you going out on a break?"

"No. I need to talk to Dr. Michaels. I'm crashing this class, I need it."

"Then you need to talk to me, I'm her secretary. It helps pay for the tuition."

Patrick grinned. "Will you help squeeze me into the class?"

"If you need it, you got it," Heidi returned.

"I need it. It sounds like its going to be a snap course and I've got some real deadlies that will take up most of my time."

"It's only a snap course, if you have an open mind," Heidi laughed. "Trust me. The 'Leprechaun Lecturer' does not use any textbook you've ever read," she promised.

"The what?"

"You're not from around here, are you?"

"No. I quite literally blew into town today."

"That's her nickname, the 'Leprechaun Lecturer'. Everyone calls her that. Dr. Michaels is a little different. If she follows her usual format, the rest of the day will be spent on minishrinks."

Patrick frowned. "What the hell is a minishrink?"

"According to Dr. Michaels," Heidi answered, smiling, "the entire basis of psychiatric medicine."

###

Fifteen minutes later, Kristen Michaels was back on the desk, again sitting Indian fashion. "The rest of this afternoon we will be discussing minishrinks."

There were a few whispered comments.

"I'm short, I'm not 'mini'," Kristen smiled, hearing the typical response.

Light laughter.

"So, what's a minishrink? Anyone?"

"A psychologist who listens to children?" Joanna Sullivan stood.

"Write that exact sentence down," Kristen told the class. She waited a few seconds. "Now. Cross out the fancy title and the age barrier. What's left? Read it back, exactly."

Another young woman stood. "A...who listens?" she laughed lightly.

"Good!" Kristen told her. "That's the exact answer. A minishrink is the term used to describe any person, place or thing that does not ostentatiously display a doctorate on its den wall and who listens, comforts or brings out emotion. Can anyone think of an example?"

"Dolls used in sexual abuse cases?" someone guessed.

Kristen nodded lightly. "The puppets used by police and psychologists in court cases are a popular example of this philosophy, but it is only an interim tool. Those are 'detached' minishrinks. The puppets have minishrink value, but they are not actual minishrinks. Like those puppets, a simple deck of cards can have an interim minishrink 'value'. Conversation over a game of cards is natural and usually enlightening, because the person is 'detached' from the conversation.

"A Minishrink already exists in the life of the patient, they are already an integral part of who they are. Most people find their own special minishrinks long before we see them as patients."

"You mean like a teddy bear?" Joanna asked.

Kristen nodded. "Very good. A teddy bear is a category two minishrink. Who or what else did you talk to or depend on as a kid? Anyone? Stand and be embarrassed."

"I had a blanket," a student stood. There were a few muffled laughs.

"A favorite doll," came another answer.

"A least some of you were normal kids," Kristen smiled. "Anyone else?"

"I talked to my dog," another student stood.

"You still do," the girl next to him put in.

Several laughs.

"Don't scoff, dogs are extremely good listeners and their value is incalculable. A category one minishrink." Kristen hopped off the desk and went to the whiteboard, turning it over. The top of the board was labeled MINISHRINKS in block letters. Underneath, the board was divided into three parts.

She rapidly wrote, "toys, blankets, dolls", in the middle of the board, "dog", on the left side. The class started writing furiously, copying the board exactly. Those with recorders borrowed pens and paper from their more prepared classmates.

Kristen turned, putting the marker in her left hand and used it as a pointer. "The ones you've mentioned are all rather common. To this list," she gestured to the middle column, "you can also add, musical instruments, finger paints, almost any hobby or sport. A place can be a minishrink. Julie Andrews sang to the mountains in the Sound of Music. Sally Bows screamed under the trains in Cabaret. A great many people have a special place that is emotionally calming, or necessary for serious thought. I have a big boulder near my home where I talk to myself for hours."

There were a few nods.

"Any other minishrinks that might fit into this column?" she looked expectantly at the class. "Don't limit yourself by a patient's age."

"The workplace," came an answer.

"The gym," came another.

"Good! Exercise is useful for getting rid of anger or sadness. People hide in their work, or use it as a sanctuary to get away from their personal life. 'Professional students' use school as a way to keep from entering the work force."

More laughter.

"Anyone here who has never pulled a minishrink from this column?"

A couple of hands went up, Kristen nodded. "I'll concede that you did not have a little blue blanket, but you may be missing the point. How do you escape the pressures of the world? Have any of you ever intentionally lost yourself in a good book, listened to a special song or watched a favorite movie just to laugh or cry? If so, you've had a category two minishrink."

The hands went down.

"Good. Now, this column," Kristen pointed to the left column that contained "Dog", "Is a different type of minishrink than the dolls, toys and places category. What else could fit here?"

"Cats?"

"Okay, any kind of pet or animal." She erased the word 'dog' and substituted 'pets'. "Start a trend. What else?"

"A best friend?"

"Excellent! At one time or another, every person in this room has been a minishrink to someone as a friend or confidant." Kristen wrote 'friends' below 'pets'. "Who else have you used as a sounding board, either as a child or adult?"

"A favorite teacher?"

"A priest."

"My Gran."

"Someone else's mother."

Kristen laughed. "Yes. Isn't it amazing how someone else's mother always seems to be more understanding than your own parent? Can you see a pattern?"

There was a long pause. "Think logically," Kristen suggested.

"Pets and people are alive," a voice answered.

"Bingo!" Kristen nodded. "Yes. They are alive. Why would a child, or an adult, for that matter, pull a minishrink from this column, rather than the other? Shout out an answer."

"Loneliness," came an answer.

"Fear," another voice.

"Strength in numbers?"

"Acceptance?"

"To get a different perspective."

"Love."

Kristen nodded encouragement. "I'm impressed, you guys are good." She touched both columns with the marker. "Please note that neither column is more important than the other, they are simply used for different emotional reasons. Anyone still have trouble identifying with a minishrink from either column?"

Everyone shook their head.

"Good. So far, we all agree," Kristen decided. "Finally, we come to our third column. This column is also no more or less important, just a little less understood, less common and, professionally for us, more fascinating. Here we can put in," she wrote as she spoke, "Cinderella's fairy Godmother, elves..."

"Leprechauns," came a voice.

Kristen turned slightly. "Either we have a local in the class, or someone who flunked last semester." There was a light laugh from several members of the audience.

"Yes, Leprechauns," she wrote it in the column. "Fairies, ET's, ghosts, goblins, little people, or the very popular, ever talked about, imaginary playmate." Kristen put large quotation marks around the word imaginary. "To these entities," she gestured at the board, "a child may speak freely of his pain, his fears, his dreams, his hates, his loves, his masturbation, or anything else he might consider shameful behavior or thoughts. These minishrinks are the ones you speak to if you step on a crack to break your mother's back, or if you stab an animal with an ice pick, just to see how much blood can really come out of such a tiny little hole." The amused smiles from students at the first analogy died abruptly with the last.

"Don't dismiss these minishrinks lightly, they also have a purpose. Minishrinks in this column do not have the nasty characteristics of thinking like an adult or reproachful friend, they think exactly as a child wants them to think. This is also the column you will have the most difficulty understanding or accepting."

Kristen put down the marker and resumed her place on the desk. "As a general rule of thumb, you can label these columns one, two and three, left

16

to right. As we study psychological patterns, you will note that the more tangible or acceptable the minishrink, the less open your patient will be with his confidences to that minishrink. A category one minishrink, a pet or friend, will learn less about the troubles of a patient than, say, a doll from category two. A doll will learn less about the troubles of a child than an invisible friend in category three. An animal's lifetime can be ominously short, a friend or teacher may tell your secret to someone else, or give you advice you don't want to hear, a stuffed toy will always keep your secrets, but it may be lost or accidentally discarded. Invisible friends, on the other hand, never judge, never tell, are trustworthy and stick around for as long as they are needed. Children instinctively know these facts and respond accordingly.

"My purpose here is to help you find the hidden minishrinks of your patient, whether they be fuzzy blue blankets, or invisible playmates and, more importantly, believe in their value. Don't be fooled by your credentials into thinking you can replace any minishrink, or that you can successfully transfer a child's dependence from them, to you. If you get rid of the minishrink, you are not doing anyone a favor. Parents may take a child's blanket away with the misinformed belief that they are helping the child grow up, you do not have that luxury. For you to do so would be at the very least unethical, at the most, bordering on malpractice.

"If, at the end of this course, you magnanimously believe that fantasy and imagination are fine, within responsible and grown-up boundaries, then I will strenuously suggest that you change your major, or become an 'adult' psychologist. Children have no mental boundaries, if you can't get rid of yours, your patients will be past your comprehension. I do not mind competent competition in my field, but I will be damned if I want bumblers that will give me more patients due to their own incompetence."

Kristen again looked at her watch. "Your first assignment, due Thursday, is a more complete list of the three categories of minishrinks and why you think a child would turn to those minishrinks for help. I want you to relinquish all your adult prejudices and return your minds to your own childhoods. Try and remember something you believed in then, that you might not believe in today. If you need help, rent a few DVDs this weekend. I suggest Drop Dead Fred, Pete's Dragon and The Three Lives Of Thomasina."

The majority of the students had also looked at their watches, they were silently gathering their belongings, waiting for the bell that was already two minutes late in ringing.

"One last point," Kristen went on. "I do not accept hand written reports on any assignment. I will accept a verbal recording, personal itune, flash drive or a typed report. If your report is computer generated and printed, I appreciate a size 18 font or larger.

"That's about it, this lecture is officially over. Thank you for your attention, my ever efficient secretary, Heidi Schaeffer, will have your Tuesday schedules posted by tomorrow. You are now... dismissed." The bell sounded almost instantly after her last word. Kristen looked in the direction of the bell and added in a quieter voice, "thanks for the extra time, Jory."

The students packed up their notes and books, most everyone moved toward the exit putting on snow jackets to walk rapidly to their cars or other classrooms.

Patrick McClary turned toward Heidi Schaeffer, who had sat next to him during the second half of the class. "You were right, I don't recognize the textbook. Is she kidding, or what?"

"About what?"

"That minishrink stuff. Learning to think like a child. She sounds like a bit of a nut."

"Don't let any of the locals hear you say that, Kristen Michaels is one of their sacred cows."

"I'm not knocking her ideas, just her priorities. She's putting too much importance on one simple subject."

"Maybe the subject isn't that simple," Heidi suggested. "You might be surprised."

Patrick looked at her suspiciously. "Are you a local?"

Heidi nodded. "Yes. My dad was stationed at the base when I was a kid. We moved when I was twelve, but I came back for the college and the skiing. Both have the best reputations in the world."

"Why is Dr. Michaels a sacred cow?"

"Oh. Her father was the country doctor, he delivered four or five generations of Claren townsfolk. Everyone you meet has known Kristen Michael's since she was a baby. She runs the crisis house and the 'Little People's' clinic just outside of town. She's eccentric, but most small towns like their eccentrics. She's also pretty well thought of in most psychology circles, she's published at least twice a year in all the major journals."

"Wow. Why the bit about verbal reports or large type?"

"As she said, she has a vision problem."

"How bad?"

"The prognosis is that she will be completely blind before the year is out."

18

Chapter 2

Prospero: ...I find my zenith doth depend upon a most auspicious star...

The conference room at the PSR institute was polished and comfortable, used only by the major players of the Institute.

Dr. Neil Davidson, Head of Psychiatry, was forty-three years of age, six foot one, one hundred sixty two pounds, brown hair, brown eyes. For this meeting he wore a three-piece gray business suit with a conservative tie. Neil was classically handsome, had no distinguishing characteristics with the exception of a dimple in his left cheek that was only noticed when he smiled.

It was rarely noticed, for he rarely smiled.

Dr. Davidson had very impressive credentials and had joined the PSR institute two years earlier after making a fortune in a private practice he hated, catering to the neurosis of celebrities and corporate icons. He had several files in front of him and a large mug of herbal tea near his right hand.

Dr. Denise Parker, chief of surgery of the medical facilities at PSR, sat across the table from Dr. Davidson. She was in her mid-thirties, five foot eleven, one hundred forty-five pounds, dramatic auburn hair, hazel eyes and a brilliant smile that she used quite often. She was wearing a blue dress that was mostly covered by a white lab jacket, but did not distract from her very sensual (and well appreciated) figure.

Dr. Parker was well known in all the important medical journals and had been published an average of three times a year for her contributions in cardiac surgery before joining the PSR team. She was armed with two medical files, a set of x-rays and a mug of strong black coffee.

Two seats down from Denise Parker sat L.R. (Lloyd Rudolph) Simmons, Head of Security for the Institute. He was forty-eight, sandy hair, five foot eleven, one hundred ninety pounds, gray eyes and a complexion that freckled in the sun, giving him a look of youth that he often hated.

Lloyd had a degree in law and passed the bar with flying colors, but never bothered to continue with that career. He had an innate nature that made him suspicious of everyone he met, which made him ideally qualified for his calling in security. He approved of any secret, as long as he was in on it. As always, he was prepared for the meeting and had his ever present notebook and a list of the new patients who had been admitted over the weekend.

Dr. Matthew Jeffers was nearing seventy. His posture when he entered the conference room was military straight, his stature gave the impression that the ebony cane he used was a bold affection or a weapon to be used on cheeky subordinates, not a necessary crutch for his weakening, tired legs. He sat down heavily at the head of the large mahogany table.

Jeffers' secretary of twenty years, Phillipa Moore, followed him into the room. Phillipa's dress was conservative and mild, like the woman herself. She was the consummate professional, no one present had ever heard her make a personal statement, she never called in sick, she was never a minute late when checking in for work.

Matthew made himself comfortable at the head of the table, taking his time, watching while the other three resumed their seats. Matthew enjoyed Monday morning briefings, they gave him a hint of the week to come.

"Well, Lloyd," Matthew Jeffers looked at L.R. Simmons, "how many new guests have graced our exclusive five star hotel over the weekend?"

"Four. Admiral Elias Fielding, Ms. Teresa Lawson, Secretary Hopster and..." Lloyd looked at the list, "Miss Lindsay Cummings, Senator Cummings daughter." He looked up at his boss. "Dr. Parker has been given the medical files on Miss Cummings and Admiral Fielding, Dr. Davidson the medical and psychiatric files on Miss Cummings and Secretary Hopster."

Matthew frowned. "Who is Teresa Lawson? State Department associate?"

"No. The current victim of our favorite Supreme Court Judge," L.R. answered tightly.

"Fuck." Matthew Jeffers frowned at Doctor Parker. "How bad?"

Denise handed over the x-rays and a photo of Teresa Lawson. "She'll be fine. A broken nose and jaw, two cracked ribs, eighteen stitches over her right eye."

Matthew shook his head at the photo of the obviously abused girl. "How old is she?"

"Not yet seventeen," Denise answered.

Matthew studied the photo. To him, the girl looked pre-pubescent. A child dressed up for Halloween. "Prostitute?"

"Yes."

He handed the photo back to Denise. "I think it's time for a little constructive blackmail." He turned to Phillipa Moore. "Get some heavies on it. Judge Cooper either places himself under 'voluntary' observation and psychiatric treatment, or the media goes public on his hooker bashing. Eventually I suspect he'll decide that a dead hooker is less likely to talk than a live one. The man is out of control."

"Yes, Sir," Ms. Moore made herself some notes.

"Neil?" Matthew Jeffers looked expectantly at Dr. Davidson. "Do you want him?"

"I'll assign him to someone on my staff who hasn't met his previous victims," Neil answered.

20

Matthew Jeffers nodded, one problem solved. "What's the poop on your two new patients?"

Neil Davidson opened the files in front of him. "Secretary Hopster will probably be short term, it looks stress related, but I'd pull his security clearance permanently, it's his third incident. Miss Cummings is new to PSR. She is fourteen years old and has seen three different child psychologists in the past year. I don't have their files yet. She's been at a private hospital the last four weeks for an automobile accident. Evidently, she has become abusive and destructive. They can't handle her, so we got her."

"What caused the accident?"

L.R. looked at his notes. "According to the case report, she drank to excess, stole Senator Cumming's car and wrapped it around a telephone pole. Since no one else was injured, the local police agreed with the Feds to lose the file."

Jeffers nodded and turned to Neil. "Who do you want to give her to?"

"No one on my staff is comfortable working with juveniles. I suggest we transfer in a child psychologist for evaluation, then ship her off to a private juvenile detox center."

"Any preference on child psychologists?"

Neil Davidson shook his head. "I don't think it really matters, I interviewed the girl, anyone our security clears can handle her evaluation. As soon as her medical injuries heal, we can ship her out and be rid of her."

"What's her medical condition?" Jeffers asked Denise Parker.

Denise looked at the file. "Broken right tibia, various cuts that required stitching. We've got her in a walking cast. I'm ready to release her whenever a psychologist signs her off."

"Senator Cummings must be so proud of his little girl," Matthew Jeffers frowned. He turned to Phillipa. "Make a note for a child psychologist." He turned back to Denise Parker. "What's the story on Admiral Fielding?"

"Ventricular Tichardia. I've scheduled him for a bypass as soon as he's stable."

"Prognosis?"

Denise nodded. "Looks good."

"That takes care of the new inmates," Matthew Jeffers decided, feeling slightly let down at the normalcy of it all. "Any new traumas or breakthroughs on our other guests?"

"Ambassador Denning might be breaking out of his apathy," Neil Davidson offered. "Security tells me he had an episode during his sleep last night. I don't know if its medical or psychological, I haven't viewed it as yet."

"Denning?" Matthew Jeffers repeated. "I hope its something positive, the State Department is breathing down our necks, they want him back. The conference at the UN is less than a month away."

"He isn't stable. If we release him too soon, I cannot guarantee his behavior," Dr. Davidson answered.

"Let's view the tape," Jeffers suggested, looking at L.R. Simmons. "What time was the episode?"

"0432 hours," Simmons told him looking at his notes, "then again at 0435 hours."

Phillipa was already calling security to have the tape played on the large television screen at the end of the conference table. "It will be a few moments," she told Dr. Jeffers.

Jeffers nodded and looked directly at Denise Parker. "Denise, you are the medical advisor on the Denning case, what is your opinion of his physical condition?"

"Physically, the Ambassador could be released in two weeks, unless there are complications."

Matthew looked annoyed. "I see. No lung disorders, secondary infections...?" he asked hopefully.

Denise shook her head, her red hair catching the light in a blaze of incredible color. "None. The damage was fairly extensive, but we used a sandwich implant and covered it with a myocutaneous flap and he's doing beautifully, better than we had first hoped. His lung expansion is nearly normal, the implant is maintaining a healthy rigidity. I foresee no further complications. With normal precautions, he should be able to resume work, checking in only as an outpatient."

Matthew placed his cane across his lap, absently twirling the heavy wood. "If you looked very hard, could you find a complication?"

"I don't follow," Denise admitted, looking at him curiously.

Matthew Jeffers decided to be blunt, Denise was new on his staff and didn't know all the tricks of the trade. "Do you have any ethical problems with advising the State Department that the Ambassador will be unfit for his job for another four or five weeks?"

"Oh." Denise thought about it. "No," she decided. "The heart surgery I performed is still relatively tricky, I would enjoy observing his physical progress during the added time."

"Good."

"The video is ready," Phillipa told Dr. Jeffers, putting down the phone.

"Good. Excuse us, Phillipa. I'll call you when it's over."

"Yes, sir." Phillipa quietly left the room, closing the door behind her.

"Put it on, Lloyd, let's see what we've got," Jeffers suggested.

L.R. Simmons flipped the switch on the monitor and sat back to watch with the others.

The scene on the television was that of a bedroom at the institute. A date and time indicator flashed silently at the bottom right corner of the screen. Charles Denning was sleeping fitfully, the blue sheets of the bed wrapped around his waist. He suddenly sat up, put both hands in an outward position, growled, "you dirty, conniving son of a bitch!" and pulled the trigger of an invisible gun. He repeated "Bastard, bastard, bastard!" five times as his arms recoiled with reaction to the imaginary shots he was firing, then he nodded in satisfaction, pushed his hands stiffly into his stomach against his ribcage and fired his imaginary gun once more. With that, he smiled lightly, laid back against the pillows and returned to sleep.

Denise Parker cleared her throat nervously.

The recording fast-forwarded, stopping at the time of 0435 on the screen. Charles Denning sat up, rubbed his eyes with his knuckles, then looked cheerfully at the corner of his bed and grinned. "Hi, Chipper! Did anyone see you come in?" his voice was that of a young child and carried a slight mid-western twang. Charles listened for a moment, then shook his head. "You may be right about Grandpa, but I think Gran really does see you. Gran sees everything." He paused for a moment and shook his head again. "...No, I'm not sick. I don't know why I'm here. It's not like when I had the flu and they don't let anybody visit... I don't know anybody here." He looked disgusted. "Okay, yooou," he drawled out the word, "but that's about it. Tell me what everybody else is doing, I'm going borey in here."

Charles Denning seemed to listen for awhile, then laughed, the sound a high shrill giggle. "Oh, it's okay, I guess, I really don't remember. I think I've been here a long time, Chipper, even riding Skyeagle seems like a long time ago." He yawned. "Yeah, I'm tired, too. See you later, Chipper." He laid back down and fell into instant sleep."

The picture on the screen went black.

Matthew Jeffers was the first to speak. "Huh. Now that's unexpected," he stared at the blank screen.

"What was all that about?" Denise asked

Doctor Davidson looked to Matthew Jeffers.

Matthew Jeffers returned the look. "What is your opinion, Doctor?"

"It is the first time he has acknowledged the shooting, even subconsciously," Neil said carefully. "It could be the breakthrough we've been waiting for."

"But who was he talking to?" Denise Parker persisted.

"Someone named 'Chipper'," Matthew Jeffers grinned, "apparently."

"Who's Chipper?"

"An old friend, I'd say," he answered. "A very, very old friend."

"A classic type three minishrink," Neil said softly, frowning.

"That would be my opinion," Jeffers agreed, still smiling. "Incredible."

"What's a minishrink?" Denise Parker asked, still in the dark.

"In this case, a classic imaginary friend," Neil Davidson answered.

"Probably drawn from his own childhood," Matthew Jeffers put in. "It's not only unusual in an adult, it's potentially worth a journal of its own."

"You're giving it too much credence. He's simply dreaming about an old apparition," Neil shook his head. "Its another escape mechanism."

"Has he reverted to his childhood any other time in his therapy?" Matthew Jeffers asked.

"No."

Denise looked interested. "Will this 'mini-shrink' apparition help Ambassador Denning in his therapy?"

"If used properly, there is a chance of it," Matthew Jeffers answered.

"I disagree. If we get sidetracked by a childhood fantasy, however interesting, it could add years to his recovery," Neil Davidson put in quickly.

"It's your therapy," Matthew Jeffers shrugged. He stood and stretched his legs. "Well, it looks like we all have our day worked out for us. Is that everything?" He looked at the group. "Oh, yes. The Cummings child." Jeffers turned to L.R. Simmons. "Lloyd, I'd like you to approve security of Dr. Kristen Michaels as a consulting psychologist for Lindsay Cummings," he announced. "Her clearance should take about a week."

"Dr. Kristen Michaels," L.R. Simmons nodded and wrote the name in his notebook.

Matthew looked at the group. "Any questions? Comments?" he looked directly at the strong and arrogant face of Dr. Neil Davidson. "Temper tantrums?"

There was a minor flash of anger in the eyes of Neil Davidson, his posture had stiffened somewhat, but the shrug he gave bore no evidence of emotion. "Dr. Michaels has a habit of overloading her calendar. Teaching, working charity cases, keeping irregular office hours, maintaining a rather rigorous writing schedule. I'm sure we could find another psychologist that is closer and less in demand."

"I believe I can convince her to come here for a day or two," Jeffers answered.

"It's your call," Neil said mildly.

"Yes, it is," Matthew Jeffers smiled with a hint of malice. "You know, while she's here, Neil, you might even consider using her as a consultant on Denning. Aside from the minishrink angle, she did have his son in therapy three years ago, she might be used as an emotional catalyst, of sorts."

He looked at Neil's typically unsmiling face. "Of course, it's only a suggestion."

"Thank you, Dr. Jeffers, I'll consider it," Neil Davidson answered coldly.

"If that's everything, I suggest we all get back to work," Matthew, dismissed the group. He waited until they filed out of the room, turned his chair toward the window behind him.

Kristen Michaels. He'd finally get her here. With a little work, maybe, this time, he could talk her into staying.

###

SECURITY FILE #61940

TO: D.B. HASTINGS, FS HQTRS
FR: L.R. SIMMONS, FS 0215, PSR

Dr. JEFFERS has requested the immediate security clearance of one Dr. Kristen MICHAELS, of Claren, Colorado (see attached stats) for the preliminary evaluation of Lindsay CUMMINGS, Senator E. CUMMINGS daughter.

TO: L.R. SIMMONS, FS 0215, PSR
FR: D.B. HASTINGS, FS HQTRS

A forty-eight hour priority one security clearance for Dr. Kristen MICHAELS has been ordered by this office, as per regulation 116. Dr. MICHAELS has been cleared for security reasons previously, a simple update will be all that is necessary. Put on your vest, Lloyd, the coming fireworks at PSR should be interesting.

TO: D.B. HASTINGS, FS HQTRS
FR: L.R. SIMMONS, FS 0215, PSR

I don't follow.

TO: L.R. SIMMONS, FS 0215, PSR
FR: D.B. HASTINGS, FS HQTRS

You will...

May I intrude?" Denise Parker had knocked once, then cautiously poked her head around the door to Neil Davidson's office.

Neil looked at her sharply, then relaxed. "You are never an intrusion," he answered graciously. He sat back in his chair and looked at her appreciatively. "Just an incredible distraction."

"Good to hear," she grinned and came the rest of the way into the room. She nodded at the folder that was open on his desk. "The Ambassador?"

Neil nodded. "It's a tricky situation."

"What is?"

"The entire therapy," Neil responded simply. "Time limits, medical problems...the whole thing is problematic."

"Oh." She nodded at the chair in front of him. "May I sit?"

"Of course." He looked at her curiously.

Denise sat down crossing her legs comfortably. "That imaginary friend he talked to in the tape. How unusual is that?"

"Its unusual in a non-schizoid adult personality."

"What was the name of the consultant Dr. Jeffers wants to bring in on the Cummings child?"

The electric shock Neil Davidson felt at the question did not come through in his voice. "Dr. Kristen Michaels."

"Do you know her?"

"We've met," Neil answered.

"Is she any good?"

"She has an excellent success rate."

Denise looked at him speculatively. "Okay, but do *you* think she's any good?"

"Her chosen field is child psychology, my opinion is not relevant. As I said, she has an excellent success rate and is well-respected by her peers."

"Where does she teach?"

"Claren University. Colorado."

"Impressive. Is she the one they call the 'Leprechaun Lecturer'?"

Neil gave a light grimace. "Yes. That would be Dr. Michaels. How did you hear about that?"

"When you used the term 'minishrink', I thought I remembered something from some journal, but it wouldn't come to me."

Neil nodded. "If you've heard about minishrinks, you've read one of Dr. Michaels' articles. She publishes a lot. She first coined the phrase, oh, seven, eight years ago. I believe her doctorate was based on Santa Claus, the Easter Bunny and the movie 'Harvey'."

"Oh, I loved that movie," Denise smiled.

Neil Davidson looked tired. "Most people did. It was an enjoyable diversion, even if it did put psychiatry in a bad light. Dr. Michaels loves imaginary friends. She is obsessed by them."

"Why 'obsessed'? I would think the use of fantasy would be a natural tool in child psychology," Denise argued mildly.

"If held in check, you're probably right. Unfortunately, Kristen Michaels uses fantasy in both her psychological therapy and her personal life. As a therapist, she ignores standard theories. She is stubborn, opinionated, obstinate, childish and exceptionally naïve."

Denise felt her heart lurch, but answered gamely, "I think I like her already. I could use a little fantasy in my life. Big bad cynical adults are beginning to wear a little thin."

"Enjoy it while it lasts, she'll be out of here less than forty-eight hours after she arrives," Neil promised firmly.

"I see," Denise answered softly. "You don't like her," she speculated.

"I don't agree with her. There's a difference."

"Do you think she can help the Ambassador?"

"No," Neil answered flatly.

"The Senator's daughter?"

"Probably," Neil shrugged. "As I said, she has a good success rate with children. "

"What does she look like?"

"Kristen? She's..." Neil looked at Denise sharply. "Your curiosity seems a bit high this afternoon, Dr. Parker. May I ask why?"

"Oh, as a cardiologist, I'm always alert to possible heart problems. Am I mistaken, or was this Kristen Michaels one of your past love affairs?"

"Are you asking as my cardiologist, or as my current love affair?"

"Both, I expect. Jealously is a nasty emotion, but I am human. Did you have an affair with her?"

"Tell you what, Dr. Parker, if Kristen Michaels does find time in her busy schedule to bless us with her royal presence, why don't you ask her if we've ever been lovers? I'd be curious to hear her answer, myself." He smiled at her calmly.

Denise looked disgusted. "It's really annoying how you manage to control your emotions, do you know that?"

Neil looked surprised. "I don't control my emotions, I simply face them, accept them and learn to live with them. I am also human, Denise."

"Take me home and prove it," Denise suggested.

Neil raised one eyebrow. "You are feeling insecure, aren't you?" he asked.

"Don't psychoanalyze me, Doctor. Just take me home and screw my brains out."

Neil gave her an appreciative smile. Denise was the perfect woman. She represented reality, sexual satisfaction and emotional stability from a partner that knew his needs as well as he knew hers.

She was exactly what he needed.

Kristen Michaels and Matthew Jeffers could both go to bloody hell.

###

SECURITY FILE #61941, PSR FILE #213, 5/25
TO: D.B. HASTINGS, FS HQTRS
FR: L.R. SIMMONS, PSR

The clearance of Dr. Kristen MICHAELS has been received, in part. I am not satisfied with a simple update of Dr. MICHAELS, I would prefer a full background disclosure of her from day one for my files. The clearance she received for Dr. JEFFERS three years ago was from another administration and might very well contain some discrepancies. We all know how slip-shod some of their methods were.

TO: L.R. SIMMONS, FS-215, PSR, 5/26
FR: D.B. HASTINGS, FS HQTRS

Enclosed is the original background check of Dr. MICHAELS and as much of the subsequent knowledge we have on her that we can give you. Sorry about the holes, Lloyd. Some files were sealed for national security and it will look like some of the dates are screwy. It's an intentional security measure. Kristen Michaels has dealt with the kids of VIPs up to the president, and the powers that be figured if the dates were wholly accurate, someone might figure out which political yokels were having family problems. Personally, I think all politicians are crazy, even if they left in the dates, it would be a crap-shoot.

Chapter 3

Ariel: I come to answer thy best pleasure, be it to fly, to swim, to dive into the fires...

Kristen looked at the clock on her desk, then at Heidi's block lettering on her calendar. L.R. SIMMONS, PSR INSTITUTE, LA JOLLA, CALIFORNIA, 6:30. She felt a mild sense of irritation. The large print was necessary and Heidi was hardly to blame for the use of it, but Kristen hated block letters. Back in the days when she used computers for fun as well as work, it was a form of yelling.

Well, either Heidi had the wrong day, or L.R. Simmons had decided to be a no show. It was nearly seven. Annoying, but it was probably for the best. An institute with initials preceding it was usually some bogus operation asking for "tax-deductible" funds. This Simmons character was probably a high pressure salesman ready to convince her that she needed another tax shelter.

Kristen took off her glasses and rubbed the area between her brows. It had been a very long day, she probably would have been rude to L.R. Simmons in any event. The phone shrilled at her elbow, she answered it tiredly. "Dr. Michaels."

"Kristen? I'm sorry. I expected Heidi to answer."

"She's gone for the day. She and one of my new students went up to Spruce Meadow for night skiing."

"Oh. I know you have a client, I apologize for the intrusion, this will only take a second."

"Take your time, Paul, he was a no-show."

"Really? Do you want to reconsider dinner?"

"No, I grabbed a sandwich and I have twenty eager reports on minishrinks to grade. Any other offers?"

"Want to go night skiing up at Spruce Meadow?"

"Nope. I'm too old and blind for those slopes, Mr. Prosecutor. Embarrassing as hell. The last time I plowed into a tourist."

"Serves him right, Spruce is a local spot, he should have been on the other side of the mountain. I know! How about an uninterrupted night of kinky sex and pleasure?"

"Tempting. Throw in a full body massage and I'll put off grading the reports," Kristen told him. "Is that why you called?"

"In many ways, that is the only real reason I ever call you," Paul answered. "My secondary reason is to update you on the Keenan case."

Kristen's interest peaked. "What happened?"

"Good news. Both Keenan girls are in protective custody at the state receiving home, Teresa Keenan is in the shelter and John Keenan has been dutifully arrested for child molest, rape and various other charges that were dreamed up by yours truly. I saw the judge right after your deposition, he

29

went for it without a quiver of his golden pen."

"That was fast! How did you get him to do that? I thought you said this one was going to be a real fight."

"Well, I'd like to take all the credit, but Teresa Keenan finally took your advice and came down to see me on her own. With her deposition and your psychological statement to back her up, the warrant was a cinch. I thought the judge was going to go for immediate castration."

"Good for her, I was concerned she might renege."

"Now the bad news."

"Oh oh. What?"

There was a short pause. "Keenan is already out on bail. He's more than a little pissed off at you, Kris and is fully aware that you encouraged his wife and daughters to go to the authorities. He may get nasty. Scratch that, he *will* get nasty."

"Maybe with a good psychiatrist, he'll get over it," Kristen suggested. "I have a list of some very good referrals."

"Don't be flip. The man is a bona fide asshole, Kristen, his daughters have the physical and emotional scars to prove it. You are stranded up there now that you can't drive and I don't like it. I think you should stay with me for awhile."

Kristen sighed deeply. "For how long, Paul? Until the trial, until Keenan is convicted, then rehabilitated? Come on! Keenan is not the first abusive parent I've uncovered for your office and he's no worse than any of the others."

"You're wrong, Kris. I've got a bad hunch about this guy."

"Paul, you..." Kristen abruptly closed her mouth on the sarcastic retort she had been about to make, the door to her office opened at that moment with the violent force of a gale wind. Kristen hastily put on her glasses and stared at the intruder. Framed in the doorway was the bulky form of John Keenan. He was clad in jeans, a plaid shirt and heavy snow jacket, the latter still showing traces of the weather outside. His hair was in wild disarray, also covered with flakes of melting snow. Keenan's face was florid with either anger, alcohol, the cold weather outside, or all of the above.

"Hang it up," the man suggested in a tense whisper. "Now."

"I hate it when you're right," Kristen said hollowly into the phone.

There was a shocked silence. "Is he there?" Paul asked, fear in his voice.

"You've got it," Kristen answered, her voice one of feigned cheerfulness.

"Oh, Jesus! Are you really alone in the house?"

"Not now," Kristen answered dryly.

"Okay. Keep talking as though you can't get me off the line. With this snow, it will take almost twenty minutes for the police to get to you."

Kristen's eyes had never left Keenan's face, nor had his eyes left hers. She gave the intruder a small, overworked smile, holding up one finger to let him know she would be off the phone in just a moment. "I don't think that will be necessary," she told Paul.

"Dammit, quit playing the psychologist! I don't give a tinkers damn what you think is necessary! I'm sending the police! I've already handed my secretary a note and she is calling them now. She doesn't shirk her duties to go skiing!"

"Gambling with unknowns is often detrimental," Kristen responded with measured calm, "the results can be quite devastating."

"Hang it up," Keenan broke in, his voice rising angrily.

Kristen nodded in agreement. "I'm afraid I really must hang up now," she said in the phone. "A late client just came in. Do call my secretary, Sir, I honestly believe your problem is quite minor and can be handled without any outside assistance."

"No dice, Kris. The police are on their way and so am I. Keep calm, honey, I'll..."

Kristen was spared the rest, she hung up the phone quickly at the expression of agitation on John Keenan's face.

"Mr. Keenan," she stood, her face carefully calm. "I wasn't expecting you."

"Do you know why I'm here?" he hissed.

"At a guess, I'd say you're here to blame me for all the trouble you've had today," Kristen answered. "I think we should discuss it. Would you care to sit down?"

"No!" Keenan stuck his hand into the pocket of his coat, bringing out a small gun and pointing it at her levelly.

Kristen's surprise was genuine, the gun was completely out of character for John Keenan. "You don't need a weapon," she assured him, "I am hardly a threat to you."

"I know about you! You talk, using all your warped logic and psychological terms and pretty soon you convince me that all my problems are my fault, not yours! That the destruction of MY family, the loss of MY job, MY reputation, MY friends..." his voice rose angrily with each of his losses. "YOU! Not me, YOU! You lost me my life! I had everything before you butted into our lives!"

Kristen held up both her hands in concession, turning her palms out in a helpless gesture. "Alright. I agree. My intervention cost you a great deal."

Keenan sneered with disgust. "Without this gun, you'd try to make me believe that I destroyed my own life, wouldn't you?"

Kristen nodded. "Probably. I am human, Mr. Keenan. No one would want to take responsibility for all the wrongs that have been dealt to you. I'm willing to take responsibility for my part in your troubles, are you willing to take your share of the responsibility?"

"You think I'm insane!"

"Mr. Keenan, I'm a child psychologist. I deal with children, because I've never been able to figure out the actions of adults. I am not qualified to judge your mental stability. I do know that your behavior towards your daughters is making them feel unstable."

"Bullshit! I love my children!"

"I'm sure you do. Since we both care about your children, may we sit down and talk? We share a common interest. We both want your daughters to be happy. You do want them to be happy, don't you?"

John Keenan's face underwent several changes, his eyes registered total confusion for almost thirty seconds, then they turned hard, once again. He steadied the gun more firmly. "No. He said you'd say that. I know about you. You're only dangerous when you talk. You confuse things. You twist things to make yourself look good. You're the problem, you're the one who ruined my life. Without you, my life can return to normal." He started to squeeze the trigger.

It took Kristen a near fatal split second to fully recognize the fact that he really intended to shoot. "Damn!" she exploded. "Jory!"

Simultaneously, the overhead and desk lights went out and John Keenan pulled the trigger. The sudden lack of illumination caused him to jerk his aim just enough for Kristen to quickly change her position to one of relative safety under her desk. From her standing position to the cramped one, she somehow lost her glasses, but that was the least of her worries. This was all wrong. Somehow she had perceived the situation with Keenan a hundred and eighty degrees out, Keenan had not responded to her the way his psychological profile should have had him react.

The deafening noise of another shot sounded again, Keenan firing his weapon rapidly toward where she had been standing, the shattering sound sadly informing Kristen that her specialized reading lamp was the latest casualty of his anger. How many bullets did the gun hold? In westerns there were only six, in recent spy thrillers, guns carried a seemingly inexhaustible supply. So far, Kristen counted, as the next sound informed her that the corner of the desk was the newest victim, Keenan had fired three shots. One more sounded, the telephone shattered, rang feebly with a short gurgle of sound and stopped. Several papers floated down on the floor next to where she was crouching. Was that four, five...? She was losing count.

"FREEZE!" The voice was not Keenan's and the order had the effect of freezing Kristen, but evidently not Keenan, as another shot was fired. This time the noise took off toward the unknown voice. Another weapon fired, the sound different even to Kristen's untrained ear. There was silence for a split second, then a heavy thud. More silence.

"Dr. Michaels?" the voice was not that of John Keenan.

"Here," Kristen answered, rising shakily to her feet. "You didn't kill him, did you?"

"I won't know until I find the damned light switch. Stay where you are, until I give you the all clear."

"Jory." The lights came on, Kristen glanced briefly at the blurred form of a stocky man still searching the walls for the light switch. She made her way around her desk to check on the status of John Keenan. Without her glasses, his form was an indefinite blur, but she dropped to her knees next to him and searched for a pulse at his neck.

The pulse was regular, if a little rapid. Both the color and the odor of blood led her hand to his wound. It was high in his right shoulder, bleeding sluggishly, but steadily. There was an additional odor of alcohol surrounding Keenan, giving Kristen a partial reason for his bizarre behavior.

"How bad is it?" the voice came from above her.

"He's out cold, but fair," Kristen answered. "There's a roll of sterile cotton in the right hand corner cabinet under the bookcase next to you. If you could get it for me, we can use it as a compress until an ambulance gets here."

The man found the cotton, gave it to Kristen, then watched as she applied her minor medical treatment. "Are you also a medical doctor?"

Kristen finally looked up at her rescuer, carefully maintaining the pressure on John Keenan's shoulder at the same time. "Lord, no! My father was an MD, what little I know and believe me, it is very little, I picked up from hanging around him." She concentrated on the face above her, squinting her eyes to see more clearly. "Are you new on the force? I thought I knew everyone in the Claren Police department, but we've never met, have we?"

"No and I don't work for the police department. Are you expecting them?"

"Yes. I was talking to the District Attorney on the phone when Mr. Keenan came in. Who are you?"

"L.R. Simmons, PSR Institute," he answered absently. He walked over to Kristen's desk, returned with a pencil, then gingerly picked up the gun he had previously kicked out of Keenan's hand. He put the weapon carefully on a clean sheet of paper on the top of the desk.

"PSR Institute," Kristen repeated dully, watching as much of his movements as she could. "You're my six-thirty appointment?"

"Yes. Sorry I'm late. Its been snowing pretty heavily, I wasn't sure which was road and which was open field. Don't you have snowplows out here?"

"Not very often," Kristen answered. "Once a week or so. It takes a few days to pack and the roads to the ski lifts get top priority. Locals use four wheel drives."

"But this is a medical facility!"

"A few years ago, yes, but..." what a stupid conversation. "When it's an emergency facility again, we'll..." Kristen shook her head. "Who are you again?"

"L.R. Simmons, PSR Institute. Tell me," he gestured to the still form of John Keenan. "What did you do to set this guy off? From the dialogue I overheard when I first came in, you had him pretty well calmed down. I thought he was one of your regular patients."

"I'm not sure what sent him off," Kristen admitted. "From what he said before he fired, I'd guess he was goaded into it by someone else. John Keenan is into rape and physical violence, the gun is completely out of character. He prefers to terrorize his victims with brute force, macho fashion. Nothing in his psychological profile would lead me to believe..." she grimaced wryly. "At least that was my considered opinion before today. It's glaringly obvious that my evaluation was a wee bit flawed. Pop always warned me that book knowledge was not a fair substitute for practical experience."

Simmons voice became hard. "I have had practical experience with a few wackos in my time and I think your original theory is right. This guy doesn't fit the pattern of a rapist out for revenge. Those jerks like to humiliate their victims, not simply shoot them. And that," he added darkly, "makes me a whole lot suspicious."

"He'd been drinking. He doesn't have a background of alcohol abuse, but I'm sure it was contributing."

"Handy. Diminished capacity as a legal defense conveniently covers a great many unexplained behavior patterns, doesn't it?"

"Just what kind of cop are you?"

"I never said I was a cop," Simmons answered.

Kristen squinted lightly. She wanted to see his face. All his movements, all his actions pointed to 'cop'. "Granted, you don't dress like a cop," she decided, making out a three piece suit and totally impractical shoes for Colorado weather in May, "but..."

"You don't look like a psychologist," Simmons voice smiled, "but Dr. Jeffers advised me not to go by appearance."

"Matthew Jeffers?" Kristen looked surprised. "How are you connected to him?"

"Dr. Jeffers is Chief of Psychiatry at the Institute," Simmons told her. "He sent me to find you and bring you to him."

"Matt sent you? For what possible reason?"

Simmons started to answer, then looked up sharply, listening. "Later. It sounds as though we have company. The local police, from the sounds of it."

Kristen had also heard the faint voices, Paul Beckner's the most distinctive among them. "And the District Attorney," she sighed heavily. "He must have driven like a mad man to have caught up with them."

"Let me do the talking. You make a show of whimpering, or something. Say nothing, I'll see if I can streamline this thing. That, or we'll be hung up here for days."

"As opposed to what?"

"As opposed to being in California, Thursday, when Dr. Jeffers wants you," Simmons answered simply.

"Oh." Kristen checked to make certain she had not lessened the pressure on Keenan's shoulder, then looked up at Simmons, her face doubtful. "You want me to 'whimper'?"

"Ha. Folks around here wouldn't buy that, would they?" He grinned.

34

"Scratch that plan and just keep quiet. I'll handle the cops, you get the District Attorney away from the others if you can. Lawyers always screw things up. We'll cook up some story to placate him, later."

"I don't think the DA is going to be any problem," Kristen answered. She had no time to elaborate. At that moment, the door to her office revealed several uniformed officers and one tall blond man in a business suit who took in the situation instantly, yelled, "get an ambulance!" then huskily added, "Kris!" and rushed over to her, pulling her off the floor and away from Keenan. "Are you hurt?" he checked her face carefully, "tell me if you're hurt."

"I'm fine, Paul."

"Did he touch you?"

"No. I'm fine," Kristen assured him.

"Thank God," he very possessively crushed her into his chest, kissed the top of her head, "its okay, baby, I'm here. It's going to be okay. I'm here now, he didn't hurt you, you're fine," he let out a shaky sigh. "You're fine," he repeated. "Let's go into the other room. You don't have to talk to anyone, until you're calmer."

"Until I'm calmer," Kristen repeated, hiding a smile.

Chapter 4

Prospero: I know thou canst not choose...

Kristen sat back on the old wing-back sofa and looked at the soft blurs around her, memory taking the place of healthy eyesight. The ceilings were too high to allow the fire Paul was building to warm anything but the spot directly in front of it, the flames springing into life only added the illusion of heat to the rest of the room. When her father was alive, they spent almost every evening here, discussing various cases or household matters, or simply enjoying each other's company in quiet comfort while reading journals or listening to music. The room was always hazy with smoke from the fireplace that never drew properly and the smell of cherry blend tobacco her father used in his pipe. One match. All he ever needed was one match to light it. The whole room had always smelled of cherries from his pipe and pine from the fire.

Funny. Maybe odors created a warmth of their own. The room didn't seem so cold when it smelled of cherries and pine. None of her students ever mentioned smell as having minishrink value. She should someday bring it up in class. Bayberry candles at Christmastime, chocolate chip cookies baking in the oven, cherry blend tobacco...

"Kristen? Have you heard anything I've said?" Paul was standing directly in front of her, glaring down at her small form.

Kristen blinked up at him. "About what?"

Paul kneeled down in front of her, gently touching her face under the eyes. "You're crying! Oh, Kris, I'm so sorry..."

Kristen quickly wiped her eyes. "I'm fine. My mind was wandering, I was thinking about Pop."

"You're not fine. You've been frightened badly, you're just finally reacting to it. You need some brandy, or something. Where do you keep it?"

"The glasses and decanter should be under the sideboard by the fireplace," Kristen told him. "If that fails, there's some in the usual place in the kitchen." She started to get up from the sofa, Paul gently pushed her back down.

"You sit, I'll look."

Paul found the glasses, searched the other cupboard and pulled out a bottle. "I told you you're not safe here alone. I don't know how you've managed to survive this long."

"Lighten up, Paul. I've lived here all my life, this is the first time anyone has taken a shot at me."

Paul set the glasses and the bottle on the coffee table, then sat down next to her, pouring a couple of inches of brandy in each glass then handing her one. "No, you're not safe. Last year that Wilcox kid pulled a knife on you..."

"He pulled a knife, he didn't use it," Kristen pointed out. "Kenny turned out okay. I got a letter from him last month. He's been given an internship at the Daily Press in Claymore, did I tell you?"

L.R. Simmons came into the room. He held out a pair of glasses to Kristen. "One of the officers found these on the floor."

"Thanks." Kristen took the glasses, wiped them and put them on.

Paul stood. "I expect they sent you in here to get us?"

"No," L.R. answered calmly. "As a matter of fact, I just closed the door on the last of the local constabulary." He addressed Kristen. "The cleanup crew will be by tomorrow morning, about ten. There's a small stain on the rug, but nothing too serious." He sat down heavily on the chair facing the sofa.

Paul stared at the man. "What do you mean? Are you saying that the police have left? Kristen hasn't given her statement!"

"Paul, calm down," Kristen suggested, turning politely to Simmons and studying his face. It was the first time she had seen it clearly. It was a good face, strong and reliable looking. "Would you care for some brandy?"

"Yes," Simmons answered. "It is a bit chilly in here."

Kristen started to rise, Paul anticipated her, ordered her to "stay put," then got the third glass himself, poured out a healthy measure and handed a drink to Simmons. "Just who the hell are you?" he asked with obvious hostility.

"L.R. Simmons, PSR Institute," came the mild response. He took a sip of brandy, "good! Napoleon?"

"Probably," Kristen answered. "Pop was partial to it. I'd forgotten it was even in here until just a few minutes ago. Generally, I drink the cheap stuff, in coffee, I can't tell the difference." She nodded at his feet. "You should take off your shoes and socks, they're probably soaked through."

"I've never heard of the PSR Institute," Paul broke in.

"We don't advertise," Simmons answered calmly, taking off his shoes and socks and pointing his feet toward the fire. "Oh. Nice."

"I'll get you some slippers," Kristen offered and left the room.

Paul watched Kristen leave and shook his head, then turned back to L.R. Simmons. "What are you, government?"

Simmons took a slow sip from his glass and said nothing.

Paul let out a sigh that sounded like a hiss.

Simmons smiled. "What do you know about this Keenan character?"

Paul shrugged. "He's a creep that rapes his two daughters for sport. Kris," he corrected himself, "Dr. Michaels, works at the crisis house in town and the girls confided in her. Between the two of us and a very brave, violently abused wife, we had the man sent to jail. Unfortunately, he got out on bail less than an hour after he was charged."

Simmons frowned. "Do you know his political affiliations?"

Paul looked at the ceiling for help, then back at Simmons with suppressed patience. "Generally, I find that political backgrounds are not terribly important when dealing with local criminal cases," he answered sarcastically.

"Pity. Just for the record, what are your political beliefs?"

"Usually disillusioned," Paul answered instantly. "Care to tell me what 'record' we're putting this into?"

"Mine," Simmons answered.

"Fine. Just for my record, how did you get involved in all of this?"

"Accidentally. Actually, I came to see Dr. Michaels. I generally like to stay away from crazed men with guns."

"Why did you come to see Dr. Michaels?"

"It's a personal matter," Simmons answered.

"Personal?"

Kristen came back into the room carrying a pair of leather slippers. "Here. They were my Dad's, I think they'll fit."

Simmons put them on. "They do, thanks."

"Can I get anyone coffee, something to eat?" She looked at Paul, then Simmons.

"Sit down, Kris," Paul said sternly. "Next you'll be offering to bake a pie and knit a sweater."

"Sorry." She sat back on the sofa next to him.

Paul smiled at her. "You're just over-stimulated, relax," he put an arm around her shoulders, holding her close.

Simmons looked at Kristen. "Just for my own piece of mind, who the devil is 'Jory'?"

"Jory?" Paul repeated, then gave a hoot of laughter.

"Paul," Kristen said in an undertone.

Paul looked suspiciously at Kristen. "You haven't met this guy before, have you?"

"Mr. Simmons is a friend of a friend."

"A curious friend of a friend," Simmons corrected her. "So, who is Jory?"

"Jory," Paul answered with a straight face, "is the leprechaun who lives in lights. The kid who had him, didn't want him, so Kristen took custody."

Kristen said a quiet swear word, Simmons blinked and requested, "would you run that by me again?"

"It's not important," Kristen assured him.

Simmons studied her high color and raised one eyebrow. "You called his name twice during your confrontation with Keenan."

"And the lights went out, then back on again?" Paul asked innocently.

"Yes," Simmons responded, still watching Kristen's obvious embarrassment. Strange girl. She handled the danger like a pro, now she looked concerned for the first time.

Kristen took a deep breath, then answered almost casually. "Jory is simply the name one of the kids in my first therapy group gave to the...well, whatever it is that causes lights to flicker. It upset him, so we gave it a name. Unexplained things are much more manageable when they have an identity. I tend to tack on names to just about everything, I'm afraid. My car, my radio, my computer, various knick-knacks..."

"And 'Jory' is the name you gave to the lights?"

"In a way, yes."

He nodded slowly. "So you installed one of those voice activated light switches that responds to a word of your own choosing, Jory, and your voice activates it," he concluded.

"Okay," Kristen agreed carefully.

"What a tremendously logical explanation," Paul marveled. "Every light switch in the city of Claren activated electronically to Kristen's voice. Not to mention the university public address system, the..."

"Paul, stop it," Kristen said sharply.

"Don't you have a home to go to?" Simmons added.

"I'm in no hurry," Paul told him.

"But I am," Simmons told him. "My consultation with Dr. Michaels is confidential."

"It has been a long night, Paul," Kristen stood.

Paul took both her hands and looked deeply into her eyes. "I don't care who this guy is, Kris. Government flunky or not, if you want me to stay, I'll stay," his voice was worried, almost pleading. "You've had enough tonight. You decided months ago to cut your case load, you don't need to take on any political parents who can't handle their own kids."

"Excuse me?" Simmons looked the question at Paul Beckner.

"Oh please," Paul glared at the man. "I'm approached every time Kristen needs clearance to work with some high mucky-muck's delinquent offspring," he answered.

"You are?" Kristen asked Paul. "You never told me."

"You never asked," Paul answered. He turned back to Simmons. "Am I right?"

"Yes."

"I'll call you, Paul," Kristen suggested.

Paul started to say something, shook his head, then left.

Simmons walked to the front door, watched the DA drive off, then came back into the room. "Rare man. Curious as hell, yet knows when to pull out."

"He's a very special friend," Kristen answered.

"How special?"

"Why?"

"Because I need to know if anyone will be looking for you if you leave town for a few days. In his profession, he has the resources that might create embarrassing questions."

Kristen raised an eyebrow. "How many days?"

"I'm not sure, exactly," Simmons answered.

Kristen looked surprised. "When?"

"Thursday night, after your class. Dr. Jeffers didn't want to disrupt your regular schedule more than necessary and I'd like to check out this Keenan guy a little more carefully."

Kristen nodded. "Thursday it is."

"Good," Lloyd answered mildly, hiding his astonishment with difficulty. Jeffers had told him Kristen would not question it, but he was surprised.

"Who's the patient?"

"Lindsay Cummings. The daughter of Senator Cummings."

"What's the problem?"

"I don't know, I'm not a psychologist," L.R. answered smoothly. He retrieved his briefcase from the back of the sofa and pulled a manila envelope from it. "Dr. Jeffers thought you would like to see the case file before you come to the institute." He handed her the envelope.

Kristen opened the folder and looked at the pages. They were in regular type. She frowned at the unreadable print and sighed heavily.

"Is there something wrong?" Simmons asked, feeling uncomfortable at the expression on her face.

Kristen smiled self-consciously at him. "No. I'll read them a little later."

"I'm supposed to stay with you when you read them," L.R. answered.

"Are you supposed to burn them after I read each page?" Kristen looked amused.

L.R. grinned. "Paranoia does run deep at PSR," he answered. "National Security. Sorry."

"Swell." Kristen looked vaguely annoyed. "Well, in that case, we'll have to go back to my office at the campus."

"Why?"

"I need my magnifying light to read these," Kristen answered, "and Mr. Keenan shot the one on my desk here." She looked at his surprised face. "I'm almost entirely blind, Mr. Simmons. I guess I just assumed you knew."

"No, I didn't," Simmons answered, frowning. The thick glasses she was now wearing had also surprised him. They were ugly and unflattering. When he had first seen her in her study, she looked like a tiny, but very attractive and capable young woman. Now... well, suffice it say that the glasses changed her appearance drastically. He wouldn't have recognized her from her file photo. When the local cop had given the glasses to him and stated that they belonged to Kristen Michaels, Simmons had been completely unaware that she even wore them. Her vision problem should have been in her security file

Now, all those other holes in Kristen Michaels profile seemed suspiciously large.

###

Due to the circumstances surrounding the initial contact with Dr. MICHAELS, the possibility of a security leak at PSR should be considered. Strenuous protective measures for Dr. MICHAELS will be established while she is at the institute.

An investigation of John B. KEENAN, has failed to positively determine who supplied both his bail and the weapon with which he tried to assassinate Dr. MICHAELS. The .38 SW has no registration record on file and cannot be traced. KEENAN himself is vague about the identity, stating "some guy... he knew how I felt." During a cursory investigation at the local tavern where KEENAN was drinking after his bail had been posted, both the bartender and waitress confirmed that he was drinking heavily with another man, not known in the community. Description indeterminate, medium everything. KEENAN'S bail was posted in cash, the name given to the bail bondsman was that of his employer, JOHNSON and Associates. His employer denies posting bail, but that could simply be embarrassment on his part due to the subsequent attack on Dr. MICHAELS.

It is the belief of this office that KEENAN was used by someone previously unknown to him and that further information from KEENAN will not be forthcoming. The staff psychiatrist at the hospital agrees that someone must have encouraged KEENAN into violence, stating emphatically that had KEENAN been left to his own devices, he might physically confront Dr. MICHAELS, but "she would have been able to diffuse the situation with her normal verbal spanking" (direct quote). See attached report, Claren Police Department, interview, Dr. Bernard RICHARDSON, Claren City Hospital.

###

Lloyd Rudolph Simmons frowned unhappily at the report before sending it off. The facts were there, but not his gut feelings. The very thought that Kristen Michaels might be a threat to anyone was ludicrous. If he had not seen her in action, he would have thought Jeffers was mad for wanting such a little piece of fluff on the Denning case, but now... well, Lloyd would reserve his opinion. During that first evening she had been confronted by an armed wacko, shot at, subjected to police and she had never turned a hair, except in his questioning her about the lights.

All in all, Dr. Kristen Michaels had damn near earned Simmons respect, not an easy accomplishment.

Chapter 5

Prospero: There's something else to do. Hush and be mute...

Kristen sat in the small office designated to her by the college wearing a ratty turtle-neck sweater that had seen better days, and faded blue jeans covering thermal underwear. The smoke filter was turned on high and still the room contained a light cloud of smoke directly over her head. The circular magnifying glass she was looking through attracted more wisps of smoke and she put out her current cigarette to avoid it.

The coffee in her large mug was cold. Kristen frowned with annoyance at the cup, made the decision and gulped it down quickly. She poured coffee from the thermos and sighed contentedly as she sipped the now hot brew.

There was a quick knock on the outer door of the office, a young man poked his head inside. "Dr. Michaels?"

Kristen squinted at him. "Yes?" She focused on his outfit. It was the kid who had taken Heidi out skiing earlier that day. "Patrick, right? Patrick McClary?"

"Right." He flashed a brief smile and came into the room, his head towering above the cloud of smoke. He waved at the thick air. "Those things will kill you," he nodded at the full ashtray next to her.

"I know. That's why I smoke in secret. That's also why I went into psychology, rather than psychiatry. With a medical degree, I'd have to recognize that fact professionally and I hate being a hypocrite. Why don't you open the window?"

"Okay." Patrick walked over to the window, cranked it open, a wave of cold, fresh air poured in.

"Mind you," Kristen continued, turning off the circular magnifying light and snapping on the regular desk lamp, "I am often a hypocrite, I just don't like being one when it's unnecessary." She piled the papers that were scattered on her desk into a neat pile. "I gather you brought me your psychology assignment?"

"Something like that," Patrick answered.

"I don't mean to nitpick, but it's Wednesday, the assignment was due on Tuesday."

"The dog ate my homework and then, when I was re-writing it, a huge monster came into the room and stole my pencil. He left muddy footprints all over the floor and Mommy spanked me, because she thought I did it." He grinned at her.

"Good answer," Kristen told him.

"You said, return to our childhood. That's how I got through the second grade."

"Okay, I'll accept the assignment," Kristen smiled. "Is it recorded, or typed?"

"Hand written," he answered.

Kristen's smile faded. "Again, I don't like to nitpick, but..."

Patrick walked away from the window and to her desk, flipping on the magnifying light. "This thing must give you one hell of a headache."

"I can manage." She turned off the magnifying light with an angry twist of the knob.

"You could use some help," Patrick argued. "Why don't you hire an assistant to help you?"

"I can manage," Kristen repeated flatly.

"Heidi tells me you're going blind," Patrick stated. "I'm sorry."

"Good God! Are you the villain who caused it?"

"No, but..."

"In that case, I don't think I'll accept your apology," Kristen decided. "And I'm sure you and Heidi have a great many more interesting things to do than to discuss my physical shortcomings." She reached into a drawer, pulling out a blank flash drive and handed it to him. "If you could dictate your written report, before class tomorrow, I'll accept it. If not, you're more than welcome to drop the class."

"I'd rather read this report to you," Patrick answered.

Kristen sighed heavily, put out the cigarette she had just lit, then lit another one. "Mr. McClary, I am trying to be as flexible as possible, but I haven't the time nor the inclination to listen to your no-doubt fascinating report on various categories of minishrinks. Most of the reports from your peers are typewritten, they take time. As you pointed out, I do have a bit of a vision problem. As much as I detest the emotion, I would appreciate it if you would take a bit of real pity on me and simply taped your goddamned report!"

Patrick stiffened sharply.

Kristen took a deep breath and rubbed her forehead. "I'm sorry. Swearing is the direct result of a tired intelligence and I'm tired. It's been a very busy week."

Patrick blinked. "When was the last time you ate?"

"Excuse me?"

"According to Heidi, you had two appointments this morning, you worked in your office at home for three hours, then you went to the crisis house for a group session, then you came here. Before your appointments, you were up at the crack of dawn walking around the clinic. Then there was that bit with the intruder at your house last night... I'll bet you haven't eaten more than one meal in the last twenty-four hours."

"This is too much," Kristen decided, standing. "Mr. McClary. I have no idea why you are invading my privacy and I really don't care. We. Are. Done. Leave your report. If I have a chance, I will get to it. If I don't, you will fail the class."

"Just let me read it to you."

"Not a chance. You may have been a ace student from whatever college you attended before, but..."

"UCLA," Patrick offered. "Pediatrics and special therapy. I'm eligible for a pediatric internship this year, I'm hoping to work with you at the Little People's Clinic."

"I'm not hiring," Kristen told him. "The point is..."

"The point is," Patrick interrupted her, "The Weather Bureau is predicting a storm and suggested that I read you this report so you might be prepared for it."

Kristen stared at him, them frowned and sat down heavily. "Oh, shit. How old are you? Fifteen?"

"Twenty-four," Patrick told her sharply.

"Same thing." Kristen groaned, taking off her glasses, then shook her head. "It only needed this. I gather you have a nickname?"

"Trinculo," he answered.

"Right. Catchy," Kristen said sarcastically.

"I was to mention that the same number would suffice."

Kristen nodded, pulled the phone to her, put on her glasses and punched a few numbers. She waited a few more moments and punched an additional six numbers.

"Weather Bureau," the other end answered.

"I understand there is a tempest brewing," Kristen told the voice.

"Who told you that?"

"A child by the name of Trinculo, if you can believe that," Kristen answered.

"And?"

"I'd like a weather report," Kristen answered the code words with a sigh of annoyance, "from Gonzolo, unless he drowned at sea."

"Please hold."

The delay was less than a second, a new voice came on the line. "Patrick McClary, six one, one eighty-five, auburn hair, brown eyes?"

"That sounds about right. What the hell are you guys doing, recruiting from grammar schools now?"

"They're not getting younger, we're just getting older. Hi, Ariel! It's been a long time."

"Not long enough," Kristen answered. "Is that you, Reaper?"

"The one and only. There's a new storm brewing, little bit."

"Fascinating, I'm sure. Why tell me?"

"We need you on this one."

"Damnit, I know the mail is slow, Reaper, but I sent my resignation in three years ago. Along with a medical report and some very good reasons for the resignation."

"A piece of paper."

"An *official* piece of paper."

"Come on, Ariel, where's your sense of adventure?"

"Buried somewhere in my youth, I believe. I'm tired, Reaper," Kristen answered.

"So, we sent you some help. Trinculo."

"He's a kid!"

"He can read, he can write, he can do all those picky things that are making you tired and he can be a good sounding board when you're fresh out of ideas. Don't let his youth fool you, the kid's smart. What more do you need?"

"A brain transplant, apparently."

"Knew you'd do it," the voice chuckled. "Bye, Ariel."

Kristen hung up the receiver and looked over at Patrick McClary. She pulled off her glasses and closed her eyes. She didn't need to see his face, his expression was probably eager and anxious. Hell, she probably looked like that herself when she was fifteen.

"Is everything alright?" he asked when she didn't speak.

"Peachy," Kristen answered dryly. "I've been told that you can read and write."

"Yes," he sounded defensive.

"What's in the report?"

"Do you want me to read it to you?"

"No, I want you to tell me what's in it."

"Oh." Patrick sat quietly for several minutes as he opened the envelope and read the pages inside. "It's a background of various political personnel that have been blackmailed and/or manipulated in the past, a full background on the PSR institute and a speculative report on various psychological manipulations that could be used against a current Ambassador that is staying there." he paused and started looking through he pages for the name.

"The name is not important," Kristen told him tiredly.

"The weather bureau suspects..."

"I know who they suspect," Kristen broke in.

"How? I've been told that you haven't seen this report, that you came into this cold!"

Kristen rubbed the area between her eyes. "What's your background, Patrick?"

"I'm sorry?"

"Come on! Prospero always finds people that have a particular background he thinks might be useful in the future. What's yours? Aside from pediatrics."

"I'm a psych major," Patrick answered.

"We are all 'psych' majors," Kristen answered. "Prospero doesn't delve into military types, he leaves that to less subtle departments. By Charter, we simply keep the playing field fair, without political prejudice. What did you do before the 'tuition' was suddenly available for you at UCLA? Did you have a job?"

"Uh..."

"Come on, Patrick. What did he set you up for?"

"I had a job. I worked at the National Institute for the Blind in Washington. I assisted in both physical and educational rehabilitation."

"Translation, you taught Braille and how to keep your patients from walking into traffic when using a cane," Kristen took a deep breath. "Out of morbid curiosity, when did Prospero decide that you were destined for a more prosperous future?"

"Five years ago."

Kristen nodded. "Figures."

"Are you upset?"

Kristen considered it. "Yes. Not for me, for you. A friend of mine, however caring, has obviously been planning on getting me a nursemaid for five long years, has been training a nursemaid fresh out of high school to help me... and to help himself, he always has 'one more' personal favor. You, on the other hand, if you stay in this crazy situation, will be saddled with a blind, possibly insane child psychologist, for a hell of a long time. If you're looking for adventure, trust me, you won't find it in Claren, Colorado."

"I am not a nursemaid, I volunteered and I like Claren, Colorado."

"Three hundred sixty-five days out of the year, I am exactly what I appear to be, Patrick. There are no adventures in Tempests."

"I'm a pediatrician who wants to add child psychology, not a..." he paused, not sure of a word that would fit. "I have wanted to be a doctor all my life. I'm not looking for adventure."

"Everyone is looking for adventure when they're fifteen," Kristen countered.

"I'm twenty-four!"

"You're young," Kristen told him.

"And you're short," Patrick countered. "Deal with it."

Kristen laughed. "Touché."

"Do you want to hear this report, or not?"

"That depends. Did you finish your assignment for my class?"

"Yes."

"Where is it?"

Patrick leaned over her desk, sorted through several of the mini-drives in her 'in' box and handed one to her. "This is mine. I turned it in yesterday, when it was due. Okay?"

Kristen nodded. "Alright. Just as long as you keep your priorities straight."

Patrick looked again at the pages he was holding. "Where do you want me to start?"

"At the end. When does the Weather Bureau predict that I'll be home?"

"The first stage is 36 hours," Patrick answered. "Don't you want to hear the rest, so you can plan what you're going to do?"

"No. I'm a psychologist, Patrick, nothing more. I've been given a patient. Who is the best physician of the mind?"

"The patient himself," Patrick answered.

"And, as a psychologist, what's my job?"

"To listen, but..."

Kristen was shaking her head. "I repeat. I am a psychologist. The very most I can do is make myself available, nothing more. I'm the person Prospero calls when you lose your little blue blanket and need a temporary replacement. The operative word here, is 'temporary'."

"What if your patient doesn't find that blue blanket?"

"Then I help him find another one," Kristen answered simply. "There are always more blue blankets, the world is full of unused minishrinks."

"Then you lose control of your patient," Patrick frowned.

"I never have control. Who is the best physician of the mind, Patrick. What's the textbook answer?"

"The patient himself, but..."

"No buts. If I were totally blind, right now and asked you to hold my hand, what would you do?"

"I'd hold your hand."

"You're a nice boy." Kristen smiled at him. "And if I asked you to never let it go, if I asked you to hold my hand for the rest of my life, that I never wanted to walk alone again? That I wanted you to be my permanent blue blanket?"

Patrick bit his lip. "You have to learn to walk alone, or you'll always be handicapped."

"Exactly. The rules don't change, Patrick. Not because of age, or handicap. The patient is the only physician."

Patrick let out a large sigh. "I get the idea. You don't have to push it."

"Good." Kristen stood. "Because that is next Thursday's lecture. Quite honestly, I give the same lecture every day, I just change the words over and over until they sink into the dimmest of minds." She smiled at him. "Remember it and find some words of your own. If I'm not back from California on time, you're going to have to give that lecture."

"What??"

"Did you really think that 'being my assistant' meant that you got to have shootouts with some super secret government spy network?"

"I can't give a lecture!"

"Of course you can. Prospero would never send me someone, unless they were qualified in everything I do." She stood and walked around the desk. "I'm walking to McDonalds for a hamburger and apple turnover. You're invited. Before I leave tomorrow, we're going to have to get you settled into something you can do."

"Why not just hire me as your assistant?"

"Because it's a dead end job and you deserve better. You can assist me for one month. Dr. Sumner needs an intern on the pediatric side of the Clinic starting in June. The place is a mess since Pop died, if you clean it up and get the examining rooms in line with the newer technology, I can put in a good word for you. Harold Sumner is impressed by hard work and tenacity."

"Sounds reasonable," Patrick looked slightly disappointed.

"It's settled then. Let's go." She started toward the door.

"I'll get the lights," Patrick offered.

Kristen turned toward him. "No need." The desk light and the overhead lights went out. "Thanks Jory." She looked at the shadow that was now Patrick McClary. "Leave the window, Patrick. It's going to be clear tonight and the room could use the airing."

Patrick was standing very still, looking at the desk lamp that had gone off by itself. "How did you do that?"

"I didn't do anything."

"How did the lights go out?"

"Oh. Leprechauns," Kristen said mildly. "Prospero probably didn't mention them to you, but they are part of the package, if you work with me as my assistant, or my nursemaid. Not to worry, Patrick. If things get too weird for you, you can always change your major again. At fifteen, no decision is permanently set in stone."

"I'm twenty-four!" Patrick repeated once again and followed her out of the room.

Chapter 6

Ariel: ... to thy strong bidding task Ariel and all his quality...

Kristen had waited for several minutes for the noise in the lecture hall to die down.

"Hello?" she said loudly. Several people looked up at the stage. "I'm beginning to feel like a classic category three minishrink who's invisible to the majority of the population."

There were several "shushes" in the room, the talk died down.

"When I asked you to relive your childhood, I didn't mean I wanted you to go back to throwing spitballs in the classroom," Kristen advised the group.

A young man stood. "There have been some rumors that one of your patients took a shot at you on Tuesday evening."

"Wow! That sounds exciting," Kristen responded. "That's the beauty of rumors, they are rarely accurate, but they can be fun. Unfortunately, I can absolutely assure you that none of my patients tried to shoot me on Tuesday. Actually, none of my patients have ever tried to shoot me. I'm a very good psychologist, I don't let my patients carry guns during therapy sessions. It's a little rule I have."

There was a light laugh from several students.

Another student stood. "How about the parent of one of your patients? I heard it was John Keenan."

Kristen uncrossed her legs and dangled them from her desk. "Since curiosity seems so genuinely high today, I think this would be a good time to review a key word of my chosen profession and your hopeful one." She grinned, got down from the desk and wrote in large letters on the board.

CONFIDENTIALITY.

Kristen underlined the word and put the marker down with a flourish. "Okay! Who would like to define that word for me?"

Kristen looked out at the group of faces. "No takers? Okay, does anyone have any more questions about any rumors they might have heard recently?"

The room was deadly quiet.

"Fine. Curiosity is good. You need to be curious and interested in your patients to get them to confide in you. Another prerequisite is Trust. Capital 'T'. How do we keep the trust of our patients?" She pointed at the whiteboard.

Kristen went back to the corner of her desk and sat down. "For the record, I'm not trying to be bitchy, but usually, at least once during a semester, I have to reemphasize the point that I am a working psychologist. Occasionally, during this semester, I will discuss various situations that have come up during my career. I will not reveal names or dates, nor do I wish speculation on your part. Many of those cases took place in other states, even other countries."

Kristen clapped her hands. "Okay! I have reviewed your reports on minishrinks and as a whole I am delighted with your efforts. I am pretty much convinced that you all will be able to recognize a minishrink when you hear about one. So! How do you hear about one?" Kristen looked at them expectantly. "Anyone?"

A tall student stood, he looked embarrassed. "The patient tells you about it."

Kristen nodded. "And your name?"

"Jonas Wagner."

"Mr. Wagner. What do you do when the patient tells you about it?"

He grinned. "I listen."

"And what do you do if your patient introduces you to a category three minishrink, a classic invisible friend?"

He thought about it for a moment. "I say 'hello'?"

Several people laughed.

Kristen waited until the laugher died down. "Exactly, Mr. Wagner. You say 'hello'. Common courtesy demands it. If you can not hear the minishrink's response, what do you do?"

He shook his head. "I don't know."

"Who is the best physician of the mind, Mr. Wagner?"

"The patient?"

"Who has the answers Mr. Wagner?"

"The patient."

"What do you do if you can not hear the minishrink's answer, Mr. Wagner?"

"I ask the patient what the minishrink said," he speculated.

"Thank you, Mr. Wagner."

He remained standing. "Are my dues paid now?"

Kristen grinned. "Yes, Mr. Wagner."

Jonas Wagner resumed his seat.

Kristen removed her glasses and set them on the desk next to her. "Before you all believe that we are playing a rather silly game of 'pretend' with our patients, please keep in mind that children are usually very serious about their minishrinks. Never laugh at them. The same holds true for adults who believe in something that holds no particular value for you. God, astrology, superstition, lucky medallions, family heirlooms, spirits of dead relatives, anything they might have or believe in that you don't. Recognize that the value of objects or beliefs are not subject to your appraisal.

"Believe it or not, I learned this lesson from a group of children. First year psychology. I was working at a regular daycare center, having a 'pretend' tea party with three little girls, all age four. My cup tipped over and almost simultaneously, all three kids jumped back so they wouldn't get any 'pretend' tea on them. One of the little girls was nice enough to mop off pretend tea from my skirt with a napkin."

There were a few giggles.

Kristen grinned. "It was real to them. Kids see things we do not see." Kristen looked around the room. "Who haven't we picked on?"

A tall brunette woman stood. "Monica Harper. I'm an intern at Claren General."

"Pediatrics?"

"Yes."

"Dr. Harper. You have a six year old patient with a problem. He has a monster in his closet. A big, hairy, big, nasty, big, long toothed monster with big, *really* big claws. This particular monster eats blond haired children. Your patient has blond hair. Your patient is scared to death. What are you going to do?"

"Scare away the monster."

"Do you see the monster?"

"No."

"How are you going to scare it away, Dr. Harper?"

"Yell at it, make noise..."

Kristen nodded. "Possible. Some monsters run for the hills when they hear noise. Unfortunately, *some* monsters like noise. As a matter of fact, *some* monsters, especially monsters who eat little blond haired children, grow even bigger and meaner when they hear loud noises."

"Oh."

"You have a scared little patient, Doctor. What are you going to do?"

"I don't know," she laughed lightly. "Ask for help?"

Kristen nodded. "Good plan! Who are you going to ask? Who is going to give you that help?"

There was a long pause. "My patient," Dr. Harper answered.

"Why?"

"Because the patient knows the answers."

"Even what weapon is needed to get rid of a big, hairy, mean, nasty, long toothed, huge clawed monster?"

"Yes."

"And what are you going to do when the patient tells you?"

"Listen."

"And when the secret is revealed on how to get rid of that monster, who needs to get rid of it?"

"The patient," came the answer.

"Why?"

"Because I can't rid of a monster that I can't see. Only the patient can."

"Thank you, Dr. Harper. By the way, in case he hasn't mentioned it, Dr. Sumner thinks you're a damned fine pediatrician. He says you're great at calming the kids."

"Thank you, Dr. Michaels," she grinned broadly and sat down.

"Okay. We are now up to Monsters. The flip side of minishrinks. Very often, when you find a minishrink, there will be a comparable monster lurking somewhere nearby. A monster can be a toilet bowl, a garbage disposal, a park, a tree at the window, a clown doll with a freaky face, a bad recurring nightmare, the neighborhood pedophile, or a big hairy invisible monster under the bed or in the closet similar to the one I described to Dr. Harper. Anyone notice a pattern here?"

"Three categories?" came a timid answer from the group.

Kristen grinned. "Oh, I like dealing with sharp people. Okay. Using the same criteria we used for minishrinks, yell out some category one monsters."

"Parents."

"Dobermans."

"Teachers."

"Other kids."

"Doctors."

Kristen held up a hand. "Okay, you got that. Living things. Category two monsters?"

"The basement of my Grandmother's house," came a voice.

"Immunizations."

"Marionettes."

"Blood."

"Knives."

"Scissors."

"Scary movies."

"Ski lifts."

Kristen held up a hand again. "Wow. Out of curiosity, does anyone still have either category one or two monsters currently lurking in their adult closets?"

Most of the hands in the room came up. Kristen nodded her head. "Okay. Category three monsters."

There was a long pause, a few murmurs, some quiet responses not shouted out.

Kristen nodded again. "I heard a few 'big hairy monsters under the bed' and maybe a ghost or two somewhere in there, but not much else. For adults, category three monsters are harder to remember and harder to find. You are going to need to learn to search. Those monsters are very real and very scary to your little patients. You can't ignore them, saying they don't exist doesn't make them go away.

"Anyone want to guess what your next assignment, due by Tuesday, will be?"

There were a few groans.

"Yes. Three categories of monsters. Remember your own monsters, people, places, things. You may even find that one person's minishrink, is another person's monster. Some kids love roller coasters, some kids are terrified by them.

"We're going to add a little twist to this assignment. Most of you remember or still have some category one or two monsters still hanging around in your life. I'd like you to find one of yours, then find a minishrink that could offset that monster and give me a good reason why you think that minishrink would work. For an example, someone mentioned 'scary movie'. Often that can be lessened by someone holding your hand, spending the night with you," a few embarrassed murmurs, "even outtakes at the end of the movie showing you how the scary movie was made can have minishrink value." She smiled. "By the way, I'd really like to have someone come up with a minishrink that offsets 'immunizations or shots', that happens to be one of my own bugaboos, I'd love a solution for that one." Several nods in the group, a few laughs.

"Visual aids," Kristen said cheerfully. "I suggest Poltergeist, The Exorcist, or any of the movies adapted by Steven King novels. Form a group, if you're scared to be alone. Any questions?"

"Are 'bad dreams' a category two or three monster?" came a question.

Kristen looked toward the voice. "I don't know, what do you think?"

Several laughs.

"Okay. I'm going to be out of state for a couple of days, turn in your work to my secretary, Heidi Schaeffer, or my assistant, Patrick McClary. They will get them to me."

Chapter 7

Ariel: O' the dreadful thunderclaps...

The PSR Institute was an attractive four story building perched on a cliff next to the ocean. Kristen caught only a glimpse of grassy lawns and the high fence surrounding it before she was taken into the building, walked through a brief security check, including a metal detector. She stood by with fascination as an unsmiling woman carefully checked her computer, briefcase and luggage for drugs and less obvious weapons.

The woman nodded at Kristen. "You may disrobe in that room," she nodded at a door to Kristen's right.

When Kristen walked out of the dressing room, ten minutes later, her smile was a bit forced. "What does P.S.R. stand for, Mr. Simmons, Paranoia, Suspicion and Research into the above?"

He smiled apologetically. "Pretty close. The formal name is the Psychological and Surgical Recovery Institute for Security Sensitive Individuals, but PSRISSI was a little cumbersome."

"Right."

Kristen was given a short tour of the facility where she briefly met Dr. Denise Parker, who proudly displayed the extremely modern medical labs and Operating Room. Kristen made polite comments, then turned to Denise Parker, looking up at her with respect. "I hate to admit it, Doctor, but you're talking way over my head." She admitted. "And I'm not referring to your height," she grinned at the tall woman.

"Call me Denise," she answered, smiling in return. "I'm not sure, Doctor, but I think I was trying to talk over your head."

Kristen looked surprised. "Really? Why?"

"Probably to impress you," Denise answered.

"Huh!" Kristen looked at the beautiful woman, feeling a little confused by the obviously honest, but unnecessary admission. "Well, you succeeded, Denise. And my name is Kristen. I think I'd better drop the title around here, just in case someone thinks I'm qualified to take out a splinter. I'm not."

"I've been reading some of your articles," Denise told her. "They're fascinating."

"Thank you."

"And, one of my colleagues, Jeff Klausan, thinks you're brilliant."

"Jeff? I haven't heard from him in, oh, wow. It must be six years. What's he doing?"

"He opened his own clinic in Maryland. I'll give you his email address before you leave."

"Thanks, I'd appreciate it," Kristen answered.

Kristen received an even briefer tour of the psych labs, where Simmons introduced her to Neil Davidson. Conversation was nonexistent, he gave Simmons a short nod, ignored Kristen completely and left abruptly.

"Dr. Davidson is not very social," Simmons told her, looking slightly embarrassed.

"He never was," Kristen answered, "with his talent, he doesn't have to be."

Simmons looked at her suspiciously. "You know Dr. Davidson?"

"There's a tough question. Does anyone ever really know Neil Davidson?" Kristen looked at Simmons curiously. "With the metal detectors and skin search downstairs, don't they also do even a minor background check on visitors?"

"Of course we do!"

"Oh."

"Why do you ask?"

"Because I think you missed a few things on mine," Kristen offered.

"I'm beginning to feel that myself," Simmons answered tersely. He didn't elaborate, but turned to a rather nondescript man who was hovering nearby. "Mr. Hayes."

The man took the few steps necessary and approached them. "Mr. Simmons."

"This is Dr. Kristen Michaels," Simmons introduced them.

Raymond Hayes gave Kristen a damp hand. "Dr. Michaels. I've heard of you, naturally."

"Good things, I hope."

"I'm sure they were," he answered absently and turned to Simmons. "I've been ordered back to Washington for a few days. Dr. Jeffers wanted me to inform you personally."

"Thank you, Mr. Hayes. You've left your itinerary in the security office?"

"Of course." He nodded at Kristen. "Dr. Michaels," and hurriedly walked away.

Simmons watched him walk away and shook his head minutely. He took Kristen's arm. "Dr. Jeffers wanted to see you after your evaluation of Miss Cummings," he told her. He led her down a short hallway. "We've set up an office for you here." He opened a door and gestured her through.

Kristen looked around. The walls were beige, a few scattered paintings of various ocean landscapes decorated them. There were no windows. A wooden desk with one chair on each side completed the total inventory of furniture. To Kristen, it looked like the standard interview room of a county jail. "Is there anything you need?" Simmons continued, "Coffee, food?"

Kristen walked over to the desk and looked at the file for Lindsay

Cummings that was on top of it. The only other thing on the desk was a yellow legal pad and a pencil. "I could handle a cup of coffee," she smiled at Simmons. "And a deck of cards, if you have any."

"In the desk drawer for the cards," Simmons returned the smile. "Dr. Jeffers said you'd want them. I'll have the coffee sent to you before your patient." He looked around. "It is rather sparse," he frowned.

"It's fine," Kristen assured him, "I don't plan on living here."

"I'll come to escort you to Dr. Jeffers when you've finished with your patient," Simmons told her.

"Thanks, L.R." Kristen sat in the chair behind the desk.

"Uh..." Simmons looked at her. She looked like a little child sitting behind that desk. He'd met the Cummings girl when she was admitted, he suddenly didn't want Kristen Michaels to have to deal with the brat. She should at least have a little time before jumping right into a therapy session, for God's sake, she she'd just arrived!

"I'll be okay, L.R.," Kristen smiled at him, recognizing the expression on his face. "I have done this before, honestly. "It's what I do for a living."

"Okay. Well, then, I guess I'll see you in a little while." He slowly left the room, closing the door behind him.

Kristen checked the drawer of the desk, closed it, then opened the file on Lindsay Cummings. It was a little more complete than the file she had read a few days earlier at her home. A young woman came in quietly, handed her a cup of black coffee and left. Kristen had just finished reading the file when Lindsay Cummings was brought in.

Kristen looked at her mildly. Lindsay Cummings did not especially look like the pampered daughter of a very powerful Senator. She might have been any one of several fourteen year old kids she had met that Spring at the Crisis house. Her posture was a combination of defiance and resignation, her straight brown hair was combed free of tangles, the long bangs hung over her left eye. Her jeans were cut off raggedly and accentuated her still slightly chubby female figure. Her right leg was adorned by a fresh walking cast.

Lindsay sat heavily in the chair facing Kristen, the cast stretched out to the side. "So! You're the newest shrink! Don't tell me, let me guess your very first line. 'You really care about me and you want to be my 'Friend'. That's a capital 'F' for brain Fuck. Right?"

Kristen sat back in her chair and barely blinked. "Wrong. I have no desire to be your friend." She tapped the folder next to the yellow pad with the pencil. "From what your file tells me, you're a budding alcoholic who takes her father's Mercedes for joy rides and you like to beat up on your eight year old brother for kicks. I look for friends with more going for them than that. I like both kids and Mercedes. I do have some standards."

Lindsay parted the bangs from her eyes and looked at Kristen curiously. "This is a novel approach. What's that line supposed to do? Try and make me prove to you that I'm worthy of being your friend?"

"Can you prove it?" Kristen asked in return, taking a sip of coffee.

"I doesn't matter, I'm not going to try," Lindsay smiled viciously.

"Then, if that was my intention, it isn't going to work," Kristen shrugged. "Well, we have some time to kill. How do you want to spend it? We can glare at one another, play cards, or talk. Your choice. I get paid, no matter what we do."

"Play cards?" Lindsay looked at her suspiciously.

"Exactly."

"Don't you want to discuss my alcoholism?"

Kristen gave an exaggerated shudder. "Lord, no! Not only is it a thoroughly depressing subject, I've heard more about teenage alcoholism than one person can stand. I'd be bored to death. Aren't you interested in anything other than booze?"

Lindsay stared at her, then smiled lightly. "Boys," she offered. "I like to suck their pricks."

"Whatever makes you happy. Do you want to talk about that?"

"Not especially."

"School?" Kristen tried.

"No."

Kristen sighed heavily and checked off spots on the legal pad. "Your parents?"

"NO!" Lindsay shouted it. "I hate them!"

"Christ! Don't get so defensive. Everybody hates their parents when they're fourteen. It's not that big a deal." She smiled lightly, looking at the pad and put down the pencil. "Okay then! Obviously, we have nothing to discuss, so let's play cards. Do you know how to play gin?" She opened the desk drawer and pulled out the pack of cards.

"Yes," Lindsay looked confused.

"Do you cheat?"

"No," Lindsay answered slowly.

"Good!" Kristen pulled out the duds, placed them to one side, shuffled the deck and dealt the cards. She waited until Lindsay picked up her cards, then arranged her own. A moment later she announced, "your discard, you have eleven."

"Oh." Lindsay studied her cards, then threw a nine.

Kristen picked it up and discarded a seven.

Several quiet minutes of card playing passed, Lindsay finally announced, "gin," and laid down her cards.

Kristen looked at the hand on the table, nodded and put down her own cards. "Twenty-six," she turned over a page on the legal pad and wrote down the number.

"And twenty-five for gin," Lindsay reminded her.

"Right." Kristen wrote down the additional number.

Lindsay started dealing the cards. "So! Are you new around here?" She looked at Kristen's surprised face. "I heard the nurses talking."

"I'm just visiting," Kristen told her. "I live in Colorado. I'm leaving tomorrow."

"So you're not going to be my full time shrink?"

"Not unless you're going to Colorado as well," Kristen answered. "I certainly don't plan on commuting."

"Don't you like California?"

"It's okay. I miss the snow back home. Southern California weather would drive me buggy, it's almost always the same."

"Oh, yeah." Lindsay started arranging her cards. "Other than snow, does anything exciting happen in Colorado?"

"Sometimes."

"Like what?"

"Hmm," Kristen thought about it. "Well, someone tried to take a shot at me the other day. It was exciting at the time."

"With a gun?" Lindsay asked, astonished.

"Yes."

"Why?"

"I'm guessing he didn't like me much," Kristen shrugged.

"Why not?"

"He raped his own daughter. I talked her into reporting it. He blamed me for it."

"Creepy! Did the police put him away?"

"For now. He'll get help, then get out in a couple of years. That's the way the system works, unfortunately."

"I'd cut off his balls," Lindsay decided.

"Hmm." Kristen studied her cards.

"I saw a movie like that on television. A man beat his daughter, then raped her. It was disgusting!"

"So why didn't you change the channel?" Kristen asked.

"Because," Lindsay looked at Kristen with sudden suspicion. "Why do you ask? Do you think I'd let my father rape me?"

Kristen looked surprised. "Certainly not! I never would have mentioned it, if I thought he did. Give me some credit, will you?"

"Oh." Lindsay was quiet for a time. "My dad's pretty neat. I mean he's there for me... he really does love me, I know that."

"I thought you said you hated him?" Kristen countered.

"Not because of anything like... not because of anything perverted! You said all fourteen year old kids hated their parents!"

"So I did. Is your mom 'neat' too?" Kristen asked, throwing a queen on the discard pile.

"I guess," Lindsay picked up the queen. "She's a little stupid, though."

"Oh? That's not good. Isn't she a teacher?"

"Yeah. High school. She knows books and stuff, but nothing about real things. Sex, boys... she doesn't know anything about that. I don't let her tell me what to do."

"Hmm."

"I'm going down with seven," Lindsay announced, laying down her cards. "What have you got?"

58

Kristen counted her cards. "Thirty-four. Less your seven, that's twenty-seven." She wrote down the figure and started shuffling.

"How old are you?"

"Thirty-six."

"Are you married?"

"Nope," Kristen started dealing.

"That's smart. I'm never getting married. Boys only want one thing. They'll do anything to get it. Jerks. Hell, they'll even whimper to get it. It's disgusting."

"Hmm."

"Have you ever been raped?"

"Not that I remember. Have you?"

"Hell no." Lindsay picked up the cards. "Do you know what my mother told me to do if someone tried to rape me?"

"Nope."

"Guess," Lindsay suggested.

"I dunno. Call the cops? Run like hell?" Kristen guessed, picking up the six of diamonds Lindsay had discarded.

Lindsay shook her head. "Not even close. What if you couldn't get away?"

Kristen considered it. "Well, if I couldn't run, I'd talk them to death, then probably make up a whopper and mention AIDS," she laughed. "In short, I'd probably lie my butt off."

"Would you scream?"

"Hmm. If the mention of AIDS didn't work, yeah, I'd probably scream. I think." She looked thoughtful, then shrugged. "I guess you really never know what you'd do until it happens."

"Gin." Lindsay laid down her cards. "What did I catch you with this time?"

"Uh..." Kristen looked at her cards. "Is an ace one, or eleven?"

"Since I won," Lindsay smiled, "it's eleven."

"Fifty eight, then," Kristen told her, writing down the numbers. "Your deal."

Lindsay started shuffling the cards. "Don't you want to know what my mother told me to do if someone tried to rape me?"

"What was her suggestion?" she asked, sounding bored.

"To do whatever was necessary to stay alive," Lindsay answered, "even put up with the rape, don't antagonize the rapist, just stay alive."

"That's fairly common advice," Kristen shrugged.

Lindsay kept shuffling the cards. "It is?"

Kristen nodded. "A lot of mothers tell their kids that. Deal, will you? Are we going to talk, or play cards?"

Lindsay dealt the cards. "It's a stupid thing to say. I don't care if they're bigger and stronger, I'd fight back, even if it got me killed."

"Hmm." Kristen gave her full attention to the cards, discarding a two of clubs.

Several more minutes passed as they played cards silently.

Lindsey broke the silence with a frown. "A lot of women actually like men to be stronger, to treat them like... I don't know, sex slaves or something, don't they? Stupid women, anyway. I'm not going to be like that. Boys should learn early that girls are just as tough as they are, that we do fight back, that they can't have their way with them, just by being stronger and meaner. Ricky won't ever treat a girl that way."

"Ricky?" Kristen looked up curiously. "Who's Ricky?"

"My brother. He has a sick sense of humor. He laughs when Dad talks Mother into doing something she really doesn't want to do, but I'm teaching him that it's not funny."

"Hmm." Kristen picked up the three that Lindsay had discarded, then threw down an eight.

"As a shrink, what would you tell Ricky? Shouldn't he learn to respect women? Don't we have rights, too? Shouldn't we be able to do what we want sometimes? Do we have to let them have temper tantrums and get their own way?"

"I don't know," Kristen shrugged, "I've never thought about it. What do you think?"

"I think we have rights! Men can't boss us around!"

"That sounds reasonable."

"Think about it! Look at marriage! Men think that just because they're married, they have the right to have sex, any time, any way they want it. If a woman says no, they go right ahead anyway, until she finally gives in to him! They even change their name to show they're the man's property or something! Men never take the woman's name! Is that fair?"

Kristen shrugged again. "Do you think its fair?"

"No! Fuck that shit! I'm never getting married!" She shook her head vehemently. "I'm not giving up my name or my dignity!"

"Good for you," Kristen answered.

Lindsay nodded and laid down her cards. "Gin."

Kristen frowned at the cards then looked at Lindsay with suspicion. "Are you sure you don't cheat?"

"I'm sure. You're just a lousy gin player," Lindsay told her. "What did I catch you with?"

Kristen looked blankly at the cards in her hand. "I don't know. You add them up, okay?" She handed Lindsay her cards. "I really don't want to play anymore."

"I've got you on a blitz!"

"That's one reason why I don't want to play," Kristen admitted.

"That's not fair!"

"Life's a bitch, kiddo," Kristen answered calmly.

Lindsay stood up. "You're not even a good sport!"

"Why should I play if I don't want to?" Kristen asked. "Just because you're bigger and stronger, have a louder voice, what?"

"You..."

Kristen stood up, displaying her diminutive size. "It's your call, Lindsay. I'm little, I'm nearly blind, the room is soundproof, you can probably wipe up the floor with me. So! What are you going to do? Cry, plead, reason, finally use brute force to get what you want? Isn't that the way it works? That the meanest, biggest guy always wins?"

"I'm teaching Ricky to respect women!"

"What does Ricky have to do with this?" Kristen asked the necessary question.

"He's going to turn out just like Daddy!"

"Is that what you think?"

Lindsay started shaking, then burst into tears and looked at Kristen helplessly. "Why does he do that to her? If mom doesn't want him to... why does she let him? She doesn't have to! Daddy believes in equality, it's part of his campaign! Why does she let him treat her like a... like a whore! He makes her... she cries and she cries... he laughs and then he... and she... she does whatever he wants anyway! Why does she always give in?"

"I don't know," Kristen answered, "To be honest, Lindsay, I really don't care. That's their problem, it's not yours and it's certainly not mine."

"I have to listen to it, every fucking night!"

"That's different. That's something we can talk about."

Lindsay bit her bottom lip, her chin still quivering. "Now what?"

Kristen walked around the desk. "Oh, usually, I start therapy with something stupid and very trite, like... uh, 'I care about you, I would like to be your friend'. Then, I suggest something even more silly and stupid, like a hug. It makes me feel big and strong and vastly superior."

Lindsay gave her a weak smile. "I think I'd like that." She walked the one step necessary, put her arms around Kristen, then started crying hysterically.

Kristen just held her, let her calm down, then let her talk.

From that point on, all she had to do was listen.

Chapter 8

Ariel: Pardon Master. I will be correspondent to command and do my spiriting gently.
Prospero: Do so and after two days, I will discharge thee...

L.R. Simmons led Kristen carefully through several corridors, into an elevator, then down several more corridors and to an outrageously showy office. He knocked once on the open door. "I'll see you later, Dr. Michaels," he smiled at her and steered her through the door, closing it firmly behind her.

Kristen walked a few more steps into the office, turned around slowly and let out a low whistle. "Quite a setup." She turned to Matthew Jeffers who was standing behind his desk. "Well, you conniving, sneaky old bastard, just what have you been up to?"

Matthew Jeffers walked around the desk, leaning heavily on his cane. He put his arms around her and gave her a tremendous hug, then looked at her critically. "When did you start wearing glasses?"

"Two years ago."

"They're ugly as hell, do you know that? They make you look like an owl."

"Thanks. Owls are wise and majestic. When did you start using a cane?"

"Three years ago," he answered.

"It makes you look like an old and decrepit man," she told him and kissed him on the cheek.

He grinned. "Old men can be nasty and hard," he told her.

"And rude, obviously," Kristen agreed. "Are you going to offer me a chair?"

"Sorry," he took her arm, "sit," he tapped the chair in front of his desk, then walked around behind the desk again and waited for her to be seated before he sat. "I watched the session with the Senator's daughter." He handed her several tissues.

"You nasty little voyeur."

"They always get to you, don't they? Do you think us grownups will ever know how our actions effect our kids?"

"No, or learn to soundproof their bedroom doors. Hell, even normal sexual relationships between adults can screw up a child," Kristen answered, wiping the tear smudges from her face and glasses.

"How are you, Kris?"

"Homesick. Why am I here? You could have sent Lindsay Cummings to me. She's hardly a hard-core security risk, just one confused, lonely little girl who has listened to one too many nasty adult games."

"Before we sent her, I wanted you to evaluate her."

"Why? Any one of a dozen psychologists could have done that."

"I like watching you work, you never cease to amaze me. Besides, while you were here, I thought you might be able to help on another little matter."

"Oh, really? What a surprise," Kristen said sarcastically. "What 'little matter' might that be?" She put the used tissues on the desk.

"Don't be flip, Kris, I really do need your help. Do you remember Charles Denning? You treated his son a little over three years ago. On my referral."

Kristen nodded, looking slightly confused. "Yes. Charles wrote me when his son was killed." She shook her head at the loss. "What's happened to Charles now?"

"Didn't you read about the burglary and shooting at his home in San Diego?"

"A shooting? No."

"It was covered by the national media."

"I have a tendency to fall behind on current issues," Kristen admitted. "I have a hard enough time keeping up with the news in my own profession. As for television..." she tapped her glasses. "Sorry, I rarely watch it any more."

"It doesn't matter," Matthew Jeffers told her quickly, "the incident as reported to the media was bogus in any event."

"Oh. What a shock," Kristen grinned. "Politics never change, do they? What really happened?"

"The Ambassador tried to commit suicide."

Kristen stared at him. "That doesn't make sense. What pushed Charles to that? Something to do with Danny?"

"You tell me," Matthew suggested. He handed her the official version of the incident.

Kristen opened the file, read the top line and looked daggers at Matthew Jeffers. "Whoa. Party foul, Uncle Matt. This is one of Neil Davidson's patients."

"He knows you're reading it," Jeffers answered.

Kristen sat back and turned the page. It was a computer printout, in a large font. She was silent for several long minutes while she read it, then handed it back to Jeffers. "Freaky," she told him.

"And still unexplained. Two months of therapy and even he doesn't remember what happened. He's calm and confused."

"Then it's deep and it's painful." Kristen shook her head. "It's going to take time."

"We are almost out of time."

"Politics again?"

"It's always politics," Matthew nodded. "You've read the report, give me your opinion."

"Give me yours. According to that, you had Charles in observation after Danny's death, did he learn to manage it?"

"Does anyone learn to handle a child's death? At the time, I felt he had learned to accept it." Matthew shrugged. "I don't know, Kris. I don't know if that incident is even connected. That's why I want you in on this."

Kristen shook her head. "It's not my case."

"And if it was your case?"

Kristen shook her head again. "No way, Matt. I'm not going to second-guess Neil Davidson. I'm a child psychologist, Neil is much more capable of handling Charles than I would ever be. I don't want to get involved."

"What if I told you that Neil Davidson needs your help on this one?"

"I'd say, 'Bullshit'. Neil Davidson has never needed my help on any case."

"This is different. You know Denning, you worked with his son for almost four months. Even Neil admitted that you might be used for an emotional catalyst."

"Right. And I'm sure Neil was just as enthusiastic as hell about the idea. Sell me another story, even I don't go in for that much fantasy."

"He needs you, Kristen."

"You're out of your mind," Kristen decided and stood. "Forget it, Dr. Jeffers. I tried, once, and damn near got my heart broken in the bargain. Neil is a brilliant man, but his mind is closed. I can't reach him and I don't particularly trust him."

"Okay then, Charles Denning needs you."

Kristen groaned. "Oh, good, Matt. Go for the guilt trip! Even if I could help Charles, Neil will never let me try any of my usual therapy. He'll point out, very correctly, that my expertise is with children, not adults, and block me at every turn."

"So be subtle! Tell him you want the benefit of his expertise and get around him that way! You're not inflexible, Kristen and you do have some manipulative power over Neil. Use it!"

"Give me a break!"

"No," Matthew Jeffers said flatly. "I want you to try and work with Neil on this case, using every ounce of talent you have, emotional and professional. It's a personal favor, Kristen. Please. If it doesn't work out, it doesn't."

"I don't do personal favors any longer, Matt, I have enough on my plate."

Matthew Jeffers shook his head. "A simple consultation, then. Nothing more. In many ways, I could be doing you a favor with this."

"I somehow doubt that," Kristen answered, but sat back down.

"Good girl! Two days. Give it your best shot and I'll be satisfied. After you meet with Denning and if you convince Neil to let you continue as his consultant, I'll show you another reason why you want to work with this."

"Oh, goody. I get a lollipop if I'm good?" Kristen smiled weakly.

"Better than a lollipop. I promise you." He leaned back in his chair, putting his cane across his knees. "Talk to me," he suggested.

Kristen looked at him suspiciously. "About what?"

"You?" Jeffers suggested.

Kristen leaned over and tapped the boldly printed pages of the file he had given her to read. "I'd say you know all there is to know about me."

Matthew looked uncomfortable. "I honestly didn't know, Kristen, I was advised just recently. Do you want to talk about it?"

"Nope," Kristen answered. "It's not the beat all and end all of my life and I have good people at home helping me with any issues that might arise."

He nodded with resignation. "Okay, we table that. Give me your impressions of everyone you've met here."

"Why?"

"I like to see people from your perspective. Start with Denise Parker."

Kristen thought about it, remembering the woman she had met in the medical wing. "I like her. She's quick, she smiles easily and if I ever needed surgery, I'd like to have her for my physician. She reminds me of Pop, a little. Honest and dedicated. Since she's working for you, I shall assume that she is brilliant with a scalpel, as well as being physically stunning enough to give every woman she meets an inferiority complex."

Matthew nodded. "She is. What did you think of Raymond Hayes? You met him in the psych lab."

Kristen frowned, thinking of the man who had said so little during the brief introduction. "I couldn't tell much, except that he did not want me here."

"He's Charles Denning's chief aide," Matthew offered.

"And he knows you want me to work with his boss?"

"He might."

"That explains that."

"What else?"

"I don't know. The man has secrets, but that should be natural, simply because he's chief aide to an Ambassador. I'd say he's a good schemer, like you and gets what he wants, but probably the hard way. He doesn't trust too many people, including this institute, and he thinks too much."

Matthew looked interested. "Would you trust him?"

"As what? In my line of work, I rarely need an Ambassador's aide."

"Point taken. What was your opinion of Lloyd Simmons?"

"Is that his name, Lloyd? He introduced himself as L.R. and never gave me a first name. Does he have a nickname, as well?"

"No."

"Hmm." Kristen's response was careful. "I like him, I'd trust him with my life, if that means anything, he has a good sense of humor, a well-controlled sense of the ridiculous, a gentle heart, a sweet nature and he's very sensual, but he keeps that under control as well. As a guess, I'd say he is basically honest, but breaks the rules when it suits his purpose, or he can justify it to his conscience."

"That's a rather in-depth analysis," Matthew looked at her curiously.

"I've seen him in action in Claren and I spent several hours with him on the plane and driving here," Kristen pointed out.

"You forgot to mention that he's loyal."

Kristen shrugged. "Everyone is loyal to you, you bring out the subservient in people. If I could figure out how, maybe I could get off the hook and go on with my own life."

"Then you'd never have to leave Claren, would you?"

"Don't start picking on me, Matt. Mr. Simmons gave me my return ticket. I insisted on it before I'd get on the plane. He didn't ask why. By the way, thanks for the first class."

"You're welcome." Matthew pushed a button on his intercom. "Tell Dr. Davidson we're ready for him." He clicked off the box and looked expectantly at Kristen. "Are you ready to face Neil?"

"No. I've never been ready to face Neil."

Matthew Jeffers stood up. "You can handle him."

"Ah huh." Kristen also stood. "Do you have any idea what you're setting me up for? Granted, we have some kind of perverse attraction for each other, but we mix like oil and water professionally and on a personal level..." Kristen gave a physical shudder.

Matthew put an arm around her shoulders and walked her to the door. "You can handle it," he repeated.

Kristen looked down at his legs when they reached the door. "You forgot to limp, Matt. The cane is only effective as an emotional catalyst when you lean on it heavily and force a limp."

Matthew squeezed her shoulder. "I'll remember that." He opened the door and glanced down the hall. "Oh, look. There's Neil, chomping at the bit, waiting for you."

Kristen looked at the tall dark form coming toward them. Tall, handsome, arrogant, never a public smile. Same old Neil. "Chomping, in any event," she sighed heavily.

Chapter 9

Ariel: ...Hell is empty and all the devils are here.

Kristen faced the angry look on Neil Davidson's face alone. She gave him a small, worried smile. "Hi. It's been a long time, Neil, how are you?"

"Busy and very pressed for time," he answered. "You are not here on a social visit, Kristen, so I'll make my position clear from the onset. Charles Denning is my patient and I am hardly enthused about your interference. I only agreed to this because Matthew Jeffers has given me full jurisdiction over you during your stay here. The moment I feel that you are doing my patient more harm than good, you will be dismissed. Is that clear?"

"Be of good cheer, Neil, they probably haven't even finished fluoroscoping my suitcase, yet. If you like, I'll simply pop back into Matt's office, say goodbye and leave. I am more than aware that your credentials far exceed mine. I'm not even sure why Matthew Jeffers showed me the file. I thought I was coming just to see an emotionally disturbed teenager."

"Offhand, I'd say it was a case of emotional nepotism, or your basic Oedipus. Your reasons for jumping, every time he calls, are obvious. He's a displaced father figure."

"My, my! Just listen to the fancy Beverly Hills psychiatrist talk them educated words! I do hope that before I leave, you will allow this little hayseed psychologist from Colorado to take notes, I shore would like to impress the folks back home on the farm."

"If you would read something other than fairy tales to your clients, I'm sure you would learn some of those fancy words all by yourself, Doctor Michaels."

"Ooh, a hit!" Kristen put a hand over her heart.

Neil shook his head. "As I said, I'm a bit pressed for time, Kristen, shall we try to work together on some kind of professional level?"

Kristen grinned up at him. "I'll try anything, once."

"So I recall," Neil grudgingly returned the smile, taking Kristen's arm so she could keep up with him. "Have you read the report on the shooting?

"Yes."

"Do you have an opinion?"

"My ego is no less swollen than yours, Dr. Davidson, I have an opinion on everything. In this case, however, I'd rather keep it to myself. I don't have enough facts." She stopped walking and looked up at him. "Listen, Neil. This thing is way over my head, I know it, you know it. I don't believe I can help you, Matt, or Charles Denning. My expertise is with Minishrinks, not with manic-depressive adults. I'm a lightweight here."

Neil's voice softened. "Your expertise, as you call it, is why Dr. Jeffers felt you might be useful in this case. First, however, I would like to watch a confrontation between you and my patient."

They stopped outside a door. "As you read in the report, the Ambassador has been with us now for a little over two months, both as a medical and psychiatric patient. He is lucid, in complete, if forced, control of his emotions and, even under hypnosis or drugs, cannot recall why he fired those shots into his television, or why he tried to take his own life." Neil looked at her sternly. "Here is the procedure I want you to follow. I will take you into his room, re-introduce the two of you, linger for a moment, then leave. If the Ambassador shows, in any way, that he does not want you here, you will leave with me, at my simple suggestion. Agreed?"

"You mean you might actually leave me alone with him?" Kristen asked incredulously, "without staying to watch me screw up?"

Neil took her arm angrily. "Don't push me, Kristi, your being here was not my idea. The room is constantly monitored, every movement you and the Ambassador make will be recorded. In essence, I will be there to watch you screw up."

"Big brother will be watching."

"Yes. In this instance, Big Brother can include our security chief, the Head of medical and Dr. Jeffers. If you wish to stay, I suggest you try to be just a little conventional, he does have some ethics that even you can't overcome."

Kristen peeled his fingers off her arm. "Do you patronize everyone, Neil, or just me? I don't know how to be conventional. When I see a patient for the first time, I play it by ear and never think about it. I just use my own, clumsy style. You've had Denning under observation for more than two months. If you honestly think I can harm him, don't let me see him. If you don't think I can harm him, don't tie my hands."

Neil shook his head. "I don't think you can affect him one way or another," he sighed lightly. "I'm sorry. We're all under a lot of pressure around here, I don't mean to take it out on you."

"Why change the habit of a lifetime?" Kristen asked sarcastically.

Neil looked at her sharply, then let it go. "Do it your way, we'll see how it works, then go from there. After I leave, you'll have about twenty minutes alone with him, then I'll send in someone to take him to his physical therapy. I'd appreciate it if you joined me in my office afterwards, at that time we'll discuss whether or not you can be effective as a consultant."

"Sounds fair."

Neil stared at her for a long moment, started to say something else, thought better of it, then nodded brusquely, knocked and opened the door to Ambassador Denning's suite.

The room was set up as conventional living room with sofas, chairs, a stereo, several bookcases loaded with current fiction and magazines and, oddly, a small wet bar. The floor was carpeted with gentle beige, the walls were painted a light, serene blue.

Ambassador Denning stood politely as Kristen and Neil entered, putting down the National Geographic he had been reading. He was a tall, thin man, in his late fifties, with warm brown hair graying heavily throughout. He was dressed casually in dark blue twill pants and a soft pullover golf shirt with one blue stripe across the chest. His smile when they entered was mild and vaguely embarrassed.

Neil began the introductions. "Ambassador, do you remember Dr. Kristen Michaels?"

The overhead light flickered for several seconds, demanding the attention of all three. Kristen opened her mouth as if to say something, then closed it abruptly, looking at Neil, obviously thinking better of it.

Ambassador Denning's face broke into a quick smile and he laughed lightly, his eyes openly teasing as he looked at Kristen. "You're no longer talking to Jory?" he asked softly.

Kristen returned the smile and rolled her eyes briefly toward Neil. "Not with the MP's around," she answered. "I came to visit, Charles, not to be committed for an extended stay."

"Good thinking," Charles Denning agreed. "You wouldn't believe the lack of stimulating conversation at dinner time." He tilted his head slightly. "How are you, Kris?"

"Quite well, all considering. I understand that you, however, are going about murdering innocent little television sets for sport. Are you on a private vendetta toward commercial programming, or can anyone join the fight?"

The Ambassador paled perceptively and Neil inwardly cringed. He'd been right all along. Kristen was impossible. This was one hell of an approach. No leading calmly to the subject, no gentle bedside manner, just straight for the throat, bypassing all standard procedures.

The Ambassador bit his lip and looked sadly at Kristen. "I wish I knew what I had been shooting at, Kris. Not knowing may really drive me insane. Have you come here to help me find out?"

"Nope. I came to California to see a teenage patient that's staying here," Kristen answered. "For now, I am just here as a friend."

The Ambassador's eyes filled with tears. "Danny's dead, Kris. He was only sixteen."

"I know. He was a terrific kid, Charles, a son anyone would envy. I am very sorry."

Denning took several deep breaths, his face became composed, his eyes hastily retracted the tears that had formed. "If I remember correctly, your usual first step in therapy was a hug."

Neil was astonished, but professionally, could have cheered out loud. This was the first conscious emotional response he had seen from the Ambassador since his arrival. Neil looked expectantly at Kristen Michaels. She had not made a move toward the patient, nor had she responded verbally to his obvious request. She was, in fact, studying Charles Denning unemotionally, her face was an expressionless mask. Neil's mind started yelling at her silently. Walk over to him, you stupid twit! Are you so damned under-educated that you can't take an obvious opening when it's offered to you? What the hell did you learn in school?

"As I said," Kristen responded quietly, "I am only here for a visit. I am not your therapist."

The room remained tense, then the Ambassador broke into an easy smile, walked over to Kristen, touched her face gently and re-iterated the offer. "Then may I hug you, Kris, as my friend in need?"

"Are you physically up to it?" Kristen smiled.

Charles Denning responded by picking her up off the floor in an enthusiastic hug, then setting her down gently. He winked at her, totally disregarding the presence of Neil Davidson. "Lady, I'm up to anything you might have in mind."

"Hmm." Kristen nodded. "I see the bullet wound left your ego intact."

"Well," Neil broke in stiffly. "I guess the two of you have a great deal to catch up on. I'll leave you now."

Kristen's eyes twinkled from behind her glasses as she took in Neil's not too subtle, knowing expression. "Are you sure it's safe, Dr. Davidson? Does Charles have occasional fits of uncontrolled violence, or anything?"

Neil glared at her. Was there no end to the woman's stupidity? Where the hell was she coming from? "Not since he's been here," Neil answered curtly. Evidently he'd have to teach Kristen her own profession before he could even consider using her as an emotional catalyst for Denning.

Charles Denning put one arm around Kristen's shoulders, then held up his other hand in a three fingered boy scout salute. "I promise not to shoot any defenseless appliances while entertaining company, Dr. Davidson," he promised with a grin.

"Good," Neil responded, returning the smile carefully. Well, the patient's reaction was healthy, it was the first semi-joke the man had made since his arrival. Neil looked at his watch. "Your physical therapy session is in twenty minutes, Ambassador. Dr. Michaels, would you stop by my office at that time? We do follow certain routines here."

"Certainly, Dr. Davidson," Kristen answered.

Neil left the room feeling less than satisfied, then paused at the partly open door to hear the beginning of the "private" conversation between the two.

"Evidently, Dr. Davidson wishes to discuss my case with you in private," Denning was saying. "I'm afraid the man does not believe I am altogether a well man."

"Sounds like a reasonable hypothesis to me," Kristen answered. "If you were a well man, you'd remember why you blasted your boob tube. Lighten up on the man, Charles, he has your interests at heart."

"So you think I'm crazy, too," Denning responded heavily.

"Hell, Charles, you can't go by my opinion, I think everybody's crazy. It goes with the profession."

Neil closed the door fully, suppressing yet another groan. As he walked to his office, he wasn't sure whether he should thank Kristen for defending his position, or strangle her on general principle, but he knew positively that he wished she had stayed in Colorado. Her 'therapy', if you could call it that, was foolhardy, unprofessional and more than likely very dangerous.

When he reached his office, he immediately switched on the monitor to watch the rest of the interview. During it all Charles Denning managed to keep a hand on Kristen's shoulder, her face or her hand. He never quit touching her, smiled gently at her the entire time, spoke to her like a cherished friend or lover. For the entire fifteen minutes, Neil felt more and more antagonistic toward Kristen Michaels. Damn Matthew Jeffers!

When Kristen finally arrived at his office, Neil kept his temper in check for less than two minutes. "You're right," he gave her a tight smile, "you are clumsy."

Kristen nodded in agreement. "And...?"

"And, you verge on being inept, unprofessional..."

"Do go on, I simply live for your constructive criticism." She sat down across from him.

"You told Denning you would see him after physical therapy."

"We could both use the fresh air, I thought we'd walk around the grounds. Is that a problem?"

"No." Neil frowned at her. "Have you and Denning been lovers?"

"Nope." Kristen put her elbow on the desk, her chin in her hand and watched him.

"I am not asking out of any perverse kind of jealousy, Kristen, I want the information professionally. A relationship of that nature might be useful to know when I am dealing with my patient."

"I see," Kristen shrugged. "Again, sorry, no. However unbelievable you may find it, Dr. Davidson, I do have a few professional standards. I do not sleep with either my patients or the parents of my patients."

"Who do you sleep with?" Neil asked.

"When I find the time, the District Attorney of Claren," Kristen told him. "According to all the latest psychological studies, masturbation is not considered mentally unhealthy, but I happen to find it very lonely." She looked at him curiously. "So! Should I catch the next plane home?"

Neil viciously rubbed the back of his neck and looked uncomfortable. "What excuse would I give Matthew Jeffers? You know as well as I do that you did extremely well with Denning. He openly discussed and admitted the shooting with you, a subject he has habitually avoided with me and, most importantly, he specifically asked for your help. During the entire time he has been here, he has categorically denied that he needed any help from any psychiatrist. You are clumsy, but you do get results."

"You still don't need me. So far, I've only agitated your patient. During this interview, I've supplied a catalyst, you can take it from here. I've opened the wound concerning his son, you can bandage it, or probe for the infection and stitch it up. As for the shooting... I'll talk with him about it again after his physical therapy session, but I don't think any amount of discussion with me is going to bring it out. It's too deep. I don't, as you well know, use any hypnosis or drugs in any of my therapy, nor do I work with troubled adults, except in reference to their children."

Neil looked at her steadily. "Do you want to stay?"

"No," Kristen said flatly. "I have my own patients, Neil. I have no need to horn in on yours. And, I have a class to teach on Tuesday."

"I see. You called me an MP in there, forcing the Ambassador to look upon me as the enemy. Why?"

Kristen grinned. "That was a joke. It meant you were my enemy, not his. MP stands for 'Master Psychiatrist'. Charles and I used to kid about it. When I was working with his son and I started talking to Jory... what I mean is, when Charles kidded me about some of the things I used in therapy with my kids... anyway, he used to tease me about how if the psychiatric world knew about what I..."

"I get the picture," Neil took her off the hook. "I should have known it was something like that. You never change, do you, Kristen?"

"So far, I haven't been able to convince myself that I'd be gaining more than I'm losing," she answered.

Neil nodded. "Let me see your glasses."

Kristen bit her lower lip, then took them off and handed them to him.

Neil studied the lenses between his fingers. "Amophic lens?"

"Yes."

"How bad?"

Kristen looked at the blur that was, only moments before, Neil Davidson. "My depth perception and horizontal vision went to hell about a year ago, but I can read with ultra magnification and I can still make out the expressions on my patient's faces. It's escalating pretty quickly now. Hepler's prognosis gives me less than a month of limited tunnel vision, maybe up to a year of being able to distinguish general light from dark... then nothing."

"A year," Neil repeated.

"Actually, that's the more optimistic prognosis. The other side is that I could wake up tomorrow morning with nothing." She smiled weakly. "I've been learning Braille, but even with limited tunnel vision, I tend to cheat."

Neil frowned. "Any signs of additional complications?"

"No. No neurological deterioration, just straight blindness. Despite the cheery news, I didn't feel a celebration was in order."

"Have you checked into guide dogs? I have a friend at the National Center for the Blind, he could..."

"Too many of my patients are allergic to dogs," Kristen stopped him. "I've been all over this with Hepler, Neil, I'm not looking for a second opinion. Will you please quit playing games and give me back the glasses? I feel like I'm talking to a wisp of flesh colored air."

"You've been talking to things you can't see for years, Kristen, that shouldn't bother you in the least," Neil answered calmly. He handed her back the glasses. "You haven't accepted it yet, have you?"

Kristen glared at the glasses with contempt. "Publicly, I'm a rock. Privately, I cry myself to sleep a lot, throw temper tantrums and swear loudly at the Almighty for letting this lousy thing happen to sweet little me, when there are so many assholes out there who deserve it much more than I."

"Have you started smoking again?"

"Again, not publicly and only since Pop died. A lousy crutch, I know, but it's been a bad year."

Neil stood, walked around the desk and kneeled in front of her, lifting her chin in his hand. "Why didn't you call me, Kristi?"

She looked up at him, her eyes trying to focus, then gave up and put on the glasses. "For the simple reason that you would have been warm and wonderful and practical and you would have tried to force me into accepting the reality of my blindness. Remember me? I'm the Pollyanna that believes in fairy tales and miracles. I won't accept the fact that I am blind until I can no longer distinguish light from dark. Even then, I'll probably have a credibility gap and think the lights of the world are simply on the fritz, or that Jory is just having an emotional breakdown."

Neil lightly stroked her cheek. "Ah, Kristi. Do you really think I'm that insensitive? Granted, I think people should face reality, but I'm not such a total bastard that I can't be there for you when you need a shoulder to cry on, or someone to help you swear against God!"

Kristen pulled her face away from him. "Get off it, Neil. If you think I'm going to apologize for not calling you, you have a long wait. We've been apart too damned long for me to start calling you whenever I get depressed! I do not need or want your professional assistance."

The phone on Neil's desk gave a loud shrill, Neil jumped up to answer it. "What!" he yelled into the receiver. "Yes, Dr. Jeffers, I watched the session. Yes, it can be considered positive. I'm taking Dr. Michaels out for a light dinner tonight, we'll discuss it more fully at that time... Tomorrow at nine. We'll both be there... I'll give her the message... Yes, I'll tell her."

"What message?" Kristen asked, as he hung up the phone.

"One, that he thinks you're brilliant, two, that he has set up one of the suites on the second floor for your use while you're with us, your luggage has been taken there. We have an appointment in his office, tomorrow at nine, he thinks your input might be useful in dealing with Denning's minishrink."

"Denning's what?" Kristen straightened.

"You're going blind, Kristen, not deaf," Neil answered tersely.

"Denning has a minishrink? What category?"

"Category three. A classic imaginary friend."

"'Invisible, not imaginary'," Kristen automatically corrected him. "Good God! Why didn't you tell me?"

"Mostly, because I hoped you would screw up totally with your initial interview and Matthew Jeffers would agree with me that you are a liability, not an asset."

"Oh. Minishrink or no minishrink, tell me to leave, Neil and I'll leave," Kristen told him. "Denning is your patient."

"And what would I tell Jeffers?"

"That you can't emotionally handle my being here," Kristen suggested. "He'd never believe that you think I'm a threat to you on a professional level."

Neil shook his head at her. "You're still a bitch, Kristen Michaels."

"And you're still an unimaginative bastard," she countered.

Neil pulled Kristen to her feet and circled his arms around her. "Am I?" He kissed her lightly on the lips, pulling her tightly to him. "God, I've missed you, Kristi. Are you sleeping in my bed tonight?" he asked quietly as he kissed her beneath her ear.

"Oh, damn," Kristen closed her eyes and concentrated on steadying her breathing. "You know, there is something really sick about our relationship, Dr. Davidson. We have absolutely nothing in common, we fight like cats and dogs, yet whenever we are within twenty miles of each other, we end up in the same bed."

"We're good together, Love, we always have been," Neil told her. "Some things never change. If you like, we can debate love-hate relationships over dinner."

"I'd rather discuss the Denning case."

"I'm sure you would. Psychological truths about yourself are always hard to face."

"Which truth is that?"

"That you're attracted to me because I represent reality and reality is something you have never been able to distinguish very well and something you sub-consciously want."

"Interesting. If your diagnosis is true, what explains your attraction to me?"

"Simply, you represent fantasy, something I have never been able to accept."

"Ah. And something you sub-consciously want?" Kristen asked.

"I wouldn't go that far," Neil answered.

"You never would," Kristen sighed.

Chapter 10

Prospero: My charms crack not, my spirits obey...

Denise Parker pulled the chart next to the EKG machine and studied Charles Denning on the treadmill. The pace was good, his pulse was slightly elevated, but strong. When he looked at her, he grinned.

"Hey, Doc, how'm I doing?"

"Looks good, Ambassador."

He nodded. "I feel good."

"Well, let's not push it," Denise suggested, walking over and turning down the machine. "Cool it down, for a few minutes, then I want to listen."

"You're the Doctor." Denning slowed his pace with the machine, took it down to a slow walk over several minutes, then jumped off the treadmill, smiling. He took a small towel from an attendant, then boosted himself up to the examining table, wiping the sweat from his face.

Denise monitored his pulse, respiration and blood pressure, then took the stethoscope out of her ears and patted him lightly on his chest. "I am one hell of a physician, you're almost ready for a ten K." She examined the scar on his chest. "You heal pretty, too." She pulled out the usual rubber hammer. "Let's see if you have any reflexes left."

"Let me take you out dancing, I'll show you a few," Charles suggested.

Denise looked at him suspiciously, while she tapped under his knee. "Your mood seems to have improved since this morning."

"A friend came to see me. It was a nice visit."

"A lady friend?"

"Yes. Kristen Michaels. Actually, Dr. Kristen Michaels. She's a child psychologist. She treated my son. A terrific lady."

Denise nodded. "I just met her a couple of hours ago. She seems nice. Dr. Jeffers speaks very highly of her."

Charles nodded. "A very smart lady. She's much prettier without those awful glasses. She never used to wear them. She's still pretty, more than that, she has a heart of pure gold. My son fell in love with her during his therapy."

"Did he?"

"Yup, a heavy crush, he was only thirteen, it's probably typical with kids that age. Didn't worry her, though. Do you know what she did?"

Denise shook her head and looked at him curiously. "What?"

"She allowed it. She didn't encourage him, but she didn't make him feel like an idiot, either. She never embarrassed him, never pushed him away. She encouraged him to help her out with some of her groups of little children, made him feel needed and important. She even let him help teach the little ones to ski. He loved the responsibility. The crush gradually faded away, but she left his ego without a bruise, better than it had ever been."

Denise looked interested. "How did she get the crush to 'fade away'?"

Charles shook his head. "I don't know. He talked to me about it later, but never exactly explained it. I guess he just grew up. It just changed from a boy's crush to a young man's respect and friendship for a special woman. He never forgot her." He smiled lightly.

"Hmm." Denise finished her examination and wrote the details on his chart. "I think you should try about twenty minutes of aerobics in the pool today, Ambassador."

"Alright." Charles Denning looked at her seriously. "How 'fit' am I?"

"As a fiddle," Denise said absently, still writing on the chart.

"Good. With your medical release, I'm halfway there. The State Department will be relieved. I need to get back to work."

"That wasn't a release," Denise frowned, realizing her mistake. "I'd prefer to observe you for a few more weeks, Ambassador."

Denning shook his head. "It's a luxury this country can't afford. Maybe after the conference. Once Dr. Jeffers releases me, its back to the grind."

Chapter 11

Ariel: My master through his art foresees the danger that you, his friend, are in and sends me forth - for else his project dies...

Charles Denning walked with Kristen along the expansive lawn at PSR, enjoying the warm sun and overly landscaped grounds.

Charles signed contentedly. "It's nice to get away from the cameras and microphones," he told Kristen. "That place," he nodded at the main building off to the right, "is like living in a fish bowl. Everything you say, do, think and feel is recorded and processed."

"I guess it's the price you pay when you work for the government," Kristen nodded.

"Unfortunately, they don't mention all the drawbacks when you're appointed," Charles answered.

"You can always quit," Kristen looked at him.

"And do what? I'm fifty-eight years old, Kris. I've represented power and peace for four administrations. The only thing that's left is the talk circuit and writing my memoirs. No one is interested in South America any longer, the spotlight is on the Middle East. I'd never get a booking or a publisher."

"You could teach."

"Bor-ing."

"Not always," Kristen smiled.

They walked quietly for several minutes, Charles stopped abruptly. "Ah ha! An actual sign of spring."

"Where?"

"Over by the ice plant. A butterfly. Painted lady, I think, copper and blue with Gossamer wings."

"Very poetic, maybe you would make a good writer, almost no one uses the word 'gossamer' anymore." Kristen concentrated toward where he was pointing. She finally smiled. "I see it. Mostly."

Charles looked lightly abashed. "How bad are your eyes, Kristen?"

"Terminal," Kristen answered calmly. "Very soon they'll be only ornamental, not functional. I'm going blind. A rather insidious form of RP."

"Oh, God, I'm sorry. Anything I can do to help?"

Kristen smiled. "Yes. Continue to point out anything that looks like spring and hold my arm tightly to protect me from gopher holes. I also appreciate the descriptions, sometimes I can only make out the movement and color, not the details."

"I'll take care of you," he told her. "Count on it." They started walking again., he decided to change the subject "How's that teenage patient of yours?"

"Like all kids, she just needs someone to listen."

"I know you'll do great with her."

"I hope you're right," she answered. "Talk to me, Charles. Tell me about Danny. Who killed him?"

Charles Denning held her arm a little tighter. "I don't know the actual names. I don't think anyone does. I'm fairly certain the three men that were convicted for it were only convenient scapegoats the government found to placate the State Department."

"Weren't there any witnesses?"

"Oh, sure. They pulled him out of the embassy school in broad daylight. There were lots of witnesses. Unfortunately, not one witness could remember what they looked like. The terrorist groups in that part of the world have a lot of power and exert a lot of fear over the public. Everyone keeps quiet. Danny was missing for two hours before I even knew they had him."

"What were their demands?"

"The demands were meaningless. They never had any intention of releasing him. It was a power play to test the loyalty of the peasants and to show how they were not affected by the puppet government and local laws." Charles shook his head. "They just wanted our government out of there. We've been screwing up their drug markets and they wanted to retaliate."

"In other words, you couldn't do a thing to save him."

"Not a thing. They had him for six weeks. The autopsy report was sixteen pages long. Do you want to know what they finally did to him, Kris?"

"Do you want to tell me?"

"No, I don't. You don't need my nightmares. Suffice it to say his body was a mess. They were very imaginative. I was told the injuries were post-mortem."

"But you didn't believe them," Kristen guessed.

"No. Not really."

"Okay. Tell me what you did, afterward."

"I fell apart," Charles answered honestly. "We had a funeral, I was strong and in control the whole time. It was quite a media event, lots of speeches, lots of public outcry. Thousands of people came to mourn, even the embassy police who failed to protect him. After that, I'm told I took a gun, went to the embassy range and fired every bullet I could find at a target. Then they put me under observation."

"You said you were 'told' that. Is that what you remember doing?"

Charles shook his head. "No. I remember dressing for the funeral, trying to decide what shirt to wear. I had trouble with my tie and I broke a shoelace. Then I was there, shaking a lot of hands and expressing my thanks to everyone. Then I remember going back to the embassy, washing my hands, taking my gun from the cabinet and shooting several hundred bastards who looked like everyone who was at the funeral." He sighed. "They told me I wanted to kill myself."

"Who told you?"

"The MP's who were 'observing' me. Dr. Jeffers, for one."

Kristen frowned. "Did you want to kill yourself, Charles?"

"Naw. There wouldn't have been a point to it. I think I was already dead."

"And after the shrinks were finished?"

"I knew I was alive and alone."

Kristen squeezed his arm in sympathy. "Did it get any better?"

Charles thought about it. "I think so. Peace has been breaking out all over South America, I've about convinced myself that Danny's death was a part of that. We've made great progress in the last year."

They stopped walking. "What do you remember about the day you shot your television set?"

Charles shook his head. "Nothing."

"Nothing at all?"

He shook his head. "No." He thought about it. "I remember brushing my teeth," he smiled. "Does that help?"

"It's a start. Do you remember if you had any plans for the day?"

"I was supposed to meet Luis Arturo and a few others from the Sudeste Block to discuss some demands... the usual thing."

"Right, usual," Kristen smiled. She quickly held up a hand. "Don't try, Charles, politics scare me. Okay. You remember that you had a dinner engagement."

"No, not specifically. Everything's a blank. Raymond reminded me of it after I got here. Apparently, by not attending the dinner, I created a bit of a diplomatic problem. Some of our government wheels have been clogged."

"This Raymond person sounds like a bit of a guilt monger."

Charles laughed. "Raymond Hayes is my aide. That's the political equivalent of a mother hen. He's supposed to make me feel guilty when I miss a meeting."

"How long has he been with you?"

"Ever since Danny's death. My previous aide retired, he loved Danny, couldn't handle the stress. Raymond is good at his job, but I haven't been able to establish much of a rapport with him. It takes time, I guess."

"Oh. What do you remember, on your own, without any help from Raymond or the MPs?"

Charles shook his head. "Like I said. I remember brushing my teeth. I don't remember getting dressed. I'm pretty sure I didn't get dressed." He looked at Kristen curiously. "Why didn't I get dressed?"

"I don't know, you tell me."

Charles looked confused. "I brushed my teeth. I opened the front door..."

Kristen looked at him with unfeigned interest. "Why did you open the front door?"

"Because someone rang the bell. The mailman." He frowned. "No. Not the mailman. He was wearing brown. UPS, maybe. There was a package." He shook his head again. "Maybe it was a letter. I don't know."

"Don't force it," Kristen suggested. "What do you remember after that?"

"I said 'thank you,' and closed the door."

"What then?"

Charles was silent for several long moments, then ran his fingers through his hair in agitation. "It's blank, Kristen. I honestly don't know. I remember standing there, holding the thing... then nothing. I don't even know if I opened it."

Kristen frowned. The part about the mailman was not in the file or notes of Neil Davidson, it bothered her.

"Tell me about Claren," Charles said in a more energetic voice. "I haven't been there in years. Has that District Attorney of yours convinced you to get married, yet?"

"No, I'm too old to change my ways," Kristen told him, smiling. "Marriage would only complicate my life. He needs someone who is craving a white picket fence and ten children."

"You never wanted any kids, did you?"

"Nope. I'd probably screw them up totally," Kristen confessed. "Parenting is way beyond my skills. The day to day stuff is too hard."

"Hurts when you have them, hurts worse when they're gone," Charles nodded. "Maybe it's better never to have them."

"Do you believe that?" Kristen looked interested.

"No," Charles shook his head. "But it sounds good. A year, or sixteen years, Danny was the best thing that ever happened to me. I just miss him. I miss him a lot." He put his arm around Kristen's shoulders and they walked back toward the institute.

Chapter 12

Prospero: My brave spirit! Who was so firm, so constant, that this coil would not infect his reason?

Ariel: Not a soul but felt a fever of the mad and played some tricks of desperation...

Neil finished ordering dinner for the two of them, waited for the waiter to leave, then looked at Kristen expectantly. "What did you and the Ambassador discuss on your walk?"

"The good, the bad, the ugly and the unknown," Kristen sipped her vodka gimlet. "In that order."

Neil shook his head lightly. "Okay, Dr. Michaels. The 'unknown', I can guess, I've been dealing with it for two months. What was the 'good'?"

"A nice spring day and a butterfly, a painted lady."

"The 'bad'?"

"Danny's death."

"The 'ugly'?"

"Danny's autopsy."

"Ouch," Neil grimaced. "I read it myself. Even I don't need that much reality."

Kristen shook her head. "I'm more worried about the fantasy, it's caused. Charles doesn't believe the injuries were post-mortem, which he was apparently told, but has nightmares imagining what they did to his son per-mortem. By now, he's relived every bruise and multiplied every pain beyond actual reality. That's a hell of a monster in anyone's closet."

"Very true."

"How detailed was the autopsy? What I mean is, did the doctors put it into layman's terms, or keep it in the original Greek that is known only to specialists, eggheads and other gods?"

"Parts of it were over my head," Neil admitted, "and I keep up on my journals. The kid might have been tortured peri-mortem the last two days, his injuries were horrific, but I doubt it. There were no signs of even minor healing. Did you want me to go over it with you, or something?"

"Hell no! I just wondered who went over it with Charles," Kristen answered, "and why he came to the conclusion he was alive when tortured."

"They caught the guys who did it, the details and speculations probably came out in the trial," Neil suggested.

"Hmm." A headache was forming, Kristen took off her glasses and rubbed the area between her eyes.

Neil took her hand. "It's too dark to see anything in here Kristen, why don't you give your eyes a rest?"

Kristen looked at him almost angrily. "Leave it alone, Neil."

"Sooner or later..."

"Later, then," Kristen stopped him flatly. She squeezed his hand. "Sorry. I need to handle this on my own, Neil." She put her glasses back on.

Neil was quiet for several moments, then nodded stiffly, releasing her hand as their salads were served. "When you're ready, we'll talk about it."

"Pop used to say that, we never did discuss it," Kristen gave him a small smile.

"You didn't call me during that crisis, either," Neil retorted bitterly.

"I had a lot of friends around me and a great deal of help. Pop died quietly in his sleep, Neil, my grief was minimal and natural. Occasionally I miss him, that's all." She started eating her salad.

The waiter came with the wine Neil had ordered, poured the glasses, left the bottle and took Kristen's unfinished gimlet with him.

"Have you noticed," Neil sipped his wine, "they never wait for you to taste it any more? I think they're confused as to who gets to judge it, the woman or the man."

"They could ask," Kristen pointed out, "then there would be no confusion."

"Ah. But which of us would they ask?" Neil retorted wisely. "Equality has destroyed the fine art of dining."

"I was completely unaware of the terrible side-effects that have been created," Kristen answered. "Enough small talk. Tell me about Denning's minishrink."

"I'd rather not distort any response you might make tomorrow," Neil answered.

"Okay. Tell me about the therapy you've been using on him."

Neil shrugged. "So far, it's been pretty stagnant. The first month was spent almost entirely in the medical wing, my sessions with him were naturally short."

"How extensive were his injuries?"

"Very. He's lucky to be alive. Fortune would have it that Denise Parker was on call that night. She's brilliant with a knife and she stays ahead of her colleagues in surgical techniques so he had the very best. I have the medical journals detailing the procedure at the house, you're welcome to read it."

"You're the psychiatrist with the MD after his name, Neil, I'm only a lowly psychologist, remember? Surgical journals are way over my head."

"I'll explain them to you," Neil offered.

"No thanks, just give me the highlights. Where was his main injury?"

"Heart," Neil answered. "One shot."

Kristen frowned. "No head wounds? He went straight for the heart?"

"Yes."

"Huh. A rather large psychological difference. If you really want to die, you blow your brains out, it's much more effective. A heart wound is more of a statement than a suicide attempt."

"No way of knowing," Neil told her. "So far, I've found nothing significant about where he shot himself, much less why."

"Oh. Let's get back to your therapy, then. What's the major block?"

"The actual shooting. If I had some idea as to why the Ambassador shot himself, I might be able to affect a cure more rapidly. Unfortunately, he has blocked out the entire day completely and our security people have been unable to come up with anything that might have caused it."

Kristen frowned. "No blackmail or poison pen letters found at the scene?" she asked.

"Nothing."

"Any clue as to what was on the television? A documentary of hostage situations, or a movie about someone being tortured or killed by terrorists?"

"No," Neil looked at her curiously. "It was determined that the set was on a Santa Barbara station that was showing a popular exercise program. From your speculations, I gather you think this shooting has something to do with the Ambassador's son. His kidnapping, torture and death."

"I'm not speculating, I don't know enough about it. What do you think?"

"There might be a connection," Neil nodded slowly. "Let's try it on. What did you see the Ambassador's son about? You don't have to give me the confidential parts, just an overview."

Kristen shrugged. "Except for the actual therapy, Matt knows most of the details, so it hardly matters what I tell you, those files are available to you. Danny was suffering from post depression after his mother's death. He was eleven when she died, when he turned thirteen, he caught his father in bed with his personal secretary."

"Ouch. Was Danny going through a heavy puberty at the time?"

Kristen smiled. "You have the basic picture. It was pure textbook stuff."

"How did the Ambassador respond to his son's emotional response?"

"With a tremendous amount of guilt. It was the first affair he had had since his wife's death, the entire incident made him feel like dirt. Danny was all he had left, he thought he had betrayed a trust."

"Did you council the Ambassador, as well?"

"Only superficially. His real cure came from Danny. The kid went past 'forgiveness' and right into 'understanding'." She shook her head sadly. "Honest to God, Neil, that was some kid. It took four months, but by the end of the third, I was ready to keep him for myself. He even volunteered at the clinic for awhile. He turned from a sulky, belligerent teenager, into a gentle caring son. Charles lost a great deal when Danny was killed."

"Did you get emotionally involved?"

Kristen laughed. "Yes. I always get emotionally involved, Neil, that's my main charm and my most effective tool. You can deceive adults, you can't deceive kids. That's why I keep my practice in the child category."

Neil looked at her knowingly. "You allowed Danny to 'volunteer' at the clinic. That sounds familiar. Let me guess. Did the boy get a crush on his therapist?"

Kristen shrugged. "He got over it as soon as one of the little girls at the clinic put the shoe firmly on the other foot and got a crush on him. He was very sweet to her about it. The kid had great minishrink potential, for her and for his father."

"I see." The waiter brought their main course, Neil started digging into his Salmon. "In effect then," he decided, nodding with satisfaction at his meal, "Denning's response to you was simply caused by his attachment to his son. You are a reminder of what he has lost. The emotion is good, it opens him up for further therapy. For the most part, however, I would like to stay away from his fatherly grief. Later, we can explore any lingering guilt over Danny's death, but right now, we need to find the cause for the shooting and I don't believe that it has a valid connection."

"That could be a dangerous assumption," Kristen argued. "I read the report, Neil. After Danny's death, Charles also resorted to violence and he still doesn't fully remember that incident. Shooting hundreds of rounds at the embassy pistol range does not show a light, easily cured mania. The pressures of his job might have kept him from expressing his grief more deeply, but he didn't finish with it. The pathological association is there, it should be explored."

Neil waved away that theory with a flip of is fork. "I think it's a good idea to keep his emotions high, you could be used for that purpose."

"Ah huh." Kristen started eating. "You might change the colors in his room," she suggested. "Those blue shades are too calming, try a yellow or orange. They're more energetic."

"Good idea. The blues were chosen for medical healing. Off the record, Denise has released Denning. On the record, she is holding him as long as she can."

"She is? Why?"

"The State Department wants him for the upcoming peace talks with South America. That's in less than two weeks." He looked at Kristen, giving a sour frown. "That's the job of the PSR, Kristi. It's like working in a M.A.S.H. unit. We patch them up as quickly as possible, so they can go back to work without embarrassing the good old U.S. of A. In the past, I've been forced to release patients that could have used a good three years of therapy."

"Do you ever get them back?" Kristen asked curiously.

"Constantly. You're lucky. You can sit there and talk about a kid that you eventually became proud of, I stand around holding the revolving door open for my ex-patients until they are out of the media lime-light and I can effect a real cure. Usually, they come back with more problems than when they started."

84

"So why do you stay? Why did you give up your private practice?"

"Matthew Jeffers, for one, and the fact that I know anyone else would not do half the job that I can do," Neil answered. He looked at her sharply. "You didn't know I was working with Jeffers, did you?"

"Nope. For all I knew, you were still 'Psychiatrist to the Stars'." She gave a wry smile. "In a way, I guess you still are."

"Would you have come, if you knew I was here?"

"It's a moot point, I am here."

"Yes, you are." He put a hand to her cheek. "I've missed you." His eyes became softly sensual. "Let's go home. If you're a good girl, I'll show you my therapy tapes."

Kristen gave him a tiny smile. "What a romantic idea! Why is it that you never offer to show me your 'etchings'?"

"Because, my love, I know what turns you on."

"True. That was never our problem."

"No problems tonight, Kristi," Neil promised in a quiet voice. "I need you the way you are. With all your fantasy, all your softness, all your love."

Kristen's heart skipped several beats. "And in the morning?"

"When did you become a realist?" he countered.

"Pay the check," she suggested, pushing back her chair. "I need to freshen up."

Neil stood and pulled her chair, kissing her gently on the neck.

Kristen carefully weaved her way into the Ladies lounge and sighed in relief when she saw the payphones on the wall. She slipped in a quarter, dialed a local number, waited a few moments and dialed six more numbers.

"Weather bureau."

"I'm on a pay phone."

There was a long pause. "It's secure."

"I need a weather report from Gonzolo."

"One moment."

The line transferred. "You're not due to call for another eighteen hours, Ariel," came Reaper's voice. "Is there a problem?"

"Yeah. Either I'm becoming paranoid, or the whole setup consists of idiots and replicas of real people. I'm talking to formerly 'brilliant' people who are sounding pretty damn dumb. They are more interested in my decorating skills than my professional knowledge."

"What do you need?"

"Someone on the inside I can trust. This place is a certifiable snake pit."

"That sounds ominous."

"Doesn't it?"

"Unfortunately, Ariel, you're it. You've seen the security setup, we can't get another observer in there."

"Swell." Kristen sighed and thought about it. "In that case, I'll have to use outside sources. Send any photos you have of the scene to Trinculo, will you? I need a fresh opinion before I taint it with my own. Also, pull the autopsy and incident report on Daniel Denning. I also want to know about any previous psychiatric interventions by Dr. Jeffers. Everything. Tell Trinculo to read everything. Oh!"

"What?"

"Tell him to finish grading the class reports on monsters, first. That's priority one."

"Strange priorities you have, Ariel."

"Not really. I think you might need a replacement for me sooner than you thought, it may be his first assignment, but the kid shows potential. I may not survive this one, Reaper. Mentally or physically."

"You do sound paranoid."

"Yup," Kristen hung up the phone and walked over to the mirror. She made a face at herself, pulled a brush from her purse, then started making repairs to her appearance. "Think of it this way," she told the image in the mirror, "one day soon, you can imagine any image you want. No wrinkles, no flaws." She shook her head, blotted her lipstick with a tissue, then left the lounge.

Neil stood when she returned to the table. "Everything alright?" he asked.

"Don't be nosy, Neil," Kristen suggested. "A lady does need some privacy."

"Sorry," he smiled and took her arm, leading her back through the restaurant, quietly thanking the maitre d' on the way out.

Outside, the fresh air hit like a wave of sanity, Kristen breathed in deeply. "Nice."

"Would you like to drive along the beach before we go home?" Neil asked. "Maybe a moonlit swim?"

"Is nostalgia creeping into your personality, Doctor?" Kristen smiled at him.

"Old age." He slipped an arm around her waist. "Some of my memories need to be refreshed." His pager started buzzing madly. "Damn!"

"There's a memory I haven't forgotten. The vibrating doctor. There was always someone standing on the rail of a bridge at the worst possible moment," Kristen smiled. "Are there bridges at the institute?" she asked.

"Only metaphorically. Wait here, or better still, sit in the car where it's warm." He pulled the keys from his pocket and handed them to her. "I'll call and let them know I'm unavailable."

"It might be important."

Neil kissed her passionately. "Sweetheart, I don't care if it's the President and he just bombed the White House. I'm not available."

"Want to use my cell phone?" Kristen pulled it out of her purse and handed it to him. "It's new, international satellite access, made in Germany and, just for fun, the keys are in Braille. Very sexy."

"Nice," Neil looked at it with appreciation, then handed it back to her regretfully. "Tempting, but then our security chief couldn't properly monitor the call and put the contents in his nasty little files. Cell phones are, according to him, wide open transmissions to invisible terrorists and warlike E.T.'s. With calls to the Institute, I'm required to call through a specific terminal on a land line."

"You're kidding."

"Nope, them be the rules that apply," he kissed her once more, quickly, and walked back into the restaurant.

Kristen dropped her cell phone back into her purse, watched him disappear into the building, noted a taxi waiting a few yards down the curb, then looked at the keys in her hand and discarded the idea of leaving on her own. She was a coward, yes, but not that much of a coward.

The headache was back, Kristen took off her glasses and started walking toward Neil's car to wait for him. She knew those calls, the last one she remembered took three hours. After a nine year separation, everything seemed familiar, everything was happening too fast. It was insane. *She* was insane. Neil assumed, she acquiesced, without thinking it through, falling into all the old traps, following all the same patterns.

This was stupid. She should take that taxi. "Lady, look out!"

Instinctively, Kristen moved to the side, hugging the cars in the parking lot. A car zoomed past her, her heart jumped as she moved between two parked cars, lost her balance and fell to her knees. Both legs of her pantyhose ripped with their contact to the asphalt. The skin beneath them burned like fire along with her left hand that she had extended to break her fall. The knuckles on her right hand were grazed from fisting her hand to hang on to the keys. Luckily, the glasses she was still holding were not broken. "God Damn, Son of a Bitch!" Kristen exploded in an undertone.

"Miss? Are you alright?" A man and a woman were instantly kneeling next to her. "Are you alright?" the woman asked again.

"Fine." Kristen gave the human blurs a weak, but warm smile. "Sorry for the profanity, I was just feeling a little stupid." And blind and helpless, she added to herself in a burst of self pity.

"The jerk hadn't even turned his lights on," the man told her. "It's a good thing your reflexes are good, you might have been seriously hurt."

Kristen accepted his hand gratefully, rising from the ground and grimacing as her skirt raked over her injured knees. "Thanks for the warning. It's my fault. My mind was wandering. With this outfit," she gestured to her brown skirt, "I doubt he even saw me until he was right next to me."

"True," the man responded, his voice gaining calm, "I barely saw you myself. That thing in your hair caught the light from the restaurant. It flashed right in my face." He touched the gold barrette at the top of her head.

Neil came up, looked at Kristen curiously and asked, "Kristen? What's going on?"

"I fell down and went boom," she answered. "I have an ouchie on my knee," she added in a childish voice.

"Are you alright? Do you want to go to the hospital?" Neil grabbed her hand, forcing a small protest of pain to escape from Kristen. He looked at her hand critically.

"I have two skinned knees and a grazed hand," Kristen told him disgustedly. "If you can't bandage that, Doctor Davidson, I'm going to personally tear up your medical diploma." Her eyes narrowed. "You don't use stingy stuff, do you?"

Neil responded with a quick smile. "Yes, I do. It's the best way to teach little girls to watch where they're going." He put an arm around her waist and turned to the couple who were still next to them. "Thank you for your help. It appears my patient will live." He shook hands with the man and nodded at the woman with him.

"I'm glad everything's alright," the man smiled, took his date by the hand and walked toward the restaurant, talking to her in a low voice.

"They're bad mouthing you for threatening to use stingy stuff," Kristen nodded knowingly, putting on her glasses, then taking them off and rubbing the lenses with the lining of her jacket. "Who was on the phone?"

"The institute. Nothing Earth-shattering, just a verbal prescription for a sedative." Neil answered. He walked her to his car and carefully helped her into it. "Are you sure you're okay?"

"Yes." Kristen hid another grimace as she bent her knees to sit in the car. "Except for feeling stupid, it's strictly superficial. I was daydreaming and tripped over my own feet. I do that a lot nowadays. "

Neil leaned over and kissed her. "Are you going to tell me what you were daydreaming about?"

"No," Kristen said next to his lips.

"Were you, by any chance, thinking of taking a taxi back to the institute?"

Kristen sat back and stared at him. "Am I that transparent?"

"No, just that predictable," Neil answered, frowning. He got into the driver's side and closed his door. "You have taken off on me in the past, Dr. Michaels."

"Dr. Davidson?" a loud tap on the driver's window.

"Whoa!" Kristen started violently in her seat.

"Sorry, Dr. Michaels," the voice added, "I didn't mean to frighten you."

Neil had also jerked, he turned angrily toward the voice at the driver's window and rolled it down. "And you are?" he growled.

The man showed some identification, then returned the wallet to his inside coat pocket. "I've been asked to escort you and Dr. Michaels back to the institute. My car will be following yours."

"For what purpose?" Neil asked tightly.

"A small security problem."

"Dr. Michaels in injured," Neil told him. "I think we should call it a night. Tomorrow..."

"Dr. Michaels will be cared for at the Institute," the man broke in. "I really must insist, Dr. Davidson. I have my orders, we have to follow procedure."

Neil turned and frowned at Kristen, then started the engine, grinding the starter in his agitation. "It seems we are needed at the Institute."

"Any idea why?"

"Another standard procedure. When in public, we're under constant surveillance. Our primary Big Brother obviously wants to remind us that he's watching," Neil answered tightly.

"Which big brother is that?"

"Our paranoiac Chief of Security, L.R. Simmons," Neil elaborated. "Swear to God, Kristen, the man is certifiable."

Chapter 13

Prospero: But are they, Ariel, safe?

It took twenty minutes in the PSR infirmary for an intern to cleanse, iodine powder and patch Kristen's knees and hands, then she was led politely upstairs to the office of L.R. Simmons, Head of Security. He smiled gently as she came into the room, first holding her chair in an almost exaggerated tribute, then apologizing as he walked around to his side of the desk and sat down. "I'm sorry to break into your evening."

"Do you mind if I smoke?" Kristen asked.

"No, not at all," L.R. fumbled around his desk for matches and an ashtray, found them, then barely managed to light Kristen's cigarette before she lit it herself with her own matches. "I didn't know you smoked." Another fact missing from her file.

"Occasional crutch, hospitals and iodine give me the willies," Kristen smiled at him. "Where's Dr. Davidson?"

"He's gone back to the restaurant with one of my people, there were a few loose ends there that we felt necessary to clear up this evening. He said he would see you at your nine o'clock appointment with Dr. Jeffers. Tomorrow."

Translation, she would be sleeping on the second floor tonight and not in Neil Davidson's bed. The change in plans caused an emotion in Kristen that felt suspiciously like relief.

"Would you mind telling me about your accident in the parking lot?" Simmons asked.

Kristen frowned at him. "Is that what this is all about?"

"I understand that you were nearly killed by a passing car. While you are working here at the Institute, you are technically under my protection. I take my job very seriously."

"I'm exceptionally night blind, I walked in front of a driver who couldn't see me," Kristen shrugged. "That's all there is to it." She leaned one elbow on the desk, rested her chin on her hand and asked, "don't you think you're blowing a couple of skinned knees way out of proportion?" She looked at the cigarette in her other hand, frowned at it and stubbed it out in the ashtray. The nicotine patch she was wearing was obviously doing its job, she had lit up out of habit, not need.

"Very possibly," Simmons admitted, "but, with the exception of observing you in near fatal situations, it's been a slow week." Kristen grinned at him and he tried to make his face stern. "Dr. Michaels..." he started.

"Kristen," she corrected him.

"Dr. Michaels," he started again, not taking the name.

"My name is Kristen, Lloyd," she repeated.

"Dammit, I'm trying to deal with you on a professional level!"

Kristen sat up straight and blinked at him. "Did I miss something? How will using my name keep you from dealing with me on a professional level"

"I..." Simmons stared angrily at her face for a full minute, then relaxed. "Yes. Well, 'Kristen'," he used the name self-consciously, color flooded his cheeks. "There are, evidently, a few things you should know about the security here at the institute. Most of the patients admitted here are high level government employees or members of their families. The staff, therefore, is often privy to certain political facts that are very confidential."

"Understood. What's your point, Lloyd?"

"I'm trying to say that you, everyone working here, are prime targets for the media, political dissidents, or simply wackos who are dissatisfied with the current administration. I... we have to be able to keep tabs on you. If you leave the institute, for any reason, you are required to leave word as to where you will be in case of an emergency. If you don't plan on sleeping here, let the duty officer know where you'll be sleeping." He flushed again.

"I'm only going to be here for one night, Lloyd, two at the outside. I hardly think I need your security lecture, I'm not a security risk, check my clearance."

"Whatever the length of your stay, the same rules apply!" Simmons said harshly. "Is that understood?"

"Yessir!" Kristen saluted him cheerfully.

"I wish you'd take this more seriously," Simmons told her.

"I wish you'd lighten up," Kristen countered, still smiling, "before your name has been linked to the word 'paranoia', permanently."

"Where I went to school, it was a synonym for the word 'caution'."

"Oh. Sounds like a fun campus," Kristen answered.

"With your vision...handicap, I might also suggest an escort, other than a patient, when you wish to wander around the grounds. We are within fifty yards of the ocean cliffs here, there have been accidents due to carelessness. I'll escort you myself, if necessary. I don't get out often, the fresh air will do me good."

Kristen cocked her head to one side. "Do I detect a note of pity, Lloyd?"

He was silent for a moment. "Yes, I guess you do. I'm sorry."

"Don't be, I appreciate it. Very few people are honest about pity, most skate around it, assuming no one wants it."

Lloyd looked confused and shook his head lightly. "I can't figure you out."

Kristen sighed lightly. "Then don't try," she suggested. "I'm the very least of your concerns." She looked at him curiously. "Tell me, Lloyd. Who gets hurt if I find out why Charles Denning blew holes in his television set?"

"That's an odd question."

"Is it? That's what you're trying to figure out. You think that someone deliberately gave Keenan a gun, to main or to kill me, it doesn't matter which, and that a car was deliberately aimed at me... again to frighten or kill, but ultimately keep me from further contact with Charles Denning."

"Now who's paranoid?" Lloyd smiled nervously.

"No? Then give me another good reason for your pity and overprotection," Kristen suggested.

Simmons stood. "It's after midnight, Dr. Michaels. I suggest you turn in for the night, you have a nine o'clock appointment. One of the guards will show you to your suite."

Kristen also stood and shook her head. "'Dr. Michaels' again, huh?" She looked annoyed. "We're going to have to have a great many more therapy sessions to get rid of your basic shyness, Mister L.R. Simmons."

He gave her a shadow of a smile. "Goodnight, Kristen."

"Thank you. Goodnight, Lloyd."

L.R. Simmons paced in his office for several minutes after Kristen had left. *("Who gets hurt if I find out why Charles blew holes in his television set?")*

Who indeed...

Neil Davidson. It didn't fit. What the hell did she see in Davidson? Lloyd sat at his desk and drummed his fingers on the top, the question annoying him, taunting him. He opened the cabinet near the monitor, pulled out a dated CD and put it into the DVD player, scanned through the beginning, then stopped it.

"Neil needs you, Kristen."

"Bullshit."

Lloyd advanced a few frames.

"Forget it. I tried, once, Matt and damn near got my heart broken. He's a brilliant man, but is mind is closed. I can't reach him and I don't trust him."

Lloyd stopped the recording, looking at Kristen Michaels on the screen. She was willing to sleep with Davidson, but she didn't trust him. Why? What was the background there?

Lloyd advanced again.

"I like her. She's quick, she smiles easily and if I ever needed surgery, I'd like to have her for my doctor. She reminds me of Pop."

"Raymond Hayes?"

"I couldn't tell much, except that he did not want me here. The man has secrets..."

Lloyd nodded at the screen. "Yes, he certainly does, Kristen, you are perceptive." He scanned the next part, stopped and reversed a few frames.

"Is that his name, Lloyd? He introduced himself as L.R. and never gave me a first name. Lloyd. Hmm. I like him, I'd trust him with my life, if that means anything..." Lloyd Simmons stopped the tape, freezing Kristen's face. She was staring directly at the hidden camera, the expression on her face could almost make him believe she could see him.

("I don't trust him...")

("I like her...")

("The man has secrets...")

("I'd trust him with my life, if that means anything...")

Lloyd pulled a cigarette out of his desk drawer, lit it and threw the match into the ashtray. He had quit smoking a year earlier, the habit reasserted itself almost instantly. "Shit." He took a deep drag and blew smoke at the monitor.

("No? Then give me another reason for your pity and overprotection...")

"You want reasons, Kristen?" Lloyd glared at the image of Kristen on the monitor. "Because you look like a goddamned innocent, you talk to leprechauns, you converse without fear to a man who holds you at gunpoint, because you have the perception of a trained agent... because you don't trust the right people... because you..." He stubbed out the cigarette, it was bitter and old. What was he thinking? Damn the girl!

("The man has secrets...")

She had said something else important. Something about Denning. Simmons re-wound the tape.

"What's happened to Charles now?"

Lloyd fast forwarded. "He tried to commit suicide."

"What pushed him to that? Something to do with Danny?"

Lloyd stopped the tape, pulled the phone to him, punching buttons rapidly. The other end was picked up in three rings.

"Federal Security."

"L.R. Simmons. Give me records."

He waited for the transfer.

"Records."

"I want everything you've got on Daniel Denning's' kidnap and execution."

"It's a closed file, National Security."

"Then open it."

"I'll need Hastings's authority."

"So get it. Priority one, PSR Security."

"I'll call you back."

Lloyd hung up the phone, then picked it up again.

"Security, Frick."

"Is Dr. Davidson wearing his beeper?"

"Yes Sir."

"Did he leave an auxiliary number on the check out sheet?"

"I'll check."

Lloyd lit another cigarette while he waited.

"Yes, he did," came the answer. "Another phone contact..." he rattled off the numbers.

"Thanks," Lloyd hung up the phone. The bastard. Denied Kristen Michaels company for the evening, Dr. Davidson went back to his old standby, Denise Parker. That predictable bastard. Did Kristen Michaels even know what an asshole he was?

He fast-forwarded the picture in front of him.

"I'd trust him with my life, if that means anything..." He pushed the stop button again, looking at her image. Damn!

The phone rang.

"Simmons."

"The file on Daniel Denning will be in your office tomorrow morning."

"Thanks." He hung up the phone and looked helplessly at the monitor.

"What am I looking for, Kristen? Dammit, what do you know? What can you see? What am I protecting you from?"

Chapter 14

Ariel: Since thou dost give me pains, let me remember thee what thou has promised...

Matthew Jeffers pushed the stop button on the video recorder, then looked at Kristen's excited face with avid expectation. "Well?"

Kristen was still staring at the blank screen. "Let me see it again," she decided.

"Are you going to tell us what you think, or just keep us in suspense?" Neil asked from the other side of the room.

Kristen turned to look at him and held up her hand in a stalling gesture. "Just one more time, please? This kind of development is unusual, even in my field. How many people revert to their childhood on their own without a hypnotic trigger? I've read cases, but they're always isolated moments, with extreme non-lucid patients. Nothing like this. Charles doesn't fit the criteria. Bear with me, okay?"

Matthew Jeffers finished resetting the recorder and nodded toward the television screen. "We're set," he announced, his voice showing a touch of excitement.

"This is ridiculous," Neil diagnosed.

Kristen ignored him, focusing all her limited vision on the monitor. "I might be better able to see if..." the overhead lights in the room went out, she added, "thanks, Jory, it helps."

"I turned out the lights, Kristen," Neil's voice informed her. "You can thank me. Maybe your leprechaun friend is on a lunch break. We've been at this for almost an hour."

Kristen lightly waved a hand, acknowledging his comment, her gaze still glued to the screen.

Charles Denning sat up. "You dirty, conniving son of a bitch!" his hands pulled the trigger of his imaginary gun. "Bastard, bastard, bastard!" He nodded satisfaction, pushed his hands into his stomach, stiffened with pain, then smiled lightly, laid down and went to sleep.

"I'll fast forward to the next section," Matthew Jeffers suggested.

"No!" Kristen said instantly. "Let me watch his face before he brings Chipper in."

For five minutes there was no sound, all three quietly watched a now calmly sleeping Charles Denning. Finally Kristen suggested, "look. Look there. Can you slow the picture a bit, Matt?" Kristen touched the screen with the tip of her finger. "Now. Watch his face. It softens, you can almost see his age disappear." She nodded. "Okay, look there," she again pointed to the screen. "Charles is wearing only the bottoms of his pajamas, yet he's using his right hand to fiddle with something like a button." She nodded to herself, almost seeing the button she was describing. "The size of that button is large, you can see it from the shape of his fingers. He's wearing the pajamas of a small boy, the kind with big buttons, probably horses or boats are imprinted on his pajamas," she decided. Kristen acknowledged Neil's groan of protest at her description, but went gamely on. "Okay, Matt, regular speed."

The discussion between Charles Denning and Chipper looked like a conversation that had been intentionally blocked out on one side.

"No, I'm not sick, I don't know why I'm here... I don't know anybody..."

"...Okay, you, but that's about it."

"...I'm going borey in here."

Neil finally spoke up. "Kristen, we've seen this ten times, can we give it a rest?"

Kristen held up a hand, trying to listen to the recorder.

"...I don't remember. I think I've been here a long time, Chipper, even riding Skyeagle seems like a long time ago..."

"Stop it for a second, Matt," Kristen requested. She turned her attention from the television to Matthew Jeffers. "Do you have Charles Denning's medical records dating back to his childhood?"

"I have his medical history," Jeffers answered, "not all the records. Why?"

Kristen shook her head. "Just a hunch. Does any of his history indicate that Charles was in the hospital while he was a child?"

"No, he never even had his tonsils out," Matthew responded. "Why?"

"Because I think he knows he's in a hospital. Part of this reality is seeping into his fantasy of being a child again. The two time zones could be overlapping. Also the name 'Skyeagle' sounds like a horse or a pony. I'd like to know when he had that horse, what age he was."

"I'll get more detailed information on his medical and have Lloyd check on the horse," Matthew promised.

Kristen nodded and turned back to the screen. "Okay, let's continue."

"Yeah, I'm tired, too. See you later, Chipper."

Kristen held up her hand, anticipating the fact that Matthew Jeffers might turn off the recorder again, then watched silently as Charles Denning laid back down, his face quietly peaceful as he returned to sleep.

"Now, watch his face," Kristen suggested to the two men. "Slow it down again, Matt." The picture slowed, Charles Denning's face reversed the process of the beginning of the tape. His face was young, gentle, then over a period of several minutes, it rapidly took on the countenance of a man in his early fifties. Kristen sighed, nodded at Matthew to turn off the set, then watched the screen go blank.

She waited until the lights came on and murmured, "Fantastic," sat back in her chair, removed her glasses and rubbed the area between her eyes. "Dammit," she said triumphantly, "he did it. The son of a gun did it." Her words were soft, but the excitement in her voice carried throughout the room. "He actually brought him back."

"You almost sound jealous," Neil said quietly.

"I am, Dr. Davidson. I am always in awe at the intelligence and flexibility of the human mind. Do you know what this means? This recording shows that category three minishrinks don't have to die when a child is convinced that he's too old for them, but that they can be drawn from indefinitely. It means that other adult patients who have deep psychological problems can reach back into their own pasts, find their old friends and use them to heal themselves." She laughed lightly. "I could mean that you and I may be out of a job in the future."

Neil started to say something, Matthew Jeffers held up and hand, forestalling him. "Aside from the psychological philosophy, Kristen, what does it mean to our patient? What exactly are we dealing with?"

Kristen returned her glasses to her face and thought about it seriously, her expression becoming older and more professional. "I'd say for a certainty that we are dealing with a human child, about nine. Maybe ten."

Neil finally took the chair next to her and asked, "what do you mean, 'human'?"

"Chipper is human. I'm certain of it."

"As opposed to what?"

"As opposed to an elf, a leprechaun, a fairy, an invisible animal or an ET," Kristen explained. "Children of that age group often attract fairy tale creatures instead of human playmates, Charles Denning has a human minishrink."

"'Attract'? You mean 'imagine', don't you?"

Matthew Jeffers broke in hurriedly, recognizing the set look on Neil's face and the defensive one on Kristen's. "Attract, imagine, we're talking semantics. The point is, real or not, a child brings in the playmate himself."

"Not necessarily," Kristen argued, "on occasion a child..."

"GENERALLY, then," Matthew tried. "Dammit, Kristen, I don't want to get into a religious debate, we've had more than our share over the years and we never resolved the issue. We don't have the time now, either."

"Sorry," Kristen said quietly.

"Good. Alright. Here's the problem. Neil has not been able, even under hypnosis, to break through Denning's shield concerning the shooting and attempted suicide. Given time, he will probably be successful, but that could involve years of therapy. This minishrink of Denning's already has the Ambassador's total confidence and trust, or we couldn't even classify him as a minishrink." He looked at Kristen. "My question is, can we use this 'Chipper'? Can we get Denning to tell 'Chipper' about the shooting?"

Kristen was silent for several moments. "No, I don't think so," she answered regretfully. "Obviously, Charles can only talk to Chipper when he imagines himself as a child. He wants to tell Chipper the problem, the very fact that he relives the shooting right before Chipper comes to visit points to that, but I don't think it's possible. It would be easier if Chipper was a leprechaun. Then you might stand a chance."

"Just out of curiosity," Neil put in, "why would we stand a better chance if Chipper was a leprechaun?"

Kristen turned slightly pink. "Because a leprechaun is several hundred years old. You can tell an old man virtually anything, no matter what your own age. But this friend of Charles is just a little boy, about nine years old. A man does not willingly tell a little boy his adult problems. Charles' minishrink stopped growing the day Charles denied him. Now, Charles has to create his own illusion of youth simply to talk to Chipper. You noticed that his reenactment of the shooting was completely separate from his meeting with Chipper, obviously he won't consciously, or subconsciously, share that horror with a kid who can't handle it. He's calling for help, but he can't use the help he's getting."

Neil nodded with satisfaction. "I concur."

Kristen looked surprised. "You do?"

"Yes. The Ambassador proved that to me, himself. These tapes are more than a week old." He nodded to Matthew Jeffers. "Show her the tape from Wednesday."

Matthew Jeffers frowned and placed another DVD into the recorder. It was the same bedroom scene, Charles was sleeping, then sat up abruptly. "Chipper?" He looked around the room anxiously. "Chipper? Are you here?" His face was pinched in a childish frown, his eyes filled with tears. "Chipper?" he bit his bottom lip, another frown, then, finally, an adult frown, his face growing up in seconds for the camera. He shook his head lightly in confusion and he laid back down.

Matthew Jeffers turned off the television.

Kristen turned to Neil, her face a mask of anger and suspicion. "How did you get rid of him, Neil?"

Neil looked pained. "I didn't, Kristen, don't look at me as though I'm some kind of minishrink exterminator. The Ambassador got rid of him himself. Each night after the first incident, the Ambassador had a less violent display of the shooting, after that, he had a more and more difficult time contacting his childhood friend. When he finally quit reliving the shooting, he quit finding his friend."

Kristen nodded slowly. "I get it. You tried to get him to contact Chipper through hypnosis, right?"

"Yes," Neil answered warily.

"And you said something real clever, like, 'remember your old 'imaginary' friend, Chipper? Do you remember him, Charles?'"

"Not exactly those words," Neil answered.

"But something like it," Kristen guessed. "You reminded him, under full hypnosis, that it was all fantasy. Right?"

"What are you driving at, Kristen?"

"How the hell is Charles supposed to bring back something he can no longer believe is real? By simply calling Chipper 'imaginary', you have established another subconscious block. Now he's denying both the minishrink *and* the monster in the closet."

"Oh, for God's sake!" Neil stood.

"Sit down," Jeffers requested of Davidson. "Neil, I know you are not keen on this type of discussion, but you're not exactly batting a thousand with Denning, so let's look at all the angles before we discard it." He waited until Neil had resumed his chair next to Kristen, then looked at her. "You said before that you didn't think we could use Chipper. Are you now saying that we could have?"

"No," Kristen admitted. "I'm just saying that you could have tried. He called in Chipper right after having a nightmare about the shooting. He was looking for help so desperately, he pulled himself back into his own childhood to find it."

"For the sake of argument, let's say that Denning is still having those nightmares. That he still sees Chipper. What would you do?"

Neil stiffened in his chair. Kristen looked at him quickly, then back at Jeffers. "I don't know."

"I know you, Kris. Even if there is only a tiny chance, you'd try it. Forgetting all the difficulties, how could we use Chipper?"

Kristen was stuck with wanting to pursue Denning's fantastic call back of Chipper and also wanting to drop this entire discussion before Neil started questioning her sanity. Matt was offering her no easy exits. If she had spent a night making love to Neil, his attitude toward her might be softened, but now... now she could only threaten his position with Matthew Jeffers. Damn. Either she had convictions, or she didn't.

Matthew cleared his throat and continued to look at Kristen. "Is it possible to use Chipper?"

"I've never tried using a category three minishrink in reference to an adult," Kristen answered.

"How would you try it?"

"I don't know," Kristen repeated. "I'd probably talk to Chipper, explain why it is so important for Charles to remember and see what happens. Minishrinks in this category are usually very obliging, as long as it's for the good of their playmate."

"Have you ever talked to minishrinks before?" Neil asked with a smile.

"Oh, sure. When a child comes in to my office with a friend, I can't just ignore it. For one, it would be extremely rude. I've had conversations with dolls, blankets, pet rocks and several category three friends like Chipper. It comes with the job."

Neil nodded. "The important question is, do they talk back to you?""

Kristen shrugged lightly. "I've never had much luck with pet rocks," she admitted. "Usually the child has to translate in that case."

Matthew Jeffers was nodding rapidly. "I get the idea. You go into the room while Denning is having a conversation with this friend and convince Denning that you also see Chipper."

"I don't have to convince Denning," Kristen answered, "just Chipper."

"They are one and the same, Kristen," Neil reminded her. "Denning created Chipper from his own childhood. If you talk to one, you talk to both."

"Neil," Jeffers started, panic rising, "this is not a question of..."

Neil continued to talk directly to Kristen. "You do believe that Chipper and Denning are one and the same, don't you? It's just another form of a split personality." He looked at Kristen sternly. "Right?" Kristen was biting her lip, he repeated the question. "Right?"

Kristen sighed heavily. "Wrong. That's not what I believe at all."

"You do believe that Chipper is a figment of the Ambassador's imagination."

"Wrong again. Chipper is real, Neil. Whether or not you see or hear him is moot. Charles does see and hear him." She watched his face for some kind of understanding. "Look. Whenever a parent of one of my patients with a category three minishrink comes in, I warn them of the possibility that a child who has an invisible friend might also have an invisible monster hiding in the closet that offsets that friend. Somehow, there is always a balance, even if you can't visibly see or hear it. The monster can be loneliness, fear, or something very real, like physical scars of child abuse, but there is usually a balance. The monster is very real to the child, so is the minishrink that's needed to offset that monster."

Neil nodded, taking some of the imminent storm out of the room. "Agreed. I'm a little surprised that you understand the theory, it's almost conventional."

Kristen grimaced, but kept her anger in check. "With Charles Denning, the monster is whatever happened to cause him to shoot his television set and himself. Chipper graciously returned to help his friend fight that monster." She took a deep breath. "Chipper is no less real to him than that shooting. That's why you get both, or none. Don't you understand that?"

"I understand the theory," Neil responded, "I have had some schooling, Dr. Michaels. I'm just trying to establish that you fully understand that 'Chipper' is a fantasy creation of Denning's mind, nothing more."

Kristen balled her fists, then studied Neil, her eyes blazing behind her thick glasses. "You know, old love, for a man with twenty-twenty eyesight, you are twice as blind as I will ever be. You're so goddamned hung up on Schizoids and split personalities, you can't relate to anything else! Chipper is as real as you are. If you won't believe me, prove it to yourself! Try and reach Chipper during one of your hypnosis sessions with Charles and you might, possibly, be able to find the memory of him, but not the minishrink himself. He is not an extension of Charles Denning's mind, he exists outside of it!"

The overhead lights started blinking rapidly and Kristen looked up sharply. "Dammit, Jory, stop it! I have a miserable headache and you're just making it worse!"

The lights immediately stopped flashing.

Matthew Jeffers looked with amusement at Neil Davidson. "I wish the hell I knew how she does that," he admitted softly.

Neil groaned. "You're just as bad as she is! She doesn't do anything! She takes a bit of normal, everyday haphazard wiring faults and turns them into some kind of mystical experience. Why do you encourage her?"

"Why do you oppose her?" Jeffers countered.

"Because it's a sick fantasy!"

Kristen stood. "Dammit, you leave him alone! This is between you and I, Neil, not Matt!"

"This should be between you and your personal psychiatrist!"

Kristen took a calming breath. "You know, Neil, someday, you are going to get a patient who believes in something. An unshakable belief in God maybe, and you're not going to be able to annihilate that belief before you manage to get a well-deserved black eye. You pride yourself on being able to rationalize everything, with your own brand of reality. There are realities outside your own narrow vision."

"What the hell does a religious belief of God have to do with anything?" Neil also stood.

"Get a clue! God is the ultimate invisible minishrink! When people believe that their problems are too petty or silly to bother God, or they're too embarrassed or feel too guilty to talk to him, they come to you or one of the lesser minishrinks for help. Those minishrinks are as real as you are! Chipper, Skip, Jory, Goldie, Pepe, Two Knives, Buffy...all of them, all of the names I've heard over the years. They exist! They have to exist, because we need them. If we take away the minishrinks from our patients, throw away their little blue blankets, all we have left are people like you. Master Psychiatrists that accept what they cannot change, ignore what they lack the imagination to accept and change, reject or destroy what they don't understand."

"Do you think it's better to be like you, live in fantasy and ignore reality?" Neil asked angrily. "You can't even face your own blindness! Have you made any reasonable plans, investigated your options? What are you going to do, Kristi, pretend that you're the same and go on blithely as before? Hire someone to drive you around, read your notes to you, describe the expressions on the faces of your clients? You have the time, now, to prepare for your future and what are you doing about it? You can't face the real world, so you go into your realm of leprechauns and fairies and create your own magical world! Have you ever faced reality?"

"Often! Every day I face child abuse, child molestation, teenage alcoholism, PRE-teen alcoholism, terminal diseases..."

"Not your patient's problems, Kristen, have you faced the realities of your own problems? Dammit, admit it, you can't even face your own handicap! What makes you think you can handle Denning?"

"That's not fair, Neil. I..."

Neil shook his head. "Don't whine. Life is never fair, Kristen. What makes you think you can help my patient, when you can't even help yourself? What good is Jory to you when you can no longer tell if the lights are flickering, when your vision is completely gone? This institute is part of the real world, little girl, either join the rest of us, or admit you're too damned weak to handle it and get yourself some professional help!"

The quiet was deafening.

Kristen leaned over, picked up her purse, then straightened and gave Neil a short nod. "If memory serves, those are the two options you gave me nine years ago. I didn't take either one then, I'm certainly not going to start now." She nodded at Matthew Jeffers. "Matt, it's been a slice of heaven."

Kristen walked quickly to the door and slammed it behind her.

The quiet of the room lasted for several minutes. Matthew Jeffers broke it. "Why didn't you tell Kristen that Denning had that nightmare last night, that he again was successful in contacting Chipper?"

"I don't want her working with Denning," Neil answered. "The way he talks about her, the emotions she brings in, they are not going to help his therapy. I half believe that Denning thinks he's in love with her."

"Four out of every five people I send to Kristen for help think that," Matthew Jeffers responded. "She looks too young to be an authority figure and her knowledge is too extensive to be a daughter figure. Men still haven't shaken the belief that they are superior to women, so they can't think of her as a friend or a peer, the only thing left is a sexual partner. Even Kristen finally realized it, now she never takes on male patients over the age of fifteen."

Neil looked at him sharply. "Why? What happened?"

"She was almost raped at knifepoint by one of her patients, a sixteen year old boy. She talked her way out of it, but it shook her to the core."

"She told you about it?"

Matthew Jeffers shook his head. "No. Kristen never tells me anything in reference to herself. Certainly nothing confidential concerning one of her patients. I have a few friends at the military base outside of Claren. They keep tabs on her for me, she still works in their psychiatric unit."

"I see. Tell me, Dr. Jeffers, how do you think of Kristen? A friend, a peer, or a sexual partner?"

Matthew Jeffers raised an expressive eyebrow. "I think of her with compassion. You should try it sometime. Any other way I might think of her is strictly my own concern."

"Typical." Neil shook his head. "Kristen Michaels has been indulged, pampered, catered to and spoiled, all her life. She has never faced reality, never made a total commitment, all because people like you treat her with compassion rather than good old fashioned common sense!"

"I heard the lecture," Matthew said tiredly, "you just gave it to Kristen. I don't need a repeat performance. I'm finally beginning to understand why she left you nine years ago. You're a heavy handed son of a bitch, Neil."

"One of us had to be practical!"

Matthew Jeffers nodded. "One of you was. She just walked out that door."

Chapter 15

Prospero: How now? Moody? What is't thou canst demand?
Ariel: My liberty.

Kristen was seated on the outside terrace of the cafeteria at the institute when Denise Parker found her. She was staring out at the ocean, her expression was one of someone very far away.

"Hi." Denise sat across the table from her.

Kristen turned and looked at her, stubbing out a cigarette in an ashtray half filled with former half-smoked cigarettes. "Dr. Parker. Hello."

Denise smiled lightly. "As a doctor, I should point out that smoking those things can lead to all sorts of unwelcome lectures about emphysema, lung cancer, heart disease and various other physical ailments." She gave Kristen another small smile. "I should know. I gave into peer pressure five years ago and quit."

"Thanks for the warning. If I see any Doctors running about who look like they're eager to give me a lecture, I'll pretend it's not mine," Kristen answered. She held up her coffee cup. "Any warnings about caffeine?"

Denise shook her head. "No and you didn't have to put the cigarette out on my account, either. I said I received those lectures, I don't give them."

"Ah."

Kristen was dressed in a sweater, skirt and black tights, a heavy coat was folded on the seat next to her. "You're not dressed for the beach," Denise surmised.

"No. I leave for home in a few minutes," Kristen agreed. "L.R. is taking me to the airport."

"I'd go crazy without a beach close by," Denise told her.

"I'd miss looking at the mountains."

Denise suddenly didn't want to do this. "How did it go with Lindsay Cummings?"

"Pretty well. When her cast comes off, she'll be coming to the Colorado facility. Probably in about two weeks. I gave Matt all my reports. I'll follow up there."

"Oh. You're not going to be working with Charles Denning?"

"It's a little complicated."

"Why?" Denise grinned. "So, I'm nosy. Can't you work with Neil Davidson?"

"Let's just say I usually work better alone. Dr. Davidson and I don't see eye to eye on therapy and it's his case."

Denise looked interested. "Huh." She shook her head. "Odd.

Somehow, I had you pegged as a fighter."

"Evidently, I'm not a very good fighter. I tried, I lost." Kristen put down her coffee cup and absently lit another cigarette. "It's for the best. I have a lot of work back home."

"Charles Denning is also my patient. During his physical therapy yesterday evening, he spoke of you very highly. He's a good man. I like him. If you can help him, I think you should stay and fight."

Kristen nodded. "He *is* a good man. By staying, I'm not sure I'd be doing it for his benefit, however."

"Why would you do it?"

"Monumental ego," Kristen answered bluntly. "As I said, I generally work alone. Every now and then I would like to take those pompous, self-centered, megalomaniacs that read and write all those asinine psychology books and..."

"Shove them up their respective asses?" Denise finished for her. "People like Neil Davidson?"

"Oh, yeah."

"Then fight Neil and get the job done," Denise said simply.

"No, thanks. He doesn't fight fairly."

Denise nodded. "Don't tell me, let me guess. The two of you were discussing therapy, you were winning and he threw something personal at you, your imminent blindness, probably, and left you without a retort."

Kristen just looked at her with the question.

Denise shrugged. "No, no one told me, exactly. Dr. Jeffers asked me if I knew the credentials of one Dr. Jonas Hepler and I guessed that it had to do with you when I first saw your glasses. As for knowing how Neil bested you in a verbal debate, that's easy. I've had a relationship with the man for nearly a year and I know how he fights. Neil doesn't use psychiatry on only his patients, he lives it."

"I know."

"Dammit, you've read the same books, use psychology yourself! If you want the job, I'll bet you know ten different methods to swing Neil around!"

Kristen thought about it for a moment, then shook her head. "Not without compromising my principles."

"Oh, shit! We all compromise our principles at one time or another to get what we want! When I was an intern and wanted to go into cardiology, I had to fight a male chauvinist that thought women were only good as dermatologists, pediatricians, gynecologists, or sex partners. When he wasn't fighting me tooth and nail to keep me out of surgery, he was propositioning me to go to bed with him."

"How did you handle it?" Kristen asked curiously.

"Simple. I went to bed with him. I've never regretted it. Oh, I could have reported him to the Medical Board and raised a stink, but it certainly wouldn't have endeared me to the board and the truth of it was, I wanted to work with the man. He was lousy in bed, but brilliant with a scalpel. I am now one of the ten most sought after cardiologists in the country. He calls *me* for help. I may be the one who compromised, but he's the one who learned from it."

Kristen looked at her in fascination. "You have the healthiest ego structure I've ever encountered."

"So I'm told."

Kristen laughed. "Just to satisfy my own curiosity, did Matthew Jeffers send you out here to talk to me?"

"Of course he did. Jeffers pulls everyone's strings around here, that's why this institute works." She watched Kristen carefully. "So. What are you going to do? Go away meekly, or seduce Neil Davidson into a compromise?"

Kristen took a deep breath. "A simple seduction I could handle." She considered it. "Maybe. But..."

"Am I wrong, or didn't the two of you used to be lovers?"

Kristen looked startled at the question. "Where did you hear that?"

"I didn't, really," Denise frowned. "Come to think of it, Neil said I should ask you, that he would be curious to hear the answer himself. Were you lovers?"

("Tell me you know the difference between fantasy and reality, Kristen.") Kristen looked back at the ocean, then faced Denise. "Wow. That's a difficult question, I've never actually thought of it in that context." She frowned, then sighed lightly. "Of a sort, I guess we were. Once, I think we even liked each other. Thankfully, it didn't last. We had a honeymoon in Disneyland and marriage straight out of Dante."

"Marriage?" Denise repeated hollowly.

"It was very brief. Legally and emotionally, it was annulled."

"What happened?"

"Neil wanted something that I couldn't give him."

"What was that?"

Kristen grinned. "It would be overly dramatic if I said 'my soul', wouldn't it?"

Denise looked at her tiny face, her vulnerable, almost childlike eyes behind the huge magnifying lenses and shook her head slowly. "No, it wouldn't. Not knowing Neil. I expect that was exactly what he wanted from you. What did you want from him?"

"The same thing. That's our one and only similarity." Kristen spotted L.R. Simmons standing on the other side of the glass windows inside the cafeteria. She stood, holding out her hand. "My plane leaves in less than an hour. Goodbye, Dr. Parker."

Denise took her hand. "Don't let him win, Kristen. You don't have to give him your soul, just let him think you're giving it. The man is a brilliant psychiatrist, but he's a really stupid human being. Give him enough to convince him, then hold on to the rest."

Kristen smiled gently. "Dr. Parker, have you ever seen the Rocky Mountains?"

"I've flown over them," Denise answered.

"Pity. There's a fantasy that takes place in Claren in the Spring. The snow melts, tiny splashes of green poke up timidly through the ground and the sun shimmers on the remaining snow like a thousand diamonds of every color known to man. We get rainbows on clear days and rainbows on stormy days." She grinned. "My secretary gets the biggest smile on her face after skiing and the wildest and brightest sunburn from her snow goggles that could cause Scrooge to burst out laughing. Some of my littlest patients ski in for therapy, they banzai up to the door in a cloud of powder just to impress me. My carpet gets soaked from the melting snow on their boots, my fireplace gets black from too many fires... the fire itself is beautiful to watch. I can't ski alone anymore, but, in a little while, the wildflowers will be out. The kids bring me the flowers, even weeds that they think are pretty. And they grin. Sometimes all you can see are braces and missing teeth."

"It's time to 'stop and smell the flowers', is that what you're saying?" Denise responded softly.

"No," Kristen looked surprised. "Not really. I've always stopped to see and to smell the flowers. That's who I am. A master artist loses the use of his hands through arthritis, an opera singer loses her voice, a connoisseur of music become deaf. You always lose what you will miss the most. I'm going to miss the smiles. *That's* reality. It happens all the time."

"Kristen?" L.R. Simmons came up next to her, looking at her face worriedly. "Are you alright?"

"Fine," Kristen smiled up at him. "Ready to go?"

"We have a little time, if you like."

Denise also stood. "I won't keep you," she reached out and took Kristen's hand again. "Kristen has a little memorizing to do," she told Lloyd. She turned back to Kristen. "Good luck. I mean that sincerely." Impulsively, she hugged her.

"Thank you." Kristen took Lloyd's arm and left.

Denise sat back down and looked out at the ocean. Neil had described Kristen Michaels as a nut, a child with no handle on reality, an incompetent with beliefs that were silly and downright dangerous. Well, she had seen the competence when she viewed the tape of Lindsay Cummings, she had seen some very 'adult' expressions on that little face and as for fantasy... God help her, she was losing it, if she ever really believed in it. *(We get rainbows on clear days... rainbows on stormy days...I'm going to miss the smiles.)*

"Denise?"

She turned, Neil Davidson was looming over her. Mr. Reality himself. Denise looked up at him with undisguised contempt. "You're a real bastard, do you know that?"

Neil looked at her in confusion. "What?"

Denise shook her head. "Forget it." She stood up and walked away, Neil Davidson stared after her, shook his head and went back into his office.

Chapter 16

Prospero: Hast thou, spirit, performed to point the tempest that I bade thee?
Ariel: To every article...

Kristen found Patrick McClary in her office at the university, surrounded by papers and books. "Find everything you need?" she asked calmly.

Patrick looked up at her with a scowl. "Welcome home. What the hell am I looking for?"

"If I told you, then you'd find it," Kristen answered. "Never speculate, never assume, or you might create monsters that never existed."

"Do you always give the same lectures?" Patrick asked curiously.

"I don't know. What do you think?" Kristen asked.

Patrick rolled his eyes at her and kept it to a sigh.

"Did you grade the reports?"

"No. But I did record the ones that were typed, so you can listen to them without running up your electric bill by that magnifying light." He smiled at her. "I am not your little blue blanket."

"Ah. Well, it was worth a shot." She sat down at the desk, found the ashtray under several layers of paper and lit a cigarette.

"Yes, I do mind if you smoke," Patrick looked at her. "Take it outside, if you feel you have to tar up your lungs."

"This is my office," Kristen pointed out.

"True, but at the moment, I am in it with you, working. Ever hear of second hand smoke? Or did you forget to read that journal?"

Kristen stubbed out the cigarette.

"Thank you."

"You're welcome. Are you always this nasty?" Kristen asked.

Patrick tossed a thick file on the desk next to her. "I am when I read things like that."

Kristen opened the cover. It was the autopsy report on Daniel Denning. "How bad?"

"Bad. I felt like I was taking my medical final. Almost very bone, muscle and nerve in the body was smashed, broken, pulled, exposed or slashed at one time or another. Add malnutrition and dehydration. Before they got down to the physical scars, he was pretty nearly starved to death. What the hell did the kid do to deserve all that?"

"Rumor has it he was simply the wrong nationality in the wrong place," Kristen swallowed hard. "Were the descriptions technical?"

Patrick frowned. "What do you mean?"

"You said you felt like you were taking a med exam. If you were the normal Joe Blow on the street, would you have understood it?"

"Oh." Patrick thought about it. "No," he shook his head. "Unless Joe Blow had a minimum of two years of pre-med and four years at a medical university, he would be reading Sanskrit. I looked up half of it. It made it worse. The textbooks have pictures."

Kristen nodded. "Did you get the transcripts of the trial?"

Patrick leafed through the stack of papers and pulled out a single sheet. "You mean this little thing?"

"What's that?"

"The transcript. Translated into three English paragraphs. Basically, they said, 'did you kidnap and kill this American boy'? The three defendants said 'no' and they were taken from the room. A little while later, they came back, they were asked again, this time they said 'yes', the judge said 'guilty' and they went to jail. Two days later, they were shot. No appeal, no nothing."

Kristen nodded. "Charles Denning felt that the suspects were mere 'scapegoats' to placate the State Department."

Patrick wiggled a finger at her. "Speculation."

"It is what our patient believes," Kristen answered, "therefore it can not be dismissed."

"Oh."

"Any mention of the autopsy at the trial?"

"Nope. They didn't even mention the 'American boys' name, only that he was dead."

"Ah huh." Kristen picked up a cigarette, then put it down.

"Care to share?" Patrick asked.

"Share what?"

"Whatever you're thinking."

"Charles Denning saw the autopsy report, he said it was causing him nightmares knowing what his son went through."

"Can't blame him for that. If it was my son, I'd have nightmares too," Patrick answered, then looked up curiously. "Who translated the details of the report to him?"

Kristen looked at him with interest.

Patrick beamed. "Did I find one of your monsters? A real one?"

"Possibly," she answered. "You at least found a question that's bugging the hell out of me."

"This is neat! Where else do we look for monsters?"

"They usually lurk in closets," Kristen suggested.

"The scene of the crime!" Patrick decided. He started digging through his papers.

"What crime would that be?" Kristen looked at him curiously.

"Daniel Denning's murder, obviously."

"Hmm."

Patrick stopped looking and frowned. "Give me some hints, will you?"

"We're trying to find out why Denning shot holes in his television set and himself." Kristen just looked at him. "Textbook answers, Patrick."

Patrick rolled his eyes at the ceiling. "Don't speculate, don't assume, the patient knows the answers, you do not. To find the answers, you have to listen to your patient..." he looked at Kristen. "What did Denning tell you?"

"About what?"

"About shooting holes in his television."

Kristen gave him a look of approval. "Nothing concrete. The day itself is pretty hazy. He remembers brushing his teeth. He does not remember getting dressed. He opened the front door..." she paused.

"Why? Who was at the door?"

"A man wearing brown. UPS, he thinks. The man gave him a package, or a letter, Denning said 'thank you' and closed the door. From that point on, it's blank."

Patrick started to say something, the phone rang, he answered it. "Dr. Michael's office."

"This is the weather bureau. Apparently, Dr. Michael's called for a weather report."

"This is Trinculo."

There was a short pause.

"Voice and status verified. The line is clear."

"So, how's the weather?" Patrick asked.

"United Parcel Service delivered no letters or packages to the Ambassador's home on the day of the shooting. Any other weather patterns that need verification?"

Patrick sighed. "Not at this time." He hung up the phone and looked at Kristen with suspicion. "How do you do that?"

"Do what?"

"Get things to happen on cue. No packages or letters were delivered to Denning on the day of the shooting."

Kristen nodded. "I called from the airport in Denver, they've had a couple hours to check."

"He might have been mistaken about UPS," Patrick suggested.

"Anything is possible," Kristen conceded, "but we can only speculate about 'possibilities'. What's the textbook answer, Patrick?"

"The patient knows the answers," Patrick repeated. "We do not speculate, we do not assume..."

"Which means?"

"Denning believes he got a package or a letter from someone that looked like he was from UPS."

"Question number two," Kristen nodded, "since UPS delivered no letters or packages to him, who did?"

"And, where's the package?" Patrick added. "What was in it?" He looked quickly at Kristen. "I know, I know, textbook answers."

Kristen stood. "I'm going outside for a cigarette and to watch the sunset. Why don't you dissect a few monsters and tell me what you've come up with when I get back?"

"Do you know what I'm looking for?"

Kristen shook her head, putting on her coat. "Only if I speculate. And imaginary monsters scare me a hell of a lot more than the real ones."

Kristen walked outside and took a deep breath of the icy air of Colorado. The skin on her face tightened and chilled, she put her hands in her pockets and started walking around the psych building to catch the last rays of the sun.

Snow still covered the grassy area of the quad, but someone had kept the wooden bench clear, Kristen sat, lighting a cigarette, enjoying the huge cloud of vapor created by her warm breath and the smoke. The sky was already turning orange, but several clouds covered the sun.

It was going to snow again, she could feel it in the air. The clouds and the sun were already behind the mountain, but the color remained for several long minutes.

"Its getting cold and dark," Patrick decided, sitting next to her on the bench.

"I don't mind the cold," Kristen answered.

"Charles Denning received a video from persons unknown, put it into his player, got out his gun and killed it," Patrick said knowingly. "He then turned the gun on himself. Someone came into the room, removed the video from the machine, turned off the machine and removed all evidence that it had ever been there."

Kristen turned and looked at him. "Are you speculating?"

"No," Patrick said firmly. "If I was speculating, I'd say the video was of his son, being tortured. I didn't add that part." He gave her a small smile.

"Give me your evidence then," Kristen suggested.

"Denning received something from someone at the front door, by his own memory," Patrick held up a finger. "His television was turned on and set to channel three, the station you use for playing a video tape or DVD."

"It is also a Santa Barbara station," Kristen pointed out.

Patrick shook his head. "Only if you have an antenna, Denning was on cable. The cable box was set for CSEN. It only shows active debates on the senate floor and they were not in session that Saturday, I checked. The television was on. To 'assume' that Denning was watching a blank screen on television is pretty far-fetched."

"There was no tape or DVD in evidence," Kristen pointed out.

"Ergo, it was not found, or it was removed from the scene," Patrick answered. "Since no envelope or package was found at the scene, the same rules apply. It was not found, or it was removed." He looked smug.

"And what's the motive?"

"To kill Charles Denning."

Kristen gave him a disgusted look. "Then why isn't he dead? If someone had the time to remove your suspected video, they certainly had the time to finish him off, or simply delay calling for medical assistance."

"Oh." Patrick looked crestfallen.

Kristen looked at the last remaining color of the sunset. "Now I do want you to speculate," she said. "How is it that I visit Denning for one day and, although Denning has been in therapy for two months with a professionally brilliant psychiatrist, using drugs and hypnotherapy, I find out about a UPS delivery? How is it that you look at the physical evidence of the scene for a few hours and even though his home was searched by the very best agents of the U.S. Government, you come up with leads that they have apparently overlooked or never considered?"

Patrick bit his lower lip. "I don't know. Are you saying I'm wrong?"

Kristen shook her head. "No, I'm not. The report stated clearly that Denning was tuned to a Santa Barbara Station that was showing an exercise program, for one. The fact he was on cable should not have been a real stretch of deduction for someone with professional investigative training."

"Since the cable box was still connected to the set after it was blown up and it was in the pictures of the scene, I'd agree," Patrick retorted.

"It was in the photos?"

"Absolutely. As well as the VCR/DVD player/recorder. Connected to the TV."

Kristen let out a heavy breath. "Damn."

"Whoa, a swear word!" Patrick looked at her questioningly. "Are you 'intellectually tired'?"

"Don't be cute, Patrick, we're getting into some real muddy water here and we don't know for sure who's swimming in it. Those photos are part of the official record."

Patrick sat quietly. "Meaning that National Security, security at PSR, Dr. Neil Davidson, Dr. Parker, Matthew Jeffers, or all of the above might be involved."

"Yup, and whoever their superiors are."

Patrick let out a low whistle, then was quiet for a very long time. "Dr. Michaels, I think I'm getting scared."

"Hmm."

"Do you think I'm over reacting?"

Kristen turned and grinned at him. "I dunno. What do you think?"

"I think I'm scared," Patrick returned the grin. "Are tempests always like this?" his voice was serious.

"Every storm is different, government politics are always ugly," Kristen answered, "but this one feels especially nasty."

"What do we do now?"

Kristen stood. "I buy some more nicotine patches, go back to California and sell my soul. You find me that video of Danny's execution. I doubt very much if there is only one copy. Tell Gonzolo to go through the Officinal Meteorológica in Columbia. He'll have to fight them for answers, but there has to be someone with an in to the terrorist group that took

Danny, I'm sure of it. He's also going to have to use his connections in National Security to find out why the investigation was compromised."

"Is that all?"

"No. Tell Gonzolo I'm 'boarding the King's ship and will flame amazement'," Kristen frowned. "How was the skiing at Spruce Meadows the other night?"

Patrick looked at her curiously. "Great. Why?"

"No reason. Just wishing I was a little younger."

"You're only thirty-six, that's not so old," Patrick told her.

"Right. Tell me something, Trinculo, you were only fifteen two days ago, how old do you feel today?"

"Point taken," Patrick stood, taking her arm and walking her to his car for the drive home. He finally asked her. "Are you scared, Dr. Michaels?"

She looked at him for a long moment. "Of dying, no. Of losing my soul or someone else's because I screw up... always."

Chapter 17

Prospero: Sir, I am vexed. Bear with my weakness, my old brain is troubled.

"Dr. Kristen Michaels is returning tomorrow. I am going to hold you personally responsible for her safety."

L.R. Simmons frowned at Matthew Jeffers. "Yes, sir. How long will she be here?"

"Probably until we are forced to release Charles Denning. Dr. Parker has already released him medically," Jeffers frowned. "We can't hold him for long on a psychiatric, he appears too well adjusted to an outside observer. No more than a week."

"I see."

Matthew looked at him curiously. "You seem less than pleased, do you dislike Dr. Michaels?"

"No, sir."

"I know she looks rather helpless and vulnerable, but she's really a very capable young woman," Matthew told him. "Unfortunately, I believe that someone is deliberately trying to harm her and she is in over her head."

"I agree."

Matthew Jeffers leaned back in his chair. "Your answers seem a little terse today, Lloyd. I'd like to know what it is you're not saying."

Simmons couldn't sit, he stood and started pacing. "I don't like it. Kristen Michaels is a target, suspects unknown. Even she knows she's a target, so why is she coming back here? Is she trying to get herself killed?"

"I sincerely hope not. Kristen Michaels is a good friend."

"If she's a good friend, then tell her no! Tell her to stay in her little home town and keep the hell away from here!"

"Are you saying you can't protect her?"

"I'll protect her," Simmons said flatly.

"Good. Problem solved." Matthew Jeffers stood. "Thank you, Lloyd."

L.R. Simmons marched out of the office and closed the door carefully behind him.

Dr. Matthew Jeffers, studied the door for a moment, then sat, shaking his head in mild amusement. Four out of every five men. He flipped the switch on his intercom. "Ms. Moore. Is Raymond Hayes still waiting to see me?"

"Yes, Dr. Jeffers."

"Send him in, please." He turned off the intercom and flipped several security switches off under his desk so that the interview would be completely private.

By the end of the week, the problem would be solved.

Chapter 18

Ariel: Supposing that they saw the King's ship wrecked and his great person perish...

Kristen Michaels sat in the office of Neil Davidson, feeling the first real fear she remembered in her adult life.

Damn Prospero.

When Neil came in, he glanced at her curiously, sat behind his desk and waited.

"You're right, I'm wrong, I'm sorry," she stated firmly.

"Ah, huh. I will never figure you out," he told her.

Kristen shook her head sadly. "Pity. Lately, I've been considering the possibility that I might need the professional services of a psychiatrist, your name kept popping into my head." She closed her eyes and spoke softly. "I'm going blind, you see. I am in the final stages and I keep trying to pretend that I am not. When I'm not pretending, I go through bouts of self-pity and it's affecting my judgment, my work..." she opened her eyes and looked at him.

Neil was smiling at her. "I'm not stupid, Kristi. You're trying to bargain with me. For you to even offer to accept that kind of reality, you must really want something badly."

"And I thought you didn't understand me," Kristen answered, showing her dimples.

"I don't understand you," Neil admitted, "but I do know you. What do you want, in exchange for this boon?"

"I want to work the Denning case," she told him simply.

"If you want it that badly, you could go to Jeffers and he'd give it to you. You have emotional clout with the man that far exceeds my credentials."

"You're underestimating your own clout, but that's not the point. I want to work with you on the Denning case."

"Why?"

"The minishrink angle. Denning brought back a minishrink from his own past, Neil, do you know how rare that is? I could work for the rest of my life in child psychology and never see anything like it again. It substantiates several theories I've been spouting about in my classes, it could stabilize and confirm some methods of therapy I've been using for years."

"Again, you could ask Jeffers for the case."

"Not and help the patient," Kristen answered. "Even if I am successful with Denning's minishrink, I still am not experienced enough with adult therapy to guarantee a cure. That's your expertise, Neil, I won't pretend to be up to your level. I relate to children, not adults. Please. Let me in on this, it's important to me. I can give you new angles with Denning's therapy that would never even cross your mind. We'll both gain from it."

Neil thought about it for several moments. "If I'm successful in reaching Chipper during hypnosis, you won't be needed."

Kristen smiled. "You won't find him. Chipper lives in my neck of the woods, Neil, if you want to really use him to help Charles, you're going to need me as a go-between. I give lectures on the subject, ask around. I'm the closest thing you'll find to an expert in this country."

Neil stood and started pacing. "I can still try," he muttered.

"And you'll fail," Kristen said flatly. "Oh, I know, you can make him quack like a duck under hypnosis, but his subconscious mind will always know that he's not really a duck. Without me, you'll never know if you find the real Chipper, or just a created memory."

Neil quit pacing and sat on the edge of his desk. "For the sake of argument, let's say I decide to use you. I will stay in complete control. I will be in constant charge of Denning's actual therapy."

"No question. Oh, I'll probably argue with you constantly, that's how we have our sick fun, but the final call will be yours. I will not interfere when we're together in any session."

"Your word on that?"

Kristen took a deep breath. "With one exception."

"Which is?" Neil looked skeptical.

"In regard to the minishrink, Chipper. You will not, in Denning's presence, either when he is conscious or under hypnosis, again refer to Chipper as 'imaginary'. Invisible is fine, since you can't see him, but not 'imaginary'."

"He is imaginary, Kristen."

"I know you believe that and I will not try and change your beliefs, but I need this one restriction."

Neil thought about it. "Agreed." He looked at her curiously. "Anything else?"

"No. How much time do we have?"

"Charles Denning will resume his official duties, at least partially, at the end of the week."

Kristen grimaced and muttered a silent oath. "Is there any way to extend the time?

"No, Kristen. I told you, we patch them up and send them back to the front. Our hands are tied by politics."

"Then I guess I'm here until the end of the week," Kristen answered.

"I'll set it up with Jeffers, you can discuss your involvement with the patient." Neil nodded. "Ask Denning if you can attend his hypnotherapy session this afternoon. If he refuses, that's the end of it."

"Agreed."

"Assuming Denning agrees to let you in on his therapy. For this week only, will you allow me to help you accept your blindness?"

"That offer was made as my lead-in, Neil, you weren't supposed to take it seriously."

"Nevertheless, the offer was made and I want it."

Kristen sighed. "I was right, you do want my soul."

"Don't aggrandize the situation."

"I'm not," Kristen answered. "Okay, what do you want? Full therapy sessions? To coach me in Braille? To teach me the fine art of seeing sculptures by touch?"

"No, I just want you to follow some simple guidelines."

"Like what?" Kristen looked at him suspiciously.

"For one, no more smoking. Its not a blue blanket, love, it's a monster."

"Got it covered, I'm wearing a patch."

"You lose that, too. Poison is poison, no matter how it's administered."

Kristen frowned at him. "Anything else?"

Neil pointed to her glasses. "Do the Amophic lenses in your glasses in any way prolong the use of your vision?"

"No," Kristen answered worriedly. "They simply magnify what vision I have. Wearing corning lenses outside might be helping, the jury is still out on that theory."

Neil nodded. "I want you to take them off. When you are with me and do not need your vision magnified for work, I want you to learn to accept your limited disability. It will make the transition to your total blindness easier. Outside, you will wear the corning lenses."

Kristen didn't move and Neil looked at her sharply. "We have a bargain, Kristi. You offered to accept reality. Dammit, Sweetheart, I've watched you! You're experiencing migraines, you're choosing blinding pain over seconds of mediocre sight! You're hurting yourself and it is not necessary."

Kristen sighed, took off her glasses and placed them in her blazer pocket. "Wonderful. Now you can watch me walk into walls. With your sadistic mentality, you ought to enjoy that."

"Good! Developing a sense of humor about it is going to be part of your therapy."

"I was stating a fact, not telling a joke," Kristen told him quietly.

Neil touched her face gently. "Trust me, love, I'm not out to harm you. You are losing your vision. It will soon be gone forever. That is the reality. Don't turn sight into the beat all and end all of your life, or you will not survive your blindness. Right now, you are using what little sight you have as another crutch, you're wallowing in the pain of it, trying to memorize everything you will be unable to see in the future. In fact, you are making it harder on yourself, giving yourself things to miss and agonize over."

"You're the MP," Kristen said heavily.

"Hang in there, Kris. Now. Can you see my face?"

"Indistinctly."

"What am I doing now?"

"You're leaning over to kiss me," Kristen guessed.

"Not even close," Neil corrected her. "I was holding my hand in front of your face."

"Ah, well. One bit of male flesh looks like any other."

Neil laughed. "Why did you guess that I was leaning over to kiss you?"

"Because I want you to lean over and kiss me and I was testing to see if you would comply out of sheer pity."

"Why did you want me to?"

"Because I don't like being blind and I'm scared to death. I'm perfectly capable of self-analysis, Neil, you don't have to ask me 'why' all the time."

Neil pulled her to her feet and kissed her gently. "I'm sorry. Reality is scary, love, and its hard. There are no shortcuts. That's the first thing that you'll have to admit to yourself."

"I dunno," she whispered against his chest, "this part isn't too bad. Maybe you're the one who needs to look at both sides of reality."

Neil laughed lightly, the sound rumbling deep in his chest against her. He held her tightly. "Ah, little love, you are completely impossible, do you know that? You'd find a silver lining in hell."

"Just looking for the silver lining is finding a silver lining," Kristen answered honestly. "Looking for the good side of things is always as good as finding it. At least you don't get bored and it balances your perspective."

Chapter 19

Prospero: Of my instruction hast thou nothing bated in what thou hadst to say...

Kristen sat on the grass next to Charles Denning to ask if she could join his therapy. Several yards away, she could see the bulky form of L.R. Simmons, his back to them, pretending to look at the ocean. Evidently, he was serious when he told her she was not going to roam the grounds without an escort.

Denning also looked over at the Chief of Security. "Have I become some kind of threat?"

Kristen shook her head. "He's decided I need protection from falling over a cliff, and as a patient, he doesn't believe you qualify."

"Great. This place can really zap an ego," Charles Denning frowned.

"What can I tell you?"

"Tell me you're going to stay for awhile," Denning suggested.

"Need a little comic relief, do you?" Kristen smiled at him.

Charles grinned. "Yeah. Are you going to stay?"

"Do you want me to?"

"Yes. I need a friend on my side, Kris."

Kristen nodded. "Then I'm going to stay for awhile. I've offered to help in your therapy. I need your permission."

"You have it," Charles answered instantly.

"Don't be too quick," Kristen advised him. "I rarely get involved in Adult therapy. I have an assistant that I use as a sounding board when I get stumped on some things. That means anything you tell me in confidence, you might also be telling him. I need you to know that."

"Kristen, nothing is really confidential around here. Hell, they even let security watch my therapy sessions. Do whatever you think is right. I trust your judgment."

"I also think you should know why I've offered to assist in your therapy," Kristen continued.

"Because of Danny?"

"Yes. And the nightmares you have about him," Kristen nodded. "And, partly, because you have another friend here and I want to help you find him."

"Another friend? Who?"

"I've never had this conversation with an adult outside of the classroom, so bear with me, okay? Try not to laugh at me." Kristen started pulling tufts of grass.

Charles Denning looked at her seriously. "I won't ever laugh at you, Kris."

"Thanks. I can't discuss my patients with you, so I'm going to tell you a little bit about me. In case you haven't noticed, I have a few psychological abnormalities."

"I've noticed," Charles assured her, smiling.

"Yeah, well, like everyone else, I blame them on my childhood." Kristen reached over and squeezed his hand. "When I was a very little girl, we lived in the same house where I am now. One side was a medical facility. I'd sneak into the examining rooms, talk to the patients, hold their hands, play games, anything to keep them from being scared." She looked at him. "I was terrified of shots and doctors, I just figured everyone else was, too."

"You were a psychologist, even as a baby," Charles smiled.

"Sort of. In any event, I got sick a lot. I caught everything from the flu to meningitis. Scared the hell out of my poor dad. I was open to every virus known to the clinic, he couldn't keep me away. So, I ended up spending a lot of time, sick, in bed and very lonely." She looked at Charles Denning, her face serious. "I had one friend. It was a friend only I could see, a six inch fairy named Goldie."

"You had an imaginary playmate?" Charles looked delighted.

"That rather depends on who you're talking to," Kristen said quickly. "My mother was Welsh, fairies and little people are real in her culture, no one in my family questioned it when I talked about Goldie. I never even considered that she might be 'imaginary', I just knew that not everyone could see her. That was okay with me, her being invisible made her more special, somehow. When I got better and started playing with my other friends, Goldie just sort of faded away."

"You didn't need her any longer, so the fantasy ended," Charles determined knowingly.

Kristen nodded. "Invisible friends are good about that. They very politely leave when they're no longer needed. They are there to help, not cause more problems."

"Did you ever see her again?"

"Thankfully, yes. When I was five, my mother died and we went to Mom's hometown to bury her. Daddy was called back for an emergency. I stayed for a few weeks, alone, and was extremely lonely. While I was there, trying to get over the loss of my mother, I was molested by one of my Aunt's neighbors, a registered pedophile."

Charles touched her arm with gentle sympathy. "Oh, God, Kris, I'm so sorry!"

"Thank you, Charles," Kristen gave him a reassuring smile. "Like most kids I was incredibly resilient and found a balance. Goldie came back and helped me through it. She was with me, mentally and physically, and never left me. During the worst assault, we flew off to her castle in the sky and only my body stayed behind to be abused. I was pretty badly hurt, but I

121

never sub-consciously felt the pain. In the hospital afterwards, she kept me from being frightened of the doctors. It sounds strange, I know, but I owe my life and my sanity to that little fairy."

Charles looked serious. "It doesn't sound strange. You needed her, she came back to help you."

"True. When I got back to Claren, I went into therapy. A well-meaning psychiatrist told me that I had a 'lively' imagination and that 'pretending' was okay, but only to a point." Kristen shook her head. "Mostly, he wanted me to face the reality of the abuse and learn to realize that Goldie was not real and wanted me to admit it. Sad. If I had chosen anyone, he is the one person I thought would believe me."

"Except he had already labeled you an 'imaginative child' and he didn't."

"Exactly."

"What finally happened?"

"I was a child, I trusted the psychiatrist, he was an adult, he knew more than me. So, per his instructions, I denied Goldie entirely. It took a long time. I really did believe in her. I had to literally pretend I couldn't see her and she was sitting right there on my shoulder. She'd talk in my ear, she'd kiss my cheek and still I pretended she wasn't there. She used to pull my hair..." Kristen pulled a small lock of her hair with her right hand. "It hurt, and I pretended I couldn't feel the pain. Each time, she'd become a little more faint, a little less real, until one day… she wasn't there at all." Kristen shook her head. "My very best friend, the one and only friend who was there for me during the worst trauma of my life and I sent her away without a thank you, or kiss my butt."

"Hurt, didn't it?" Charles said quietly.

"Yes. It hurt a lot. Dealing with the reality of the abuse was a lot tougher after that. There wasn't a balance of good memories to offset it. No more castles in the sky to fly away to."

Charles nodded and was quiet for a time. "I had a friend like Goldie." He smiled self-consciously. "Only his name was Chipper. One of his teeth," Charles pointed at his right front tooth, "was chipped, that's how he got his name. Ha," he looked up, "I haven't thought about him in years. I don't remember exactly when he showed up, or even why. I think I was eight. It was right after my parents were killed and I moved in with my grandparents in New Mexico. I was one lonely kid." He shook his head. "Funny. Right now, I can actually remember him better than my real friends. Chipper and I did everything together. Horseback riding, chores, everything was an adventure..." he stopped.

"And you weren't lonely any more and the death of your parents seemed less horrific," Kristen said quietly.

"Exactly."

"Sounds like a 'real' friend to me," Kristen pointed out.

"He was," Charles answered with a little surprise. "Unfortunately, I got rid of him the same way you did. I had to fit in, my new friends thought I was nuts. I pretended he wasn't there, until he wasn't. It felt like I killed him."

Kristen nodded. "We both became fairy killers, because the 'real' world is not ready for fairies. That's why I became a child psychologist. Children have a natural way of dealing with trauma and I happen to think it's healthy and necessary. As adults, we forget that memories, dreams and thoughts are real. It doesn't matter where they come from, only that they are here. Our invisible friends are very real, or they couldn't have helped us. On the flip side of that coin, nightmares are real, or they wouldn't haunt us. Our memories, good and bad, have true substance, or we wouldn't hold on to them so tightly and they wouldn't cause us psychiatric problems."

"Like reliving Danny's death, instead of his life," Charles nodded. "Point taken. Why do you suppose adults hang on to bad memories and banish the good ones?"

Kristen looked at him curiously. "I don't know, Charles. What do you think?"

Charles thought about if for a moment. "Because that's what we're taught to do when we grow up. We think in black and white, no colors, no grays, no balance. We really do grow up to be pathetic poops, don't we?"

"Hmm," Kristen looked at him with raised eyebrows.

Charles Denning looked at Kristen with amusement. "And, I think this has been a therapy session to help me put Danny's death into perspective."

Kristen looked interested. "Why do you think that?"

"Because there is more to life than nasty reality. Danny was a part of my life for sixteen years. There was more to Danny than my nightmares of his torture and death, but that's all I ever talk about in therapy. I never tell anyone about the good things any more." He looked at her almost guiltily. "Those memories are real. Tangible. I haven't even talked to you about them since you got here."

"Why?"

"I don't know. Once Dr. Davidson went over that autopsy report with me, that's all I could think of. I believed it was all he wanted to hear."

"Ah."

Charles looked determined. "I need a stronger balance. I've given his death more substance than his life. I've been ignoring the love, friendship and fishing trips that were more a part of my relationship with Danny. We really did become friends, Kris. We really talked. He was a great kid. I need to believe in my own memories, I need to remember the real Danny." He looked at her seriously. "I need to talk about those memories with you and everyone else who will listen."

"Hey, there's a good idea."

"Yes, it is," Charles smiled in return and gave her a gentle hug. "Thank you, Kris. I promise to make an effort to mix some of my nicer dreams with the nightmares."

"It might help," Kristen told him seriously.

Chapter 20

Ariel: Your swords are now too massy for your strengths and will not be uplifted...

"Talk to me, Dr. Michaels."

Kristen looked at Lloyd Simmons with interest. "Talk is my life," she smiled, "and my name is Kristen. What would you like to talk about, Lloyd?"

"Damn." Lloyd looked around the dining area and felt surrounded by his own security systems. There was no possibility of privacy. "Let's go for a drive," he suggested, standing.

"Okay," Kristen stood.

Lloyd took her arm, walked her down the steps, across the grass and into the parking lot. Without thought, his steps picked up, they were nearly running when they reached the car. Anger. At the moment, all he felt toward Kristen Michaels, was anger and when he unlocked the passenger side of his car door he jerked it open violently.

Kristen looked at him with mild concern, sat in the seat and barely got her legs in before he slammed the door.

Lloyd walked around the car, got in the driver's side and started the engine, revving it loudly.

"Problem?" Kristen asked curiously, as he backed out of the parking space.

"You are so damned..." Lloyd shifted into drive and started speeding toward the entry gate, "...trusting!"

"Oh."

Simmons glared at her. "Fasten your seatbelt," he ordered, then tapped his fingers on the steering wheel as he waited for the security guard to open the gate out of PSR.

Kristen sat quietly and watched L.R. Simmons expressions go from anger, to professional detachment as he passed the security guard and nodded. His face returned to a mask of black anger as he kicked the car back up to speed and started driving down the coastal route.

They were on the coast highway before Lloyd spoke again. "Why did you come back here?"

"Supposedly, to help Charles Denning," Kristen answered calmly.

Simmons rapidly pulled over to the side of the road and stopped the car in a cloud of dust. He jammed it into park, turned off the engine and turned to face her. "What do you mean 'supposedly'?"

"Why do you ask?" Kristen responded.

"You are in danger here! You're almost blind, you trust everybody, you're...."

"Go on," Kristen suggested, fascinated.

"You were married to Neil Davidson."

"Good. I guess your background check on me finally came through."

"No, it didn't. Denise Parker told me about the marriage."

"Hmm. Well, I guess if you get an annulment, it really does mean it didn't happen," Kristen decided. "Interesting."

"How long have you known Matthew Jeffers?"

"All my life. He and my father used to be colleagues."

"Why does he want you here?"

"Several reasons, I suspect."

"What reasons?"

"You wouldn't believe me if I told you," Kristen answered.

"Try me."

"Why should I?"

"Because, damnit, I'm trying to protect you!"

"From what?"

"You were almost shot, you were almost hit by a car..."

"The father of one of my long-term patients got out of control, blind little me accidentally stepped in front of a moving car. Sounds pretty tame, Lloyd," Kristen pointed out. "Almost? What's that expression, 'close only counts in horseshoes and hand grenades fights'?"

"Denise Parker is sleeping with Neil Davidson."

"Okay."

"You're not surprised."

"Not especially, she's extremely attractive, Neil never entered the clergy, she's just his type. Beauty, brains, a good heart. Why are you telling me?"

"Because..." Lloyd hit the steering wheel with his fist. "Damnit!"

Kristen looked at him curiously and remained silent.

"I feel like my hands are being tied."

"That's an interesting analogy. Why do you feel that?"

"Just..."

Kristen unfastened her seatbelt, turned in the seat and faced him, pulling her legs up to a semi-lotus position. "Seriously, why? What is tying your hands, in reference to me? Tell you what, let's play a game. I'll play psychologist, you try and think like the head of Security. What is tying your hands, Lloyd?"

Lloyd gave her a startled look. "What?"

"You're angry, you're frustrated, I might even go so far as to say you're a little frightened. Why? Snap answers, Lloyd, don't even think about it."

Lloyd Simmons studied her face for a long moment. "I'm angry because... you agreed to come in this car with me and you didn't even think about it. You don't know me. You don't know who I am, you don't know what I can do. You trusted a man you do not know."

"Okay. The frustration?" Kristen asked softly.

"Every time I try and find out something about you, there's a hole in the records that shouldn't be there."

"The fear?"

"Unless I know what's going on, I can't protect you."

"Ah. And what's the result of all this?"

"I can't do my job efficiently," Lloyd Simmons answered, his voice again tinged with anger.

"Hmm."

Lloyd looked at her suspiciously. "Again, you don't seem very surprised."

"I'm not. That's probably one of the reasons I'm here."

"What? That makes no sense at all!"

"It makes a lot of sense," she argued. "I'm one hell of diversion, Lloyd. Think about it. I've been made into a fascinating character, just for you. Despite the fact that I have had an extensive background check done on me every year since I was twenty-three and started playing with the children of VIP's, somehow there are unexplained holes in my record, even a marriage and annulment that can easily be accessed by public record. Being the person you are, suspicious and thorough, you're going to start digging madly to find answers that should already be there. True?"

"True," Lloyd agreed slowly.

"I'm little, I'm almost blind, I look vulnerable as hell, cute as a button and I bring out the macho in you because I'm not naturally wilting under the strain and you feel I need protection from villains unknown, because I'm too naïve and innocent to see the danger for myself."

"You're not that cute," Lloyd answered.

"Sure I am," Kristen argued. "You're the romantic hero, I'm the damsel in distress and there's an unknown but deadly dragon stalking me. If you work at it, you might even convince yourself that you are falling in love with me. I'm the only person in your field of vision right now."

Lloyd felt himself blushing.

"You're being manipulated, Lloyd. And someone is doing one hell of a job."

Lloyd shook his head. "If anyone is being manipulated, it's you and possibly, Neil Davidson."

"Oh, I agree," Kristen nodded. "I can say, without modesty, that I'm the only person in the world who can rattle Neil Davidson to the exclusion of all else. Whatever momentum he had with Denning is probably already lost. Neil's need to control me, especially when I'm vulnerable, takes precedence over everything whenever I'm within five miles of him. Ergo, he can't do his job either."

She smiled cheerfully. "I, naturally, fight Neil on every issue to the exclusion of all else, because that is my usual behavior, so I'm rather useless, too. With luck, we can drag Denise Parker into all this with an extreme case of jealously, because she's had a sexual relationship with him for nearly a year." She frowned lightly. "Personally, I don't think the woman has that small an ego, but it would be nice icing on the cake. In any event, the conclusion of all this is that we are all so caught up in our own personal affairs, that Charles Denning and everything else will fall by the wayside."

"Ah huh," Lloyd responded.

"Ah huh," Kristen agreed.

Lloyd nodded skeptically. "And whose master plan is this?"

"Gee, Lloyd, I don't know. What do you think? Who's left?"

L.R. Simmons was quiet for several minutes, then he looked at her seriously. "You're serious about this, aren't you?"

Kristen looked at him curiously.

Lloyd shook his head in denial, stared out the windshield for a few moments, then took a deep breath. "Why would anyone sabotage the recovery of Charles Denning?"

"I don't know, Lloyd. What do you think?"

Lloyd started the car. "I think I should do some serious and very quiet investigating." He pulled the car around and started heading north on the highway, back to the PSR institute.

Kristen refastened her seatbelt, noting thankfully that Lloyd had not reminded her of it. "By the way, Lloyd, who found Charles Denning after the shooting?"

"His aide, Raymond Hayes."

"Hmm. Did he do everything according to the book?" Lloyd looked at her sharply, she elaborated. "I mean, I know certain security measures are necessary when dealing with government people like the Ambassador. Did he do everything he was supposed to do?"

"He made a few errors," Lloyd answered.

"Really? Was he new at the job?"

"No, he's very experienced. Charles Denning is the third Ambassador he's worked for."

"Hmm." Kristen looked innocently out the window. "I really enjoyed our drive, Lloyd, thank you for asking me."

Lloyd turned to Kristen again, right before they reached the gate. "By the way. You are a little cute."

Kristen grinned. "Thank you, Lloyd."

Chapter 21

Prospero: It was a torment to lay upon the damned...

Control. Neil Davidson was a master of control. Kristen knew the words, had studied the journals, taken the classes, watched the instructors and even subjected herself to hypnotherapy, but nothing compared to the skill she now witnessed in Neil Davidson.

Strange that in all the years she had known him, she had never watched him work. Of course, Charles Denning was pre-conditioned, he had been in therapy with Neil Davidson for over two months, but Neil took no shortcuts. He was slow and patient. He was a consummate professional, calm, strong... professional was the only word. Part of Kristen felt very much like a fool and an amateur. Somehow, she had a feeling she was supposed to feel like an amateur.

Charles Denning was fully under, relaxed, his eyes still closed.

"Charles, Dr. Michaels is here with us. I want you to respond to her voice. Are you comfortable with that?"

"Yes. I trust Kris."

"We are going to go back to the day of Saturday, February fifteenth. Can you do that?"

"Yes." Charles Denning's fingers on his right hand started moving slightly in a silent snapping movement.

Neil was watching Denning's hand, then looked at Kristen and back again. She nodded. "Be comfortable, Charles. Everything is fine." Neil nodded at Kristen again. "Go ahead," he suggested.

"Charles? This is Kris. You are not alone. All your friends are here. Do you understand?"

"I understand, Kris."

"It's Saturday, February fifteenth. Where are you?"

"I'm home."

"It's early in the morning. Look around. What do you see?"

"Myself. In the mirror. The water's running. Ah..." his hand started silently snapping his fingers again.

"Do you hear the water?" Kristen asked quickly.

Charles nodded.

"Do you hear anything else?"

Charles Denning raised his head slightly, his fingers stopped snapping. "Doorbell."

Neil looked sharply at Kristen.

"Do you hear anything else?" she asked.

"Just the doorbell. That's the second time. I can't find my robe." Charles looked from side to side. "I left it on the bed." He looked sharply to the right. "Doorbell again. Where the hell is Raymond? He was supposed to come over this morning. Idiot bell. Alright, I'm coming!" Charles yelled.

Kristen jerked in her chair, Neil reached over and touched her knee reassuringly.

Kristen let out a slow breath. "You heard the doorbell, Charles. What are you doing now?" she asked in a calm voice.

Charles started manically snapping his fingers and didn't answer.

Kristen bit her bottom lip, frowned at his hand, then skipped a step. "You're at the door, Charles," she said quietly. "What are you doing?"

"Looking through the peephole. It's UPS. Idiot. He's pushing the bell again."

"Paint the picture, Charles. Kristen can't see very well. Tell her what you see, tell her what you're doing. Describe everything," Neil put in, his voice coldly clinical.

Charles hesitated. "I'm opening the door. He says, 'good morning. I have a package for Ambassador Denning'. I'm in my damned pajamas. 'I'm Ambassador Denning'. He tells me to sign, 'no, just initial it'. I'm in my damned pajamas I need my robe, it's cold." He shook his head. "I take his clipboard, he hands me a pencil. 'Line six'."

"Charles, look at person in the UPS uniform. Describe the person," Kristen said quietly.

Charles frowned. "He looks young. Moustache. Too young for a moustache." Charles shook his head. "I don't know. I'm in my damned pajamas! They all look like kids, Kristen. Like Danny. They want to grow up so fast. They are all so young..." he shook his head again. "So young…"

"Don't push it," Neil told Kristen quietly.

Kristen nodded at Neil. "Keep moving forward in time, Charles. You have the clipboard and the pencil..."

"I initial line six, give the man the clipboard. His hands are cold. He gives me the package. 'Thank you'. I close the door."

"You're doing very well, Charles. Keep moving in time. You have the package. Describe the package."

"Feels like a video tape. Old type, VCR. Envelope is blank. Doesn't even have my name on it. Where the hell is Raymond? He's supposed to preview these damned bids." He shook his head.

"Keep moving in time, Charles. Where are you now?"

"I'm in the living room. I'm putting the tape in. I need my robe, it's cold in here."

"Keep moving in time, Charles. Where are you?"

"My bedroom. That's better. The phone's ringing. Shouting."

"Who's shouting?"

"I don't know. Shouting in the living room. The television. The phone's ringing. 'Where the hell are you, Raymond? No, I said here, not the office.

129

It's Saturday. Fine. Fax it over and I'll see you tonight. Five thirty, we have to go over the bids'. Idiot." His fingers started snapping again.

"Move along in time, Charles," Neil said patiently, shaking his head at Kristen. "Where are you now?"

"Kitchen. Coffee." He lifted his head in annoyance. "Shouting. What the hell is that?"

"Where is the shouting, Charles?" Kristen asked softly.

"The television."

"Keep moving in time, Charles."

Charles shook his head, his fingers were snapping frantically.

Neil looked at Kristen and gave a light shake of his head. "He's blocking," he told Kristen in a whisper. "Keep moving in time, Charles. Where are you?" Neil tried again.

Charles shook his head.

Kristen touched Neil's arm, asking permission to again do the questioning herself, Neil shrugged, but nodded.

"Charles," Kristen said gently, "all your friends are with you. You can't see us, but we are with you." She took his right hand, calming it with light strokes. The fingers on his hand stopped snapping. "I won't leave you. Keep moving in time. You are not alone. Feel my hand. You are not alone. I'm in here with you. You don't have to face this alone, I'm here if you need me."

Neil looked at her curiously.

"Oh, my God!" Charles said in a harsh whisper. "Oh, God. Oh, God!" He pulled his hand out of hers and put his hands over his ears. "No!"

"What's happening, Charles?" Kristen asked calmly. "What's upsetting you?"

Denning's face was a mask of horror. "Oh, God. DANNY! I'll kill you! You bastard, you bastard, you bastard, you bastard, you bastard, you bastard, you..."

"Charles?" Kristen again took his hand.

"You God Damned bastard, you bastard, you bastard, you..."

"Sleep, Charles," Neil broke in quickly. "You're back in the present. You're at the institute. You're safe." He slowed his words. "Breathe easily, you are very calm. Breathe in, breathe out, you are very calm."

Charles relaxed, he started breathing softly.

"In a few moments you'll awaken feeling fine. You will remember only what you want to remember. Sleep now." Neil spoke quietly to Kristen. "We've never gone that far. We've pushed far enough today." He looked at her with concern. "Are you alright?"

Kristen was still holding Charles hand, tears were streaming down her face. She nodded.

"I am going to bring him out of it. I need for you to be composed and calm. No negative emotion. Can you do that?"

"Yes." Kristen wiped her eyes and sat up firmly. "I'm fine," she said in her normal voice.

130

"Charles," Neil started. "I am going to count to three. On the count of three your eyes will open. On the count of three you will be wide awake, vigorous and perfectly refreshed as though you are awakening from a long rest. Here we go now. One. You are waking up now. You feel the energy flowing through your arms, flowing through your legs. Two. You are more and more awake, more and more awake, more and more awake. Your eyes are ready to open. You are about to wake up."

The overhead lights flickered.

"Wait," Kristen said quickly. She looked with amazement at a point to the left of Neil Davidson.

Charles Denning opened his eyes and instantly looked at the same spot where Kristen was staring. "Chipper?" his voice held astonishment.

"Three," Neil Davidson said quietly.

Chapter 22

Ariel: Lingering perdition--worse than any death...

Neil Davidson looked calmly at Charles Denning. "How do you feel, Ambassador?"

Charles Denning looked at him sharply. "Fine. Good." He reached over and squeezed Kristen's hand. "I'm fine, Kris. Better than fine." He looked back to Neil Davidson. "It was a rough one, wasn't it?"

Neil nodded. "How much do you remember?"

"Most of it. Some sadistic son of a bitch sent me a tape of Danny's execution," his expression became hard.

"His execution?" Kristen asked, not showing her astonishment.

"Yes."

"Do you want to discuss it?" Neil asked him.

Charles shook his head. "Maybe tomorrow. I think I'd like to assimilate some of the facts myself, first."

Kristen looked at him curiously. "What 'facts', Charles?"

Charles gave her a tight smile. "Don't psychoanalysis my every word, Kris, you sound like an MP. I simply mean I need to digest all of this before I'm ready to talk about it. Okay?"

Kristen shook her head. "Charles, you..."

"Dr. Michaels," Neil said sternly, standing. "Our patient has asked for some time. And, since it's nearing the dinner hour, he could also probably use a break."

"So could you, Kris," Charles smiled at her. He looked up at Neil Davidson. "Tell you what, Doc. Why don't you take my favorite child psychologist out to dinner, something really fancy, on me. Maybe a walk along the beach so she can see the colors of the sunset. Top Of The Cove. That's one of my favorite restaurants. The fish of the day is usually excellent."

"It sounds like a good idea," Neil smiled at him.

Kristen also stood. "When did I become the patient?"

"Just go, Kris. Please," Charles said seriously.

Kristen eyes flashed with concern, but she nodded.

Neil took Kristen's arm. "I'll see you in the morning, Ambassador," he told Charles.

Charles nodded, his expression grim.

Neil led Kristen out of the suite and into his office. He closed the door and immediately picked up the phone. "I've got a critical in suite six, full suicide watch. No visitors until further notice. Hold off escorting him to dinner until the first crisis has passed." Neil hung up the phone.

"Suicide watch?" Kristen asked.

Neil turned on the monitor on the wall, punched in a few numbers and the picture of suite six flashed on his screen. Charles Denning was sitting on the sofa, taking deep breaths, his hands nervously combing his hair. His breathing became slightly choked, he drew up his knees, held them and started rocking slightly. He then put his head on his knees and started crying hysterically.

Kristen watched Charles without emotion. The monster was coming out of the closet, now was the time to confront it.

Neil looked over at Kristen, his face was pinched in a frown of concentration. "It's a good sign, Kristi."

"Yes, it is," Kristen nodded, took off her glasses and put them in her jacket pocket. "So why aren't we in there with him?"

"He couldn't do that in front of you," Neil told her. "He identifies with you as his friend, Kris, not his doctor."

"I see. You want me to pull out of his therapy?"

Neil shook his head. "No. But we need to set up some signals. There are going to be times when I will want you out of the room, away from him. He's a proud man and he wants to be strong for you. He has cast you as 'friend', maybe even as a potential lover, that is the role you have to accept."

Kristen nodded. "Alright. I see your point. So you're going in there with him alone. I'll wait, I won't even monitor."

"No. I'll give him the time he asked for."

"I don't understand."

"We're done for the day. Now, we are going home, we are going for a walk along the beach, I am going to fix you dinner and we are going to make mad, passionate love either before, during or after. I'm not choosy."

Kristen looked at Neil suspiciously. "He got to you."

"I am a professional, I am detached from the situation. You are the one who needs to relax."

"Bullshit."

"Watch your language, little girl, you work with children, remember?" He looked at the screen where Charles Denning was still crying hysterically. "But I tell you, after the jerk who sent that tape gets out of surgery, I like to get him into therapy. His problems are a lot deeper than those of Charles Denning."

"Why would he need surgery?"

"Because when I find him, I'm going to beat the living crap out of him."

Kristen nodded. "Spoken like a truly detached and professional psychiatrist," she decided.

The phone on Neil's desk started ringing furiously. "I have the distinct impression that the therapy I need from you is about to be postponed," he told her darkly.

Kristen looked back at the screen and Charles Denning, her expression unreadable.

Chapter 23

Prospero: ...discord shall bestrew the union of your bed with weeds so loathly that you shall hate it both...

Matthew Jeffers was beaming when Kristen and Neil entered his office. "Well done! I watched the session with the Ambassador, I couldn't be more pleased!" He shook Neil's hand, then Kristen's. "I knew, if you tried, the two of you could work this together." He gestured to the two chairs in front of his desk. "Sit. Let's talk about where we go from here."

Neil held Kristen's chair politely, then sat himself. "It's pretty standard, from this point," he told Jeffers. "Now that we know the problem, we can deal with it."

Matthew Jeffers nodded. "I've been down this road before. The guilt Charles Denning feels about the death of his son is, quite obviously, not over."

"I disagree," Kristen said quietly. "We're not dealing with guilt here, but pure grief. And, something else."

Matthew looked at her curiously. "What else?"

Kristen shook her head. "I don't know. I almost understand shooting at the television, but not the suicide attempt. It doesn't add up."

"It adds up," Neil argued. "The man saw his son being executed, it was simply more guilt than he could bear. He's a protective man, he will feel the guilt."

Kristen shook her head. "No. Not Charles. It's not guilt. I spoke with him about it. He knows there was nothing he could do to save Danny, he understands what happened, even if he doesn't like facing it. What he feels is anger, even hatred toward Danny's killers and toward the system that allowed it, not guilt. You don't attempt suicide when you're angry with something else. You look for answers, you look for justice or revenge. Killing yourself is counter-intuitive."

"I have to agree with Neil," Matthew Jeffers was shaking his head. "After Danny's death, the Ambassador was also suicidal. Whoever set him up this time, must have known that."

Neil looked at Jeffers suspiciously. "Speaking of which, how is it that all this information, the tape, the clues that must have been left behind, have been overlooked?"

Jeffers shook his head. "I don't know. Lloyd tells me the scene was compromised by media and local police, but even so, there should have been something. He's checking into it as we speak. There is a possibility that Raymond Hayes is involved."

"That's fairly obvious," Neil nodded.

"Too obvious," Kristen frowned. "He doesn't strike me as a stupid man."

"Lloyd will figure it out," Matthew Jeffers said confidently.

"If he finds that tape, I'd like to see it," Neil told him. "It could help me determine how deeply I should go in his therapy. If Kristen is right and we're dealing with anger, not guilt, it will be easier to affect a cure."

"Chipper might help," Kristen said quietly.

Neil looked amused, Jeffers smiled broadly at Kristen. "Chipper! I'd almost forgotten him! That was quite a surprise! He actually saw him and he didn't revert to his childhood!" He reached over the desk and patted Kristen's hand. "Quite a coup for you, Kris. I hope you get the chance to follow up on it."

"So do I."

Matthew Jeffers tilted his head. "Did you see him as well, Kristen? At the end of the session, it actually looked as though you saw Chipper yourself."

Kristen glared at him and tried to contain her anger. "I didn't see much of anything, Matt. I have a bit of a vision problem."

Neil felt her anger, even he was annoyed by Matt's patronizing attitude. "The patient was emotionally projecting his delusion, Kristen probably felt that projection," he suggested.

"'Felt his projection'?" Kristen looked interested. "Sounds intriguing." She thought about it. "Actually, it sounds somewhat dirty."

"You know what I mean."

"You mean you think I'm psychic in some way? How terribly 'new age' of you!"

"No, I think you feel the emotions of your patients much too deeply," Neil answered tightly. "Given the opportunity to imagine what the Ambassador saw on the television screen, or seeing his childhood playmate, you also chose the more comfortable apparition."

"Ah," Kristen nodded. "You mean I'm a starry-eyed wimp with delusions of Disneyland dancing in my head. I forgot. You're the detached and professional psychiatrist who feels nothing."

"Don't fight, children," Matthew Jeffers put in. "It was a good session, very positive and you're digressing."

"So it seems," Kristen responded.

"I admit the room was emotionally tense," Neil offered. "Chipper aside, I think we can get to the bottom of all this using conventional methods. The Ambassador needs to face the fact that someone played a horribly cruel mind game with him, get the details he might have missed in this session and help him face his emotions."

"The devil is definitely in the details," Kristen nodded.

"Yes." Matthew Jeffers became more businesslike. "What's your prognosis, Dr. Davidson? Will we be able to release the Ambassador for his meeting on Saturday? It's your call."

136

Neil Davidson nodded. "If all goes as I expect with the next few sessions, I think we can upgrade him to an outpatient. I don't want to release him entirely. Until we know everything, he may still contemplate suicide."

"Kristen?"

"It's Neil's case," she answered, "but I wouldn't put a gun in his hand any time soon, or the fate of a peace treaty. He has a lot to work out."

"I concur. I would prefer that we go slowly this time," Matthew Jeffers looked concerned. "I may have pushed him too quickly when I had him in therapy the last time, the man needs to resolve any lasting guilt he has over his son's death." He smiled at Kristen, then looked hopefully at Neil. "Although you don't like the possibility of using 'Chipper', Neil, I hope you might let Kristen work on that angle, as well. If nothing else, it's a valuable and publishable cynosure that demands additional consideration."

"Certainly," Neil answered, surprising both Kristen and Matthew Jeffers. "Kris has already been invaluable in the Ambassador's therapy, I believe it is due to her that he was able to open up in the first place. I am looking forward to her assistance in the future."

Kristen stared at him. "Thank you, Dr. Davidson."

Neil grinned at her. "You're welcome, Dr. Michaels."

The room was silent for several long seconds.

"Well!" Matthew Jeffers stood. "Surprisingly, we are all agreed. Tomorrow, maybe we can finally start a cure. For all our problems."

Chapter 24

Prospero: They are both in either's powers...

Matthew Jeffers had been silently taking rounds with Denise Parker, nodding encouragingly at her intelligent diagnoses, looking at medical charts with interest and his own extensive knowledge of her surgical procedures.

It was a rare pat on the back for Denise, she was softly glowing under the praise. Matthew Jeffers was an icon in medicine and psychology, his accolades could only strengthen her own reputation.

Matthew spotted L.R. Simmons in the hall, he gestured him over to join them.

"Dr. Jeffers, Dr. Parker," Simmons nodded at Denise. Denise nodded in return.

Matthew Jeffers looked at Simmons expectantly. "Where's Doctor Michaels?"

"She's checked out for the evening."

"Checked out?" Matthew Jeffers looked worried. "She hasn't gone back to Claren?"

"No, Sir."

"Then where is she?"

"Dr. Michaels checked out with Dr. Davidson," Simmons answered brusquely.

"Oh." Matthew looked at his watch and nodded. "Time has gotten away from me, it is past dinner. I'm glad Neil at least has the decency to feed the poor child. When she returns this evening, let me know, I need to discuss Lindsay Cummings' transfer with her. I'll be here until about ten."

"Dr. Michaels has checked out for the evening," Lloyd told him. "She will be in again about nine tomorrow morning."

"She's with Neil for the night?" Jeffers looked surprised.

"Yes, Dr. Jeffers," Simmons looked quickly at Denise Parker, who was concentrating on a chart she was holding.

"Hmm." Matthew shook his head gently. "I see. Thank you, Lloyd."

"Yes, Sir," Lloyd nodded at Denise Parker and continued walking down the hall toward the security wing.

Matthew Jeffers turned to Denise. "I probably shouldn't keep you any longer, either. I'm sure you have plans for the evening."

Denise nodded, her smile forced.

Matthew Jeffers leaned heavily on his cane and limped toward the elevator.

Denise Parker walked back to her own office, carefully filed the charts of her patients, then pulled the chart on Teresa Lawson. Such a mess. Seventeen and already hard as nails. She'd been beaten before by friends of her pimp, the poor child probably never had a normal existence. It was incredible what women would do to survive. What stupid things women would do to find love.

Actually, she should be studying the chart of Lindsay Cummings since Dr. Jeffers was planning on transferring her soon. The cast was about due to come off, they could set up a simpler brace so the girl wouldn't be too uncomfortable for the trip. The teenager had actually come around a great deal since her session with Kristen Michaels, she was even pleasant to the staff. Kristen Michaels was, apparently, quite effective as a therapist. Nice lady. Pretty in her own way. She had that little-girl effect on men--people. Strong. Nice lady.

Denise looked at the clock on her desk. It was late, she should get some dinner and go home. Nothing was that pressing and she had that bypass in the morning if the Admiral remained stable. It was a simple procedure, but it was best to be fresh, complications always seemed to lurk when she anticipated a simple procedure.

Denise nodded to herself, filed the chart on Teresa Lawson and pulled the file on Admiral Fielding. She'd take it home and study it, just to make sure there weren't any surprises she couldn't anticipate. She put the file in her briefcase, stood and looked around the office, sure she had forgotten something. Didn't matter. If something came up, they'd call. She clipped the pager to her waist, took off her work shoes and put on the heels that matched her dress. She carefully hung up her lab jacket.

Denise looked around again to make sure she hadn't forgotten anything, then walked out of her office and locked the door behind her. The halls were empty. Walking toward the exit her heels clicked loudly.

It was actually very natural, Denise decided as she walked toward the parking lot and her car. Kristen Michaels brought out a passion in Neil Davidson that had been lacking when he was with her. Anger, frustration, annoyance, all of it. He was never calm and collected around Kristen Michaels, even if he was only talking about her. And they had been married, once. That kind of bond was rarely broken by a divorce or annulment. He was probably still in love with her. Perfectly natural.

Three tries, Denise was having trouble putting the key in the car door. "Damnit!" What the hell was wrong with her?

"Dr. Parker?"

Denise turned and looked at L.R. Simmons.

"He did that on purpose, you know. He wants you to be jealous."

"What? Why would Neil..." she left the question hanging.

"Not Dr. Davidson. Dr. Jeffers. May I buy you dinner? Not here, up the coast at bit. We'll take separate cars. I think we need to talk."

Denise looked at Simmons critically. He was wearing a blue suit and matching tie, he looked strong, reliable, and oddly comforting. "You know the Crow's Nest?"

"Yes."

"I'll meet you there," Denise offered. The key slipped into the lock easily, she gave Lloyd a brilliant smile, got in her car and drove off.

They met at the front of the restaurant and walked in together. Denise waited until they had been seated. "Do you want to tell me what this is all about?" she asked Lloyd.

During the drive to the restaurant, Lloyd had cursed himself for every kind of fool. The scenario Kristen Michaels had laid out for him seemed a little ridiculous in retrospect, but it clouded his judgment. When Matthew Jeffers had more or less forced him to reveal the fact that Kristen and Neil Davidson were spending the night together, he had looked at Denise Parker and felt a wave of protection for her.

It was stupid, really. Dr. Parker was not a fragile woman, but strong and extremely reliable.

"I think I spoke out of turn," Simmons said with light embarrassment.

Denise touched his arm. "You're probably right, you know. Dr. Jeffers likes to shake people up. I've noticed that about him. A lot of older people play God later on in life, PSR is his little planet and we are all his subjects."

"I guess so."

"You care about Kristen Michaels, don't you?" Denise guessed.

Lloyd smiled. "I do seem to be losing my perspective," he admitted.

"Now that's refreshing," Denise smiled in return. "A man with feelings, who actually admits it. You are a dinosaur, Lloyd. Protective and gentle." She looked at him curiously. "How come we never talk to each other?"

"It's never come up."

Denise nodded. "Are you going to make a play for Kristen Michaels?"

Lloyd shook his head. "No. She has someone back in her hometown."

"It can't be anyone too important, or she wouldn't be with Neil."

Lloyd pictured Paul Beckner with Kristen the day he had first met her. From his viewpoint, it had been a long term, comfortable relationship. He remembered his own opinion of Paul Beckner as well. A good and solid man, someone he would choose for Kristen himself. Lloyd shook his head. "No, he's extremely important to her. The relationship she has with Dr. Davidson is not the same. Not as real." He looked at her curiously. "You're not jealous, are you?"

Denise frowned. "Actually, I thought I was. It certainly felt like it, for a moment there." She shook her head. "Evidently, I'm more shallow than I thought. I respect Neil, but I don't love him. Huh! Imagine my surprise!" She sat back and looked at Lloyd critically. "You, on the other hand, are not a shallow person. You play for keeps. If you want her, Lloyd, work at it. Put your heart and soul into it."

"No, I don't think so." Lloyd thought about his answer. Kristen Michaels, the damsel in distress. She'd been right. That's why he had been attracted to her. It was another manipulation, another con. She was a nice lady, he liked her, but that was all. "I really don't want to hunt her down, Dr. Parker. It's not exactly my style and I don't think she needs any more complications in her life. I like her, but that's all." The last thing he needed in his life was a damsel in distress, what had he been thinking?

"Oh." Denise smiled. "In that case, let's just enjoy dinner."

Matthew Jeffers dutifully turned off all the surveillance equipment in his office and waited for the call. Explaining Charles Denning's breakthrough to his superiors was not going to be easy. How Kristen seemed to bring out patients was always difficult to explain, especially when he didn't understand it himself. This time she had broken through an intentional hypnotic block and succeeded almost easily. She didn't do anything that he could put his finger on, but she always managed to do it in record time. She should never have been able to break through that block. It was uncanny.

Kristen was confused about not going back to Denning to help him through his pain, he saw it in her eyes. At the very least she probably thought Davidson was incompetent, at worst... hell, he couldn't imagine what she thought. After Lindsay Cummings had broken down, Kristen had held the brat for nearly a half an hour, let her cry, tell the worst of her story, Kristen didn't leave her until the storm had passed and the monster fully exposed. It wasn't her way. Confront the monster. Take it down.

Kristen never left a patient alone after they broke down. She never left anyone in pain. It was Kristen's normal routine, he knew it and she knew he knew it. By not saying anything when they came to his office, he had officially co-signed Davidson's bullshit therapy. Of course Kristen probably already thought he was incompetent. Only God knew why she was still his friend.

The call came through, the first question chilled him to the bone. "How's our favorite Ambassador doing?"

Matthew kept his voice calm. "He's had a bit of a breakthrough," he answered.

A slight pause. "How big a bit?"

"He remembered receiving the tape and he remembers what was on it."

A longer pause. "Not good. How much did he discuss?"

"Just that it was a tape of his son's execution. He did not go into details." Matthew hesitated. "He's not a stupid man. He'll realize that Hayes removed the tape before the authorities got there."

"Not a problem," came the answer. "National Security, Hayes did what he was told, he can cover himself. Do you want to explain how all this happened?"

"Natural course of therapy. It would have come out sooner or later. No real damage done."

"There will be if he discusses it with anyone prematurely."

"Dr. Davidson has that covered. Ambassador Denning will be on suicide watch until he leaves Friday night. He won't be talking to anyone of consequence."

"How much does this untimely breakthrough have to do with your little child psychologist?"

Matthew kept his voice very steady. "She might have been a catalyst, nothing more. Dr. Michaels is a lightweight."

"You should never have allowed her into his therapy."

"I have full autonomy on who I hire, as long as they pass security," Matthew answered tersely. "You wanted the Ambassador to be able to resume his duties with the appearance of normalcy, now he can. Her involvement has helped him become more calm and more personable. Before she came, he was acting tense and close to an obvious breakdown. He was speaking in short sentences and was constantly distracted. He could never have attended that conference in his previous condition. Kristen Michaels has solved that problem."

"By creating a new one. She's a dangerous liability and you can't control her."

"I disagree. Neil Davidson has her under total control," Matthew Jeffers assured the voice.

"She's still a liability."

"She's also the best child psychologist that's available to wayward children of this or any administration. Dr. Michaels has been fully cleared by the State Department. She's on staff at the military base in Claren, Colorado, with a full Top Secret clearance. She's worked with kids of UN Security Council members and received *their* clearance. There is no way you can discredit her, don't even think about it. Even mildly suggesting that she's a liability to this administration would cause extremely awkward questions no one needs or wants to answer."

A very long pause. "Agreed," the line disconnected.

Matthew Jeffers hung up the phone and sagged with relief.

Chapter 25

Prospero: ... The time 'twist six and now must by us both be spent most preciously.

Kristen stood on the balcony, looking out at the ocean. The sunset had been blurry, but brilliant, more spectacular than any she might see at home. Neil always could choose a home with a view. The ocean had its own magic, its own memories.

"Getting cold?" Neil came up behind her, wrapping his arms around her waist.

"It must be seventy degrees out here. Californians don't know the meaning of 'cold'."

"It's closer to sixty. Your blood has thickened since you moved back to Colorado," Neil told her.

"I prefer the cold and snow. You can't make a decent snowman with sand," Kristen told him.

"Very true," Neil admitted. "Are you still building snowmen with your patients?"

"Not lately, snowmen seem to be going out of style. Now my kids would rather ice skate or ski." Kristen smiled "I tend to agree with them. I went skiing at Spruce Meadows the other night," she told him. "Heidi and her new boyfriend flanked me. Unfortunately, they kept me on the bunny slopes. It was fun, but slow."

"You always were the better skier," Neil hugged her to him. "You were lucky that you didn't break your neck. I could never keep up."

"You were always too careful. Afraid to take a chance."

"I'm not the one who ran away," Neil pointed out.

Kristen continued to look at the ocean. "Are we going to fight?"

"No. We're supposed to be fixing dinner."

"Then let me wear my glasses. I can't see to cook."

"So you'll make some mistakes," Neil shrugged. "Are you planning on hiring a full time maid and cook later?"

"I'll manage."

"We're talking basics here, Dr. Michaels. Stir fry and rice. You can do this."

"I know I can. I just don't want to prove to you that I can."

"I'm not going to fight with you, Kristi."

She turned in his arms. "Yes, you are."

"Okay, we have a pattern. If you want to fight about dinner, we'll fight about dinner."

"No, that means we're fighting about my handicap. I want to talk about Charles Denning and Chipper."

"There's nothing to discuss. The Ambassador had a breakthrough. Now we're just mopping up."

"You're ignoring Chipper. He was there, Neil. Charles saw Chipper and he didn't have to revert to being a boy to see him. He desperately needed to talk. If not to Chipper, then to us."

"The fantasy life of Kristen Michaels," Neil smiled. "I was wondering how long that would take. He was coming out of hypnosis, Kris. With the right conditioning, he could have seen pink hippos. You told him 'all' his friends were there. Naturally he saw his friends, including Chipper. No magic, nothing strange, he saw exactly what you wanted him to see. What you think you saw yourself."

"There is a lot more to it than that. We shouldn't have left him alone. He needed a friend, not an empty room."

"I disagree," He looked at her. "My question is, how did you get him to believe that Chipper was real again? How did you get him to believe it was 'okay' to believe in invisible friends again?"

Kristen bit her lower lip.

"I'm not complaining, whatever you did, it worked. He opened up, we now know what caused his behavior and suicide attempt. Now that he's faced it, the worst is over."

Kristen looked doubtful.

"Fess up, Kristi. What did you do? Give him the minishrink lecture from one of your classes?"

"No." She watched his face with concern. "I told him about Goldie and how she helped me."

"Goldie. I see." Neil released her waist and looked at her, his expression blank. "And did you tell him *why* she had to help you? Did you tell him that you were ripped apart and it took two years of reconstructive surgery to put you back together? Did you tell him how that psychotic destroyed your life and took away your chances for a family?"

"No," Kristen answered, "I told Charles that I had once had a minishrink and that she helped me through a difficult time during a childhood molestation."

"Molestation? Is that what you called it? Did you conveniently forget the four days of rape, torture, knife wounds, broken bones, permanent physical scars? Did you mention that you were forced to watch the torture and murder of another child during this minor little 'molestation'?"

"No." Kristen rubbed her arms vigorously. "I don't discuss the grisly details of my past with anyone."

"Then it's about God Damned time you did!"

Kristen took a deep breath, it was an old argument. "Let it go, Neil, I'm fine. The man is dead. Uncle Wally made sure of that."

"Then Uncle Wally died saving you, making your guilt and grief even more substantial!" Neil answered through clenched teeth. "But you don't discuss that with anyone, either, including me."

"We're talking about something that happened more than thirty years ago, Neil. You talked to Pop about his guilt demons, I don't have any." She gave him a gentle smile. "And you helped him, you really did. He never understood why we couldn't make it. He really loved you, Neil."

Neil's eyes softened and he touched her face gently. "And I really loved his daughter. I still do. I always will. I never fully understood why we didn't make it, either." A basic fact of life that would never change, Neil admitted to himself. He kissed her gently.

Kristen looked up at him. "Is your hysterical rant over?"

"I was not hysterical," Neil told her.

"No, just wonderfully protective of a little girl you never met," Kristen answered. "Good thing you didn't go into child psychology, you'd be a basket case by now. You really have blind spots when it comes to kids, Neil."

"How do you deal with the kids that come to you after being molested?"

Kristen thought about it. "I've been curiously detached," she answered. "Those kids need help too badly for me to fall apart."

"Healthy attitude," Neil grudgingly admitted.

"I'm a very healthy person," Kristen answered. "With a few exceptions. If we're finished with ancient history, can we get back to Denning, now?"

"And 'Chipper'?"

Kristen nodded. "And Chipper. The timing is wrong, somehow. Chipper showed up after Charles remembered the tape of his son. Not during, not before."

"So?"

"This is going to sound weird," Kristen told him.

Neil started laughing. "Right. You always sound so logical, Dr. Michaels."

"I'm serious. When Chipper showed up, the first thing I thought was it was like one of those annoying commercials where the guy says, 'but wait, there's more!'"

Neil looked at her curiously. "More than the tape?"

"Yes," Kristen nodded. "Weird, huh?"

Neil frowned, then started pacing. "I don't like your style, Dr. Michaels, and I think you're really overboard with your minishrink stuff and all the other fantasies you peddle...."

"But?"

"But, you have instincts. God knows where you got them, but they are there. You were right about the connection with Denning's son. I honestly didn't think there was a connection."

"I'm curious about that, too. The only other time Charles showed violent tendencies was after his son's death. It seems like such a natural connection."

Neil shook his head. "Not really. He's been through a lot more than you know about. He's lived in a very violent country for the past three years, Kris. During therapy he's talked about a lot of human suffering, women, children, violent coups, even cock fights that he found emotionally unsettling. Succession from one president to another usually involves assassination and several attempts were made while he was there."

"But,"

"Plus, his last therapist was Matthew Jeffers. Jeffers is an icon, Kris. He doesn't do things half way. If he believed that Charles Denning was mentally competent after his son's death, then his opinion has to be respected."

"You were protecting his reputation?" Kristen asked quietly.

Neil shook his head. "No. Matthew Jeffers is only human, he makes mistakes and admits those mistakes."

"Not since I've known him," Kristen answered.

"We are speculating, Dr. Michaels and making assumptions."

Kristen frowned.

"Yes, we are," Neil told her. "We are breaking one of your sacrosanct rules. If you want to know why Charles Denning saw Chipper after discussing the tape, what is the Kristen Michaels textbook answer?"

"Ask the patient."

Neil smiled. "And the patient is not here. You can ask him as soon as I take him off suicide watch."

"And until then?"

"We quit speculating. We came here to relax, eat dinner and make love. Make a great deal of love, I hope. Are you hungry?"

"Yes."

"Do you want dinner?" Neil smiled.

"Not if you're going to make me cook it using the Braille method."

"You don't need sight to cook. It takes a sense of taste, smell and a little dedication."

"Hmm." She grinned. "Tell you what. If you cook dinner, I'll make love to you using the Braille method. I promise to use my sense of taste," she kissed him softly on the mouth, "my sense of feel," she circled his ear with a fingertip, "and a lot of dedication."

"Not fair, you always did," Neil answered.

"Hmm. But this time, we'll leave the lights on and you can see what I can only sense."

"You're escaping again, Kristi," Neil told her.

"So escape with me, Neil," she stood on her toes and whispered in his ear. "Take me where we can dream together."

Neil smiled lightly.

"I love that dimple," Kristen told him, kissing it. "Have I ever told you how much I love that dimple?" She grinned at him.

"You are such a brat," Neil picked her up in his arms and carried her into the bedroom, depositing her gently on the bed and lying next to her. "I'll fix dinner a little later. If you fail this test, Dr. Michaels..."

"I'm not making dinner," Kristen said firmly. "I'll just keep taking the test until you decide I've passed."

Neil pulled off her sweater, kissing her between her breasts, unhooking her bra at the same time. "You are so beautiful, Kristi."

"And you say I live in a fantasy world," she sighed heavily. "Either that, or you're going as blind as I am," she decided.

Neil traced the scars on her neck and chest with his fingertips. "All I've ever see is you."

"I know. With all my nasty, realistic flaws, you see both what I am and what I could have been. I've never understood that," she admitted.

Neil gently pulled off the rest of her clothing, touching her everywhere. "God, I've missed you," he told her softly.

"Neil, I," Kristen let out a heavy sigh. "Can we get under the covers now?"

"No. Stay in the light with me, sweetheart. I love you. I love who you are, not your idealistic version of who you might have been," Neil ran his hands down the length of her body, kissing every scar. "Don't hide from me, Kristen. There's no need," he told her. "There has never been a need for you to hide."

Kristen closed her eyes, responding easily to his touch. "Please, love. I'm not hiding, I'm cold."

"Oh, Sweetheart," Neil kissed her eyelids. The earlier conversation about Goldie and her childhood attack had made her more vulnerable than usual. He wouldn't push it, he had already gone too far. He tried for a lighter tone. "You are also just as stubborn as every other female and you make false promises," he told her, pulling back the sheets, letting her hide what she thought she needed to hide. He undressed and joined her under the covers, pulling her to him.

Kristen tried to focus on his eyes, finally deciding that memory would have to take the place of eyesight. "As I recall, you preferred me just about here," she moved almost completely on top of him. "Or was it here?" she corrected the position only slightly, making the obvious connection.

"Oh, God, there," Neil put his hands tightly on the sides of her tiny waist, his heart skipping a beat. It always did with Kristen, his feelings took his breath away. "Sweetheart, I prefer you anywhere, as long as it's in my bed, with me," he told her quietly. "Where you belong."

"You always have been my favorite fantasy," Kristen also spoke quietly, "God help me, I'm afraid you always will be," she added almost too softly for him to hear.

Neil rolled over, holding her tightly, taking the dominate position. "Look at me, Kristi, see me with your heart, not just your eyes."

"I always have," Kristen told him.

"Tell me," Neil demanded, "please tell me, Kristi."

"I love you," she told him.

"Yes," Neil held her face in his hands. "Yes," he kissed her with all the passion that he could only find with her.

147

From that point on, there was no need for words.

A hour later, the phone started ringing.

Neil was still holding Kristen next to him, her head was tucked into his shoulder, he could feel her breath on his chest. It felt natural and extremely, achingly, familiar.

"Gosh, gee, the phone," Kristen told him with a light laugh. "What a surprise."

Neil kissed her on the top of her head victoriously. "Actually, if you think about it, it is a surprise. We actually beat the bell that time."

"You mean we're done? I don't remember a thing," she looked at him speculatively.

"So next time, take notes, little girl. This was a test, remember?"

Kristen started laughing. "Ah, I knew I forgot something."

The phone was up to three rings.

Neil sighed, grabbing the phone. "Do not leave this bed, I am not finished with you. I plan on making love to you all night."

"Ha! Men always say that but they never really mean it," Kristen told him, kissing him quickly and getting up, "and I'm hungry. If that's room service, I want a hamburger with everything on it," she walked into the connecting bathroom.

Neil punched the button on the phone, silencing it after six rings. "Dr. Davidson."

He listened for several moments. "No, don't bother Dr. Jeffers. I'll handle it. Fifteen minutes." He nodded tiredly and hung up the phone.

Kristen looked at him expectantly from around the bathroom door. "Are we going back to the institute?"

"No, I'm going back to the institute," he told her, pulling on his pants. "Your services are not required. At least not there," he wiggled an eyebrow at her. "I shouldn't be more than a hour, tops."

"No hamburger?"

"Not unless you make it," Neil told her. "We still have stir fry in the kitchen," he reminded her.

"I don't want stir-fry," Kristen said petulantly, her head disappeared back into the bathroom, her voice echoed lightly. "I want a hamburger with pickles. No, I want a cheeseburger with pickles. And a toy."

"No toy," Neil called back to her, "you've got me to play with."

"But you wind down too quickly," Kristen protested.

"Very funny," Neil grinned. "Okay, I'll get you a cheeseburger, not that you deserve it. Macdonald's or have your tastes improved?"

Kristen peeked around the door again and glared at him. "We had a deal. You were going to make dinner, I'm giving you an easy way out. I also want fries and a chocolate shake."

"Question answered, your tastes haven't improved," Neil decided.

"What's the problem at the institute?" Kristen walked around the bathroom door wearing a huge green terrycloth robe, it went down to her feet.

"Fetching," Neil decided, recognizing his robe, the same robe that only reached his knees. "A little big for you, don't you think?"

"I like big," Kristen winked at him. "So what's the emergency at the Institute. Charles?" she asked with concern.

"No, he's fine and I have good people watching him," Neil assured her. "Evidently, we have a new inmate. A 'very important person'," he smiled, "at least according to him. Jeffers blackmailed him into 'voluntary' therapy. He agreed to come to the institute, now he wants service."

"Blackmailed?" Kristen asked, sitting cross-legged on the bed.

Neil nodded. "In other words, he takes our Rorschach tests, or he will be exposed as a not-nice person."

"Oh. What does he want?"

"A bigger suite, someone to cater to his every whim, an office for his personal secretary, probably a playmate or two of the month who can survive his sadistic requirements. You know, the usual. For good measure, I'm sure he'll add caviar and champagne for a midnight snack."

"Ah," Kristen thought about it. "Not a Macdonald's person," she decided.

Neil put on his loafers. "If that was a reminder, I haven't forgotten. Cheeseburger, fries and a chocolate shake," he kissed her nose.

"And a toy."

"No toy."

Kristen grinned at him. "Maybe an apple turnover?"

"Don't push it, brat," Neil told her.

Kristen followed him to the front door, watched out the window until Neil's car had pulled out of the driveway, then got her cell phone out of her purse, went back into the bathroom, turned on the water and dialed the number.

"Weather Bureau."

"I'm on my cell."

A thirty second pause. "It's secure."

"I need a weather report from Trinculo."

"One moment."

Kristen waited, pacing, combing her hair with her fingers. She was beginning to feel like one of Neil's split personalities.

"Hey, Ariel."

"Hayes for certain."

"No surprise," Patrick's voice told her. "Are you okay?"

Kristen sat on the floor of the bathroom, her back to the tub. "Just peachy. I want a more controllable tempest. Tell Prospero I have enough drama around here without his interference, he has too many players. I need room to maneuver. I'm pretty sure security and medical are clean, but I've had to improvise to keep them out of my way. FYI, Hayes is going to rabbit after the conference, Denning more or less gave him away during his session today, even Jeffers couldn't deny the possibility of his involvement.

My guess is that Hayes is hearing about it now, from Jeffers. For a while they'll probably be able to cover it under National Security, but it won't hold long."

"Another one down," Patrick said mildly.

"Not until you find the tape he has."

"Sorry, Ariel. I have a copy of the boy's execution, but not his torture. Evidently, the torture was never taped." Patrick informed her.

"Then we're still in the game. The execution is the one you want, according to the patient."

"And he knows the answers," Patrick finished.

"Exactly. How bad is it?" Kristen asked.

"Tell you the truth, Ariel, it's grim, but not that bad. More or less a simple execution. The major damage to the kid was done well before that, it looked more like a mercy killing. They simply hauled him up, tied him to a post and shot him. Extremely grainy, you can barely make out his face."

"Could you make out the bad guys?"

"Nope, except for a few village folk, the bad guys wore masks. They could be anyone, including the three guys they actually convicted."

"Hang on." Kristen thought about it. Something was missing.

Yelling.

She visualized Charles in the therapy session. *(Bastard, bastard, bastard!)*. Charles was snapping his fingers, putting his hands over his ears… "What was the audio like? Did Danny say anything?"

"No. I doubt the kid even knew what was happening," Patrick answered.

"Any yelling?"

"The usual crowd stuff, nothing spectacular."

It couldn't be the same tape. "Are you sure that was the only tape made?"

"Yes."

"Damnit!" Kristen tapped her fingers. "We need the tape they took out of the machine, maybe it was doctored or something. What we have is a great big hole. I need something that will elicit more anger than a simple execution of a grainy victim."

"Watching my son get shot would bring out a hell of a lot of anger in me, Kristen."

"Except you don't sound especially angry," she pointed out.

"It wasn't my kid," Patrick countered.

Kristen frowned. "Reading the autopsy report made you angry."

"That was different. It was a total betrayal of everything human," Patrick answered. "That autopsy report made me angry enough to kill the bastards."

"Don't move, don't talk," Kristen demanded. Betrayal. Neil bringing up the explicit details of her childhood injuries, her father's death, her own blindness. Trying to dredge up her insecurities, her fears, her anger, her hurt. Words could hurt, or words could help. Only a few people in your life could use words that might affect you. Parents, teachers, friends, husband, therapists. Words that injured, words that crippled, words that frightened....

...Words that created monsters in the closet. *(keep moving forward, Charles...)* fingers snapping.

Fingers snapping. An intentional post hypnotic block by an expert. Every time he hesitated or fought on an answer, his fingers were snapping uncontrollably. She hated herself for say the words. "Davidson is a certain," she told him firmly.

"Are we speculating?" Patrick asked.

If only she was. "No. He translated the autopsy for Charles."

"Part of therapy," Patrick suggested. "The devil is in the details."

"Really? Who has the answers, Patrick?"

"The patient," he answered instantly.

"Do we give the patient the answers?"

"No."

"Why?"

"Because we don't know the answers, only the patient does."

"So what do we do?"

"We listen," Patrick answered.

"Why?"

Patrick again answered instantly. "The patient is the only one who knows the answers. We only deal with the monsters they already have, we don't create new ones." A long pause. "Except," another long pause, "by sharing the autopsy, Davidson created new nightmares, he gave the patient another monster to deal with on top of his son's death. A hell of a big monster."

"I do like textbook answers, Trinculo."

"I don't suppose Davidson read a different textbook?"

"Not hardly, he probably helped write the old one."

"Maybe he's extremely incompetent?" Patrick tried.

"Not in the least. One possibility could be covered by his arrogance, he does believe that patients should face reality, he likes to throw it in their faces for the shock value."

"So you're down to speculation that may be mere arrogance on the part of the therapist."

"No. That was my hope until now. Tonight, Denning had a complete breakthrough, then melt down. His two supposed therapists, including myself, immediately left the room. He was then put on full suicide watch, no visitors allowed, and left to stew in his own memories, without a hand to hold, or a shoulder to cry on."

"What?" Patrick sounded shocked.

"No physical compassion allowed, surprise that I even suggested the possibility." Kristen repeated.

"Why?"

"Good question," Kristen answered. "I was ordered to leave by Dr. Davidson. I was told the Ambassador's ego would be shattered if I was allowed to view his breakdown in his presence. I was only a friend, you see. I was then complimented for being such a good little catalyst and helping the patient reach a 'breakthrough'."

"Jesus Christ! Did he also pat you on the head?"

"Damned close."

"And Davidson didn't go back in to talk him down after getting you out of the room?"

"Nope. He didn't want to hear the answers. We left the patient, we talked with Jeffers, then left the Institute for the evening. In short, with Jeffers encouragement, Davidson left the patient standing on the railing of the bridge ready to jump deciding he would come back to talk him down after we had our dinner. Assuming Charles didn't hit the ground with a terminal splat first."

There was a long pause. "You're right. Davidson is a certain, not speculation. Either that, or he needs to have his license jerked. Now what?"

"Did you get the audio translation of everything on the tape?"

"Yes, I also speak Spanish and heard it for myself."

"Anything especially nasty said?"

"No. The usual 'enemy of the people' crap, nothing unexpected."

Kristen frowned. Something was still missing. "I want a voice match of every clearly audible voice on that tape," Kristen decided.

"May I ask why?"

"The patient gave me that answer. He watched the video, but covered his ears, as though he didn't want to hear something that hurt and hurt badly."

"You don't ask for much, do you?" Patrick answered. "We're talking peasants, here, Ariel, they are all probably scattered to the winds by now. We can't get voice prints of people we can't find."

"Not the peasants, I want the executioners, the main players. Cross-reference with everyone Charles works with on an official basis. The voice I'm looking for would be clear and easily distinguished. Put a face to the voice." ("Bastard, bastard, bastard.") One bastard, one voice.

"Who am I looking for?

"A tempest in a teapot," Kristen answered. "But that's only speculation."

"And we don't speculate," Patrick finished.

"God, you're bright for fifteen," Kristen told him and disconnected the call.

Chapter 26

Prospero: Thou best know'st what torment I did find thee in…

Neil Davidson noticed the lights flashing behind him less than ten miles from his home, just a little more than halfway to the Institute. Curious, he pulled over to the shoulder, the other car parked next to him. He rolled down his window. "I'm guessing the call from work was bogus?"

"He's alone," Raymond Hayes stated cryptically into a cell phone, closed it and looked critically at Neil. "Of course. Try and show surprise when you get to the Institute," he advised, "its for your own protection."

"What's going on?" Neil asked.

"Quite simply, we're a little disappointed in you, Doctor. I thought you told us that little piece of fluff was harmless and incompetent? She seems to have done rather well with your patient." Hayes smiled without humor. "You told us you could control her."

"I have and she did nothing. The breakthrough would have happened sooner or later, now he just remembers consciously what you wanted him to remember sub-consciously." Neil shrugged. "I can contain the damage, she won't talk to him again, I'll keep him on suicide watch until I release him."

"Damn straight she won't talk to him again," Hayes answered harshly. "She's a wild card we can't afford. We've contained the situation, just to make sure."

"Excuse me? What do you mean, 'contained'?"

"Don't worry about it. Just go back to the institute, realize the message was a fake, act surprised, even worried and return home. Notify security, it would be the natural thing to do when you receive a bogus call."

"Don't worry about what?" Neil looked over his shoulder from the way he came. *Kristen.* "Jesus Christ! What the hell have you done?" his voice was horrified.

"What should have been done before the lady got here the first time. She's a liability, Doctor, one we don't need. Not your fault, it was Jeffers call, but he knew better. Too much is depending on Denning."

"You are not going to hurt her. I was assured that no one was supposed to get hurt in any of this," Neil said tersely. "That is not what I signed up for. I will not be involved in anyone being hurt, most especially Dr. Michaels."

"National Security, Doctor. You're not involved. Just continue on to the Institute," he was told, and the car drove off.

Neil started shaking. He put the car into gear. Jesus. He'd left her alone, unprotected. Neil took off, turning the car, almost hitting another and drove like a madman back toward his house. God, what had he done? Stupid, stupid, stupid!

As he drove into the driveway, he started honking his horn desperately, letting her know he was there, letting her know he was coming, letting anyone else in the house know she was not without help. Not Kristen. She'd never harmed anyone in her life. Please, not Kristen. The driveway was endless, he finally reached the end, put the car into park, opened the car door and had a moment of frustration trying to unhook his seatbelt. Running to the door, unlocking it, rushing inside. "Kristi!"

No answer.

"Kristi!" He was screaming with sheer panic.

"Here," came a soft voice from the direction of the kitchen.

Okay, she was alright. He had overreacted, everything was okay. A brisk walk to the kitchen, but he couldn't see her. "Kristi?" He looked around the room, finally saw the blood. It was everywhere, counter, floor, carpet leading into the kitchen. "Kristi?" his heart was pounding furiously.

"Here," it was almost a whisper.

He found her and almost wished he hadn't. She was sitting on the floor, her back against the refrigerator, her eyes trying to focus, her glasses nowhere in sight. Her right hand was holding a blood-soaked dishcloth against her throat, the collar of the terrycloth robe was soaked with blood. "Help?" she gave him a weak smile.

"Oh, my God, Kristi! What the hell happened?" He kneeled down to her.

"I can't get to the phone," she told him in a whisper. "I think I could use a little medical help here. Knife. Stabbed." She looked at him helplessly. "Scared."

"Oh, Jesus, baby." Neil grabbed the kitchen phone and dialed 911. "I need an ambulance at 3741 Whitecap. Now. Stab wound. Doctor on scene." He hung up the phone and knelt back down to Kristen. "Let me see, sweetheart. Show me. Tell me what happened."

"No. Compress," Kristen told him in a soft whisper. "Knife wound, bleed out, don't," her eyes filled with tears. "Please, Neil... don't." She took a shaky breath. She tried to search his eyes. "You could have just told me to go home, love, I would have...I told you I would have. I love..." She closed her eyes. "Compress, hold..." and slid down the rest of the way, landing fully on the floor, her hand slipping from her throat.

Neil rolled her over, the slash on her throat was bleeding profusely. "Oh, Jesus," Neil put his fingers to the wound, pressing tightly against the jugular vein. Jesus, God, the blood was massive. The slash against the remainder of her throat was bleeding sluggishly, he pulled another dishcloth from the counter and covered it. "Damnit, baby, I love you! I wouldn't have," Oh, God. She thought he was involved in this. *("You could have just told me to go home, love, I would have... I told you I would have.")* "Oh, Kristi, you know better! Not this. I'd never let anyone hurt you like this. Damnit, you know better!"

Still holding his fingers tightly over the vein and his palm to hold the cloth, Neil managed to pick her up and carry her to the living room, his heart pounding painfully. Doctor on scene. Yeah, sure. Hold the wound, don't strangle the poor girl, just stop the bleeding. He noticed the scrapes still on her knees. That was probably no accident, either. He should have known it, didn't even consider it. He had taken Kristen's word that it was a simple accident, that she had been clumsy because of her blindness, probably embarrassed about it *(I have an ouchie on my knee...)*. The usual Kristen tactic, denial of her handicap. The suspicions of security about a car trying to hit her he had been certain was the usual paranoia by Simmons, not relevant, probably not even accurate.

It didn't make sense. Why the hell would anyone want to hurt her? Animals, they were animals. Christ, baby, what have I gotten you into? God, don't let her die, please God, don't let her die. He gave a horrified laugh. She was right. Sooner or later, everyone turned to a minishrink. He was calling to a fantasy figure like God, of all things, and he was a devout Atheist. "Kristi, please, baby, I love you. Please, baby, I love you." The blood covered her neck, his hand was soaked with it, the cuffs of his shirt were spattered and red with it. The pulse on her neck was barely felt under his fingertips while he stopped the flow.

The ambulance arrived in less than five minutes, Neil carried her out to it, getting her in with her. "Knife wound to the neck. Take her to the PSR Institute. Dr. Denise Parker. It's the closest trauma center, they have her files," he told them.

The paramedics immediately took over. "How old is the patient?"

"Thirty six," Neil answered. "Her name is Dr. Kristen Michaels."

"Who are you?"

"Her husb..." he stopped. The title of husband had come naturally and it shocked him. Nine years and he still felt it. "Dr. Neil Davidson. A friend." A friend. Oh, yeah, he was one great friend. Lousy husband, lousy friend. Cut her up in little pieces emotionally, then allow someone else to cut her up with a knife to the throat.

Cut her. Why the hell did they have to cut her? If they wanted to kill her, use a God Damned gun. Don't cut her. Not again.

"What happened?"

"I don't know. I found her this way. She was alone in the house when it happened." His voice was dispassionate, his emotions were not, but those were not for public scrutiny.

"Was she conscious when you found her?"

"Partly," Neil told him, "for a few moments."

"Did she say how this happened?"

"No, just that she'd been stabbed."

"We'll have to call the police."

Neil shook his head. "No. This comes under the heading of National Security. Call PSR," he gave them the number, "they'll handle the

155

investigation."

"I'll have to clear that," came the answer.

"Do what you have to do, but no one walks into that house unless he's a fed." Neil told him firmly. "What's her BP?" he asked professionally, his voice calm.

"Sixty over thirty."

(Hang on, Baby, you can do this, you've been through worse than this. You can do this. Don't leave me, sweetheart, don't leave me.) Ten minutes. It should only take ten minutes if they pushed it. What the hell was taking so long?

The siren took away all other sound. He couldn't see her face, it was covered by the two paramedics leaning over her. The hem of the terry robe was hanging off the side. He felt an overwhelming need to pull it up, make sure she was covered properly, but he didn't.

"What's her BP now?" Neil asked again.

"Fifty six over twenty four. She's fighting to hold on, but it's tight."

He still couldn't see her, now her legs were covered with blankets and heating units, a tiny operating theatre with more equipment than room. They were going to smother her tiny body with all that equipment. The hem of the robe was still hanging off the side of the gurney. His robe. She always did that when they were married, she loved to put on his robe, she'd wear it like a trophy after they'd made love. Whenever he put it on, it had the scent of her, still lingering.

The paramedic was talking to her. "Kristen, can you hear me? Kristen!"

Neil knew it was necessary, but he didn't want the kid talking to her, bothering her. He certainly didn't want him talking to her in such a familiar way. Both the paramedics looked like teenagers. Teenagers, trying to take care of Kristen. The whole thing was skewed, unnatural. She took care of teenagers, not the other way around.

Before he could ask for an update again, the doors opened, a blast of night air hit him, he jumped out. Denise was standing ready. "Neil, I got an emergency page. What happened?"

"Kristen's been stabbed in the neck. They hit the jugular."

"Blood type?"

"'A' positive."

"Good, we're covered." Denise didn't bother to ask what had happened, once she had a patient, she was totally professional.

Neil hung on to that fact. Denise was not a kid. Denise was solid. Denise was real.

The gurney was pulled from the ambulance, moved quickly into the doors of the hospital, down the corridors, into the emergency room, the IV swinging madly along. Neil was forced aside when they transferred her from the gurney to the table. He could finally see her face, it was horribly smeared with her own blood, the IV tube was covered with it, her hair was matted and wet.

Denise pushed him outside the doors. "My job, Neil, stay out of here. I don't need you for this."

"She's..." *(everything that's meaningful in my life, don't let her die.)*

Denise was already back inside the operating room. "Clean her up, show me what I've got," Denise told her assistant.

"Half slash to the throat, left to right," came the answer.

"Set her up, 'A' positive, no time for a type and match. BP?"

"She's stabilizing. Sixty over forty."

"Let's stitch and seal."

That was the entire conversation Neil was allowed to hear, before pacing became his only option. Memories of Kristen flooded in without his permission. A very young Kristen, a very stupid conversation. *("Do you believe I love you, Neil?" "Yes, I believe you love me." "Then you believe in something you can't see." "No. You're wrong. I can see your love, Kristi, its in your eyes when you look at me, its in your body when we make love. I can taste it on your skin when I kiss you, I can hear it in your voice when you speak...").*

She'll be fine, she's been through worse, she's a survivor, she knows how to survive. His body was shaking. Calm down, cameras are watching, he was a professional. Look naturally concerned, not terrified out his wits.

("Love exists, Kristi, we're talking about two different things. Leprechauns and fairies do not exist. Admit it. Tell me you know the difference between fantasy and reality.")

Damn. He wanted a cigarette, he needed to go to his office, the damned California laws wouldn't allow him to smoke in the hospital wing.

("This institute is part of the real world, little girl, either join the rest of us, or admit you're too damned weak to handle it and get yourself some professional help!" "If memory serves, those are the same two options you gave me nine years ago...")

Neil turned off the memories, it was counter-productive.

("You always have been my favorite fantasy,")

Stop it. Kristen would be fine, he had found her in time, Denise was taking care of her, Denise was a professional.

After more than a hour, Denise walked out and looked at Neil. "She'll make it. What the hell happened to her?" her voice was under tight control.

"I don't know for sure."

("You always have been my favorite fantasy,")

"I went for a short drive, I came back, she was on the kitchen floor," he told her. Fear gone, tension gone, she'd survive. Neil used his practiced demeanor expertly. "Life support?"

"Not necessary, we just need to replace her plasma, watch for infection." She took a tired breath. "Someone tried to slit her throat, Neil, five more minutes, she'd be dead. Considering the wound, the blood loss was minimal. You did a good job."

"Not me. She had a compress on it when I got to her,"

("Knife wound, bleed out, don't...scared.")

Five more minutes. If he had gone to the Institute as directed, she would be dead. Neil took a deep breath, the only emotion he would allow publicly. "Kristen always did know the basics. I just kept it up until the ambulance arrived."

("don't...scared.") Don't what? Take off the compress? What was she scared of, him? God, did she really think he would let her bleed to death?

"Her larynx is whole, she'll sound a bit raspy for awhile, but she'll be able to speak when she wakes up," Denise advised him.

"That was lucky," Neil nodded, "she'll be able to tell us what really happened." *("I can hear it in your voice when you speak...")* Don't shake, keep the body still, show no emotion.

"What happened to her before this happened?"

"As I said, I wasn't there, I don't know." *("don't ...scared.")*

"No. Before that. Years ago, probably. When she was a child."

Neil looked at her in confusion. "What are you talking about?"

"She has scar tissue almost completely circling her neck, Neil. Old and thick scar tissue. It's probably what saved her life, the new cut was directly on it, the skin was tough to cut."

"Oh, that. Childhood injury," Neil answered tersely.

Denise raised an eyebrow. "That's not all. She has permanent ligature marks on her wrists and ankles. She has scars running down the length of her body, on her back down to her knees, even the inside of her legs."

"Same childhood injury." *("Did you conveniently forget the four days of torture, knife wounds, broken bones, permanent physical scars?")*

"Childhood injury?" Denise repeated too loudly. "Don't you mean wholesale mutilation?" Denise looked at him skeptically. "Did she fall into a fucking wood chipper while she was tied hand and foot? Was she the target in a knife throwing party? Those wounds are old and they were intentionally inflicted. Damnit, Neil, I'm not an idiot! What the hell happened to her?" She was angry, furious.

("I don't discuss the grisly details of my past with anyone.") "Not my story to tell," Neil said calmly. "Will she survive?"

"Yes. Evidently, she's a very practiced survivor." Denise sat down. "God Damnit! She looks like a damned baby in there, Neil. Why? She's little, she's blind, she's so vulnerable! She's no threat to anyone! Who did this to her? Why?"

"I don't know," Neil told her. "May I see her?" *(I need to see her. I have to see her.)*

"She'll be in recovery after she gets out of x-ray. She's my patient, not yours, mine," Denise told him. "You have two minutes in Recovery, then I want you out of there."

"You're sounding extremely protective, Dr. Parker."

"Apparently, somebody has to be," Denise answered tersely.

Neil looked at her quickly, instantly suspicious. "Why x-ray? Was something wrong other than the neck injury?" Damnit, what else did they do to her?

"Because I'm her doctor and I wanted x-rays," Denise told him, angrily. "Don't second guess me, Neil, I know a hell of a lot more than you do about medicine. If you want to see her, wait in recovery."

While Neil went into the recovery room, Denise started shaking. She had seen bad, she had seen grisly, nothing compared. The neck wound was nothing, but the rest... Jesus! Obviously Neil knew about it, he had been married to the woman, he had to have seen the scars, yet he was so calm, so unattached...

...nothing ever pierced his armor.

Chapter 27

Prospero: You do look, my son, in a moved sort, as if you were dismayed...

From the hazy flesh color, the aura of soft auburn hair and the heavenly scent, Kristen made an educated guess. "Dr. Parker?"

"Welcome back, Kristen," Denise's voice answered professionally. "How do you feel?"

"Pretty good, sore throat," Kristen answered hoarsely. "Got any Chloreseptic spray?"

Denise gave a light laugh. "I'm afraid this sore throat is from the outside, not the inside," she answered. "I can get you a pain killer," she offered.

"Never use them, if I can help it," Kristen answered. "The pain is minimal. Am I allowed to sit up?"

"Button to your right," Denise answered, looking down on her patient worriedly.

"I know where I am," Kristen smiled, "so I won't ask that cliché question, but 'when' am I? What day is it?"

"Thursday. About ten-thirty in the evening. "I've kept you under for twenty-four hours, you needed the time."

Thursday. Damn, Patrick would be furious. Kristen managed to rise several inches with the help of the designated button. "Did anyone find my glasses?" she asked next.

"Yes. Hold on," Denise left, coming back in a few moments and handed them to her.

"How bad was it?" Kristen asked, putting on her glasses and focusing on Denise. "Oh! Hello! It's a miracle! I can see again!" Denise had her hair in a severe bun and was wearing the usual green physician's scrubs, her expression was not one of amusement.

"The jugular was nicked, most of the damage occurred over old scar tissue, it could have been a lot worse. You were lucky," Denise told her.

"Always have been," Kristen smiled.

"Apparently," Denise answered professionally.

Kristen frowned. "Oh." She sighed. "Sorry about that. Now you know why I choose turtlenecks as my permanent fashion statement. I really am sorry, that must have been a little horrifying for you. As a rule, I try to keep my shock value down to a minimum."

Denise sat in a chair next to her bed. "Can you tell me what happened?"

"Not a lot, I'm afraid. Neil went out, I was almost to the kitchen, someone came in through the balcony, evidently my neck got in the way of his knife. Before you ask, no, I don't know who it was, I didn't have my glasses on and he came at me from behind. I'm assuming it was a he because I felt face stubble when I reached up. One or two day beard, I'm guessing. I felt the breeze when the balcony door opened, that's how I know he came in that way."

Denise nodded, it wasn't really the question she wanted answered. "And your other injuries?"

"My other injuries?" Kristen asked. "What else did he...?" The light bulb flashed. "Oh. Those. A childhood trauma." She looked at Denise worriedly, concerned that she might bring out a side to her that she didn't want to see, the same reaction Kristen had seen far too often in the past.

"What kind of a childhood trauma?"

"A very sick man. I survived, he didn't." Kristen noted the look of horror on Denise's face and felt like a louse.

"I am so sorry."

"Please don't be, you weren't there, you couldn't have changed a thing." Kristen answered. "I have no lingering traumas about my injuries, Denise, just some very natural unhappiness about the death of one little girl who was still alive when I walked into the situation and the death of a very wonderful man who tried to save me." She smiled lightly. "I admit to being more than a little self-conscious about the scars. I'm vain to the core."

"Your entire neck is circled with scar tissue. What specifically caused it?"

"Bailing wire. It took awhile to cut it off."

"Oh, God. How old were you when it happened?" Denise asked softly.

"Five."

"Five?" Denise covered her mouth with her hand, her eyes were filled with instant tears. "You were a baby!"

"It's okay," Kristen smiled gently at Denise and put out a hand to touch her. "Kids are survivors, Denise, we have all kinds of built in mental protections and I had mine. Adults are the usual causalities in this old horror story." She continued to look at her with concern. "Don't become one of them. I'm not five anymore, I grew up. I survived."

Denise nodded, quickly trying to change her expression, pulling back her tears, catching several that had already fallen with the back of her hand. "How much does Neil know about your childhood?"

Kristen gave a short laugh, then put her hand to her throat. "Ow. Sorry," she swallowed quickly and cleared her throat. "I've never talked to him about it, I was never his patient. Unfortunately, I'm in quite a few medical journals and police files. He found out what he thought he wanted to know. Trust me, he didn't. Now he's created his own monsters about my injuries and I can't help him with that, I'm not his therapist, either."

Denise gave her a weak smile. "Are you telling me to mind my own business?"

Kristen looked genuinely shocked. "Certainly not! You're my doctor, I'm your patient, I *am* your business. You can ask me any damned thing you want. If I know the answer, I'll give you the answer."

Denise was surprised at the vehemence of the response, but tried not to show it. "In that case, do you mind if I make a medical observation about your old injuries?"

"No." Kristen looked interested.

"The twenty odd bones that were reconstructed after the trauma healed well, but your doctors really screwed up on some of the other surgeries. I'll be generous and assume they were more interested in saving your life, than making you look pretty, but I deplore the lack of basic follow-up. With laser, most of the scars can still be removed or lessened considerably and it can be done painlessly. I've already cleared most of the large scar tissue on your neck, in a couple of months and with a little makeup, you can probably quit with the turtlenecks. They haven't really been in fashion for a few years, you know."

Kristen started laughing, holding her hand to her throat again to minimize the pain. "Dr. Parker, I think I love you."

"Doctor/Patient crush," Denise answered sternly, "you'll get over it. You need to get some rest."

Kristen hesitated. There was still the problem of Patrick, probably waiting by the phone. She looked at Denise Parker hopefully. "I will rest, I promise, but I have to call my office." She looked at her less than enthusiastic face. "I really do. I have a patient who is in near crisis, maybe even suicidal. My assistant is handling it for me, but he's still pretty new and I promised I'd check in. I'm overdue calling him."

Denise looked at her with concern. "A child?"

"I am a child psychologist," Kristen reminded her, avoiding the question.

"A short call," Denise decided. "I'll have a phone brought in."

Kristen frowned. "I prefer a cell phone," she told her, "I still like at least the feeling of confidentiality and I know the phones around here are bugged and recorded. L.R. does not need to know the problems of my patients."

Denise took her own cell out of her pant's pocket. Use mine. Free long distance." She handed her the cell phone. "Make your call, then rest, or I'll keep you for a week," she promised.

Kristen smiled thankfully, watched her walk away and punched in the number.

"National Weather Bureau."

"Heidi, hi, Its Dr. Michaels," Kristen said into the phone. "I'm supposed to call Patrick, about our crisis patient. I'm on someone else's cell, I don't know how long the connection will last," she added.

"Checking." Several long seconds. "The cell is secure, Ariel," came Reaper's voice, "I'm guessing you're not?"

"Not in this fish bowl," she answered.

"The kid's fresh to this game, want me to monitor in case he doesn't catch everything?"

"Sure. Tell him to take off his boots and get to the phone, will you, Heidi?"

"You have a cold, Ariel?"

"Sore throat, nothing terminal."

"Meaning it was meant to be terminal," Reaper decoded. "Did you accidentally trust a patient?"

"We all have our blind spots," Kristen admitted, fighting tears.

"Sorry about that, I knew this one would be nasty. Certainty one or two or three?"

"They all play for the same team," she tried to sound detached.

Patrick came on the line, his voice was young and worried. "You're late. Are you alright, Dr. Michaels?"

"I'm fine, Patrick, just a minor mishap. How's our patient?"

"If he's hearing voices, he doesn't know any of them," Patrick answered.

"Are you sure?"

"Yup. No voiceprint of anyone Denning has worked with matches the major players. You did suspect a tempest in a teapot, as I recall from my lit classes, that means you really didn't expect me to find anything."

"True, but it was necessary to confirm the original diagnosis that was given to us by the referring physician. We take nothing on assumption or speculation. Do you remember?"

Patrick thought about it. "Do you mean you want me to look at the original information we were given by the Weather Bureau?"

"Yes. The synopsis."

Patrick started noisily shuffling through papers. "It was a speculative report on various psychological manipulations that might be used against a current Ambassador for political gain and other possible issues of the same kind," Patrick answered.

"Exactly."

"Okay, so we've confirmed the original diagnosis, I'll send our confirmation to the Weather Bureau. Now what? Are we done with the assignment?"

"Not completely, we still have a patient," Kristen told him. "We've set the forest aside for demolition, now we have to concentrate on which trees to save."

"Unfortunately true. I repeat, now what?"

Kristen thought about it. "Can you question the parents? Compare the stories?"

Patrick was silent for several seconds. "Uh, you're jumping around on me. Let me think."

Kristen gave him a few necessary seconds, hoping Reaper wouldn't break in. The kid was bright, she needed his intelligence, she needed him to be confident in his abilities.

"Do you mean do I have the original tape the Ambassador saw and did I compare it to the tape that I saw?" Patrick finally asked.

"Yes." Smart kid.

"No on both answers."

"Can you contact them?"

"No. If it still exists, it's available to a political player, not an umpire."

"If we fail, we still need proof for the powers that be."

"Or we can't prove that somebody's cheating," Patrick finished for her. "I get the idea, Dr. Michaels, I'm not that raw. I'll keep digging," he told her, "but I'm not real hopeful. We don't know where to look."

"Then the ball remains in our court," Kristen said calmly. "Textbook, Dr. McClary, what's my next step?"

"Talk to the patient."

"Why?"

"Because he knows the answers, you don't."

"And if I can't talk to the patient?"

"Are they keeping you away from him?"

"In more ways than one," Kristen frowned.

"Then you're screwed," Patrick answered simply. "If you can't talk to the patient, you can't listen to the patient. If you can't listen to the patient, you can't find his hidden monsters. You're the only one who has the necessary rapport to get the information you need and the only therapist he currently has that you know you can trust."

He was right. Point, set and match for the wrong team. For the first time, Kristen started feeling handicapped. Except… the therapist should not be the invalid, only the patient had that privilege. You didn't give up because you had a sore throat and couldn't make a session. There had to always be a backup plan.

"Try again," Kristen suggested, "that answer is pure speculation."

"And we never speculate, we never assume" Patrick finished for her. "Shit, Dr. Michaels, you're killing me here."

"Don't swear, Patrick, it's the product of a tired intellect. You're only fifteen, you can't be tired, yet."

"I'm twenty four and aging fast," Patrick considered it. Kristen could almost hear his frown, feel his concentration. "Okay, try this. Does he have a little blue blanket?"

Kristen considered Chipper, then rejected his usefulness. That particular minishrink was suffering from childhood narcolepsy. She'd love to play with the possibility, but it was too uncertain, too hit or miss. "Unfortunately, not a useful one at the moment, it's in the wash."

Patrick sighed. "Then you need to find another little blue blanket for him. The world is full of nice, clean, little blue blankets, remember?"

"Thank you, Doctor, I like textbook answers," Kristen told him, "they make me feel secure. Even when I can't figure out what the hell to do with the textbook answers."

"You'll figure it out. If all else fails, trust your patient. Remember that left alone, the majority of the populace will find their own minishrinks."

"Whoever said that is an idiot," Kristen told him.

"Those are your words, Doctor, lecture one."

"Great, now I feel better," Kristen answered sarcastically.

"You should. Either I'm beginning to have faith in your lectures, or you've completely brainwashed me," Patrick assured her.

"Ah, faith. A category three minishrink," Kristen smiled sourly.

"No, a category *one* minishrink, I believe in you," he corrected her.

"Thank you. I'm glad one of us does. The next time I call, I'm going to need you to help me with a refresher course, my brain is foggy and I'm getting cynical. I'm too tired right now."

"Done," Patrick answered. "Dr. Michaels, what happened to you? What kind of 'mishap'? Are you hurt? Why didn't you check in?"

"You can find out all of that for yourself. My doctor is Denise Parker, PSR Institute."

"Your Doctor? Why did you need a doctor?"

"Calm down, Patrick. You are listed as my next of kin. I suggest you call her. I've waived all confidentiality on this incident to you."

"I'm your *what*?"

"It's all routine, Patrick. One other thing. Before you take Heidi skiing, check the weather bureau. The last time she almost got frostbite."

"In short, after I talk to this Dr. Parker, you want me to write up a report on your 'mishap' and send it in."

"Verbal will do, paperwork is so tedious."

"And traceable," Patrick finished. "This 'mishap'. It was bad, wasn't it?"

"I got careless," Kristen admitted, "but I'll get over it."

"Okay, I'll handle the report. You start knitting a blue blanket," he suggested, his voice slightly shaky. "If not for the patient, for yourself," he added. "Damnit, be careful."

"I'll knit, you keep looking for the parents," Kristen answered. "I'll check in later."

Patrick hung up the phone, Kristen waited.

"Thanks, Ariel, we'll need that report, we need to know how far they're willing to go to protect themselves. Thank God you survived," Reaper's voice answered. "The kid's good, never missed a step. You going to keep him?"

"I quit doing consultation work for that hospital, remember?"

"Oh hell, Ariel, that resignation hit the shredder before anyone ever opened it. We just gave you a rest. I repeat. Are you going to keep the kid?"

Kristen sighed. "Yes, I'm going to keep him. He deserves better, but he's a great minishrink," she turned off the phone, put it on the nightstand, lowered the bed and fell asleep.

Chapter 28

Prospero: I had forgot that foul conspiracy of the beast...

Matthew Jeffers looked like he had aged twenty years in the past two days. His lips when he spoke were tight, under strict control and he kept the anger out of his voice, but it was clearly in his eyes. He looked around the conference table. "I won't be here Monday, I'd like an update on our current 'guests'."

Denise started. "I've released Ambassador Denning, subject to normal follow-up. I've also released the Senator's daughter, Lindsay, she can be shipped out tomorrow. Admiral Fielding needs about a week more of physical therapy, Secretary Hopster was released yesterday. As for Doctor Michaels,"

"Table Kristen for now," Matthew said tightly. "Anyone new?"

"I'm expecting a transfer from Bethesda, they're still playing with giving me the name. Follow-up on a triple bypass," Denise answered.

"Neil?" Matthew barely looked at him.

"I've taken Charles Denning off suicide watch, he leaves tonight, under my protest. He still needs more therapy, possibly long term. The State Department is tying my hands, Dr. Jeffers, I don't think he should attend that conference tomorrow."

"Politics, no choice," Matthew Jeffers shrugged. "The breakthrough you and... you had with him could make the situation less volatile, but I will note your protest with the State Department and add my own. Are you releasing anyone else?"

"No and like Dr. Parker, I have a few new patients being transferred in, one child abuse perp, two domestic violence, but I haven't been given the particulars, not even names."

"Another child abuse, it's becoming a common disease with our National bigwigs." Matthew sighed heavily. "Whose the child's doctor?"

"As I said, I've been given no particulars, Dr. Jeffers, I don't know. Why? Did you want to give another patient to Dr. Michaels?" his voice was tinged with anger.

"Don't push me, Neil," Jeffers answered quietly, finally looking at him fully. He turned his anger onto Lloyd. "As I recall, Mr. Simmons, you advised me that you were capable of protecting Dr. Michaels. What the hell happened?"

Lloyd Simmons took the question and the anger as his due. Kristen Michaels was under his protection and he failed her. "Normal procedures are obviously not adequate. Once Drs. Davidson and Michaels advised security they were in for the night, we discontinued full surveillance. We were advised that both would be returning at 0900 the next morning, surveillance would have resumed thirty minutes before that time, as per regulations. It was not anticipated that Dr. Davidson would be leaving without our notification. He, on the other hand, believed that we had notification, since he thought the call he received was from the institute." It sounded incredibly lame, even to him. "Human error, mine," his voice was professional, the look in his eyes was not. After listening to the conversation between Kristen and Denise Parker in the ER, he had looked up the childhood attack she described. He found the pictures, he read the story and medical journals long into the night. Just the thought of what had happened and could have happened to Kristen Michaels gave him nightmares. He wanted to kill the perp all over again. Lloyd forced himself to answer Dr. Jeffers questions, forced himself to remain in the present. "It is an obvious hole that was not anticipated."

"What changes need to be made?" Matthew also tried for a professional tone.

"I'm working on it, but it's problematic. I only have enough manpower to follow the staff home, or while they are out in public and to escort them to work. Twenty-four hour surveillance has been rejected by every member of staff. We have set up full security systems in all private homes to guard against burglaries and break-ins, but the alarms were not set for the evening." He looked at Neil Davidson. "I expect it was too early for them to be set?"

"Yes. That's my error," Neil put in. "The usual entries were locked, but the balcony door was still unlocked, we had been out on it earlier. I should have called back to verify the call from the Institute, but I didn't. I didn't even consider setting the alarms, I was only going to be gone a short while and it was still early, we hadn't retired for the night. I should have known better, but I wasn't expecting any trouble."

"Why did you go back?" Matthew asked curiously.

Neil shook his head. "I'm not exactly sure. Kristen's not used to the house, I just decided that I didn't want to leave her alone," he lied. "Pure Luck."

"Luck," Matthew looked skeptical, "hell of a way to protect Kristen," and turned back to Lloyd. "What have you found out about her assailant?"

"It's still an open investigation. No prints, he was probably wearing gloves. Apparently he came in through the balcony door, no tool marks, no useable footprints. Dr. Michaels couldn't give us a good description, just that he was male, probably about six foot. With her vision handicap, she couldn't see much and she wasn't wearing her glasses. I'm guessing a pro. Unregistered cell call to Dr. Davidson, it won't be easy to trace, if we ever do. We do have the voice on the surveillance tap of Dr. Davidson's home phone, that's our only real lead. I think I'm more interested in finding out *why* someone would want to kill Dr. Michaels. This is the third attempt on her life and I don't understand why she's that important to someone."

167

"Third attempt?" Neil questioned loudly. "What do you mean, third attempt?"

Lloyd turned to him. "Once in Colorado, when she was shot at, once with the car incident at the restaurant and this one. That makes three."

"What do you mean, 'shot at'? Who shot at her? What the hell are you talking about?" Neil had lost all his professional calm, he was glaring at Lloyd with hatred. "Why wasn't I told?"

"The shooting in Colorado may not be connected, Dr. Davidson, but the timing is suspicious. The shooting occurred the day we were scheduled to meet. A parent of one of her sexually abused patients pulled a gun on her at her clinic. Dr. Michaels was surprised by the attack, she assured me that her attacker was into physical violence, but that any weapon was not part of his psychological profile. He's more of a 'hands on' creep." Lloyd looked at Neil with a slight feeling of superiority, "As for not telling you about it, it was a security issue, not your concern. I also assume that Dr. Michael's would have mentioned it to you had she felt you needed to know."

"Oh, sure. Kristen tell me anything," Neil answered furiously.

"In short, everyone failed to protect her," Matthew Jeffers turned to Denise. "With the obvious exception of Dr. Parker," he smiled lightly at her. "What's Dr. Michaels' medical condition?"

Denise also smiled, trying to break the obvious tension between the men, the protective testosterone floating around the room could be cut with a knife. "I took her off the critical list within the first twenty-four hours, she's stable and getting stronger. She's a tough lady, very feisty, even calling her clinic back home to consult about some of her patients. Her prognosis is excellent, I can release her as an out-patient as early as Sunday, since I'm sure she has the resources for follow-up treatment in Colorado. Keeping her longer would do more harm than good."

"Back to her damned cloistered walls," Matthew Jeffers looked unhappy.

"Better there than here," Neil put in quietly, "assuming she doesn't misread another damned parent."

"She should have been fine here!" Matthew Jeffers retorted.

"Oh, sure, just 'fine'. She only got her throat slashed, no harm done." Neil answered, annoyed. "Let's keep her a little longer and see if we can finish the job."

"You're the one who left her alone, Dr. Davidson." Matthew Jeffers retorted.

"I'm not the one who brought her here in the first place, Dr. Jeffers." Neil shot back, his voice under only minimal control. "You just had to stir things up, didn't you? Bored, were you? She's a lightweight child psychologist who believes in leprechauns, for Christ's sake! This place is a political rat's nest. She's not cut out for intrigue."

"Do you think I wanted this to happen to her? I didn't stitch that child up so some other animal could fillet her! You left her alone to God knows what dangers!" he repeated. "What the hell were you thinking?" his voice was no longer under control. "Don't you think she's been through enough in her life?"

"You," Neil paused, translating his words "You 'stitched her up'?" He stared at Matthew Jeffers, the knowledge hit him like a brick. "You were her doctor when she was a child." he decided softly.

Matthew sighed heavily and nodded. "One of about two dozen on the surgical team, yes."

"You didn't publish," Neil told him, accusingly.

"Of course not! She was the daughter of a friend," Matthew looked daggers at him. "A perfect, exquisite little girl that was made to look like a nightmare by some psychotic pervert. Do you think I'd lay her out for public scrutiny?"

Neil nodded slowly. "Were you also her psychiatrist?" he asked quietly.

"Psychiatrist?" Matthew repeated with irritation. "That's a matter of opinion." He rubbed his forehead viciously. "On paper, yes, I was her psychiatrist."

"So she has talked to you about it," Neil sounded hurt.

"No," Matthew Jeffers shook his head. "Not really. She didn't remember much of anything when I got her. A bit about the other little girl and her uncle's death, nothing about herself or what she went through. Hell, she was unconscious half the time during the attack, there was no reason for her to remember anything."

"Nothing?"

"Nothing. At least, not at first." Matthew shook his head. "I took care of that, though. I told her what happened to her, every single grisly detail." He smiled harshly at Neil. "I made that monster *real*. Made her look it right in the eye. I did a hell of a job. It took me almost a year to destroy her fantasies and replace them with violent, horrible reality. It was for her own good, of course, even though she was little more than a baby. Standard procedure in those days. Reality is good. We need to face our fears. Fantasy is bad, it's a crutch we need to get rid of." He looked at Neil critically. "Isn't that what you always say to her, Doctor? Isn't that what we want her to believe?"

Neil nodded. "Goldie," he answered, almost gently. "You're the one who got rid of Goldie."

Matthew Jeffers took a deep breath and let it out slowly. "Yup, that was me. I'm real proud of that one," he told him sarcastically. "I tried to replace a fucking fairy. Good old Uncle Matt. I worked with her father. He was my closest friend. I'd known her since she was a baby. She knew me, she *trusted* me, she *believed* in me. In return I broke her heart, took away her only companion." He shook his head regretfully. "She was the first child I took on as a patient and the very last. I lost her. She withdrew completely. I never did find out how she finally overcame my 'therapy'."

Neil looked at Matthew Jeffers with near pity. "Knowing Kristen, she

169

probably just found herself another minishrink to use," he told him. "Lecture one of Doctor Kristen Michaels, 'the world is full of unused minishrinks' and most patients find them for themselves."

Matthew sighed heavily. "Hopefully, she's right."

Neil looked at Matthew knowingly. "That's why you brought her here, isn't it? Even with all the crap going on, knowing all the dangers. You tried to pay her back with Denning's Chipper. A category three minishrink, brought back by an adult. You just couldn't resist. You thought you might be able to help her bring back Goldie, the way Denning brought back Chipper." He shook his head. "Stupid. She's not a child anymore, she survived, she grew up. That was really stupid, Matt."

"I don't know what I was trying to do," Matthew took a deep breath, "I just know that I failed her again."

Neil shook his head. "Join the club. I fail her every time we meet. I don't even know how to look her in the eyes anymore," he admitted.

Matthew nodded. "Quite a pair, aren't we?"

"Yes, we are. Bastards to the core. You also know that she's completely ethical, her patients are her number one priority, she doesn't play political games with any of them, she doesn't break any of her own rules. She never has. She never will."

"I know."

Neil looked at him seriously. "She's got good instincts, Matt. That's why she's a target. You can't keep her here. She doesn't fit in."

Matthew Jeffers nodded. "I know that, now."

Lloyd Simmons had watched the exchange with more than professional curiosity, not sure what he had just heard. The silence lasted for several minutes, he finally asked. "I feel like I'm really missing something important here. Who is Goldie? You know why Dr. Michaels is a target? Anyone care to enlighten me?"

Matthew looked at Lloyd Simmons with real concern, Lloyd always did see too much. The conversation between Neil and himself should never have taken place with anyone else in the room. It probably never should have taken place at all. "No. Old news, nothing relevant to what's going on now. This tape you destroy, Lloyd. Immediately. All the tapes. Nothing said here leaves this room. Ever. Kristen's background remains completely confidential."

"Yes, sir," Lloyd showed no emotion, but felt an almost overpowering need to punch his fist through a wall.

"And, this time you protect her. Twenty-four seven, until she's safely home in Claren."

Lloyd nodded seriously. That was one order he had already given himself.

Denise Parker had carefully kept as quiet as a piece of furniture. Strangely, while she had not understood the entire conversation, she did finally understand Kristen's message to her. Three adult, professional men in the room, all of them emotionally traumatized by something that happened to a little girl thirty years earlier. *(Adults are the usual casualties of old horror stories. Don't become one of them.)* Amazing.

Best advice she had ever been given and she hadn't even known it. Until now.

Chapter 29

Ariel: Thy thoughts I cleave to. What's thy pleasure?

Patrick McClary was sitting in Kristen's office, buried in paperwork. Every lecture she had ever given, every article she had published, every textbook he could find that she referred to and several of her classified patient files. He had been shocked when Heidi had allowed him the patient files, until he opened them. No names, no dates, no locations. The damned files could be put on the internet and still not violate confidentiality. The woman was a consummate professional.

He was not going to be able to help her. There she was, stuck in a hospital with a knife wound to the neck and he couldn't help. A knife wound! For what? World peace? It had all seemed so simple when he took the job with the Weather Bureau. A couple days a year he might get a call from Prospero. All he had to do was observe and recommend. Simple. Always a referee or an umpire, never a player. Keep the playing field fair, make sure everyone played by the rules, never take sides. Easy. So easy, he was going to screw it up royally.

So easy that a tiny blind psychologist had been stabbed in the neck and almost killed.

Patrick dove back into the paperwork. The question remained. How did you get the patient to find a little blue blanket when you couldn't see the patient, couldn't talk to the patient, had absolutely no contact with the patient? It was impossible.

She was going to call in an hour and he had only one answer left. Trust the patient. Left to their own devices, most people will find their own minishrinks. There was no way Dr. Michaels could get control, she couldn't even see the patient, much less talk to him. The conversation he had first had with Dr. Michaels flashed into his mind.

("Then you lose control of your patient.")

("I never have control. Who is the best physician of the mind, Patrick. What's the textbook answer?")

The patient himself. Trust the patient.

The phone rang, Patrick looked at his watch. It was too early. It was the private line, she wasn't supposed to call this early. He grabbed the phone. "Dr. Michaels office."

"Weather Bureau."

"This is Trinculo," he said worriedly.

The usual pause. "Voice identification verified. We have an update."

"Tell me something terrific," Patrick sounded almost desperate.

"Is everything alright?"

"Oh, just dandy. My boss is in a hospital with her throat slit, remember?" He still couldn't believe it.

"Ariel will be fine," Reaper's voice came across the line almost gently. "She's a pro at this, Trinculo, she knows what she's doing, or we wouldn't have paired you with her. You're a good team."

"Right. So, have you got good news, or what?"

"Double edged sword," came the cryptic answer. "Once the Feds knew of the video tape, they were able to find it. Filed under National Security, naturally."

"Naturally. Could you get a copy?" Patrick asked hopefully.

A long pause. "Of course."

"And?"

"It isn't good."

Patrick's heart sank. "How bad?"

"The tape was tampered with."

"Tampered with how?"

"President Arturo's voice was dubbed over one of the executioner's. If the Ambassador heard the tape, as Ariel suggested, he probably believes it. A amateur job, pure voiceover, background noises cut out with the overlay, but initially it would be damning."

"Oh, not good. The Ambassador leaves the institute today. Anyway to stop him?" Patrick asked.

"Even if we could, we can't. It's not our job, Trinculo. If Denning accuses Arturo, the best we can hope for is full disclosure and an apology after the damage has been done. Referees can't call the game until the player commits a public foul. Disengagement or observation only."

"That will take weeks, the treaty will fall by the wayside, the chances of it ever taking place in my lifetime are nominal."

A short silence. "Anything else we can do for you?" Reaper asked.

Patrick sighed heavily. What else, what else, what else? "Can you postpone the conference until Denning knows the truth?" he tried.

"No. Same rules apply, Trinculo."

Damn. Patrick knew the lecture, at one time it even made sense to him. Thought versus deed. Thinking about a starting war, was not the same as starting a war. Lots of countries hated each other, but they played nice internationally when they had to, or worldwide condemnation or sanctions would apply. "Damn!" Until Denning or another official connected to the conference publicly accused Arturo of committing a crime he didn't commit, there was no harm, no foul. Thought versus deed.

"Anything else we can get you?" Reaper's voice asked again, breaking into Patrick's black funk.

"Not at the moment," Patrick admitted.

The line disconnected.

The fireworks could start that very evening. Denning was being released, the first thing that would happen would be a media blitz. If not to the media, Denning would denounce Arturo openly at the conference. There was no time to stop him.

Speculation. That was mere speculation. We never assume, we never speculate. There had to be an answer. Patrick looked at all the paperwork on the desk and dove back in, aging another year in the process.

The phone call he was dreading finally came. "Ariel's on the line, voice confirmed, secure line, she's not."

Another game of figure out what she was saying, without her actually saying it. "Hi, Ariel," he tried for a calm note.

"You don't sound too happy," Kristen decided, "any news about our patient?"

Well, he'd fooled her for less than half a second. He was going to have to work on his delivery. "Nothing good."

"You talked to the parents?"

Patrick groaned inwardly. "Yes. The weather bureau got a copy as soon as the Feds had to admit there was a copy."

"Did they compare the stories?"

Patrick paused. "Yes."

Her heard her sigh. "Who?"

"Arturo," he hated saying it, "bogus voiceover."

"Oh," a moment of silence. "That's bad."

"To say the least. Is there anyway you can let the patient know the truth?"

"Even if I could, I can't," Kristen answered.

Déjà vu. He was getting a little tired of that answer. "Why not? I don't understand."

A long pause. "Who has the answers, Patrick?"

"The patient, but…"

"Do we ever give the patient the answers?"

"No, but…"

"Why?"

"The patient has his own monsters, we don't create new ones for him. But in this case, Dr. Michaels, it's a fake monster!"

"Is it? Are the big toothed hairy monsters living under beds real, Patrick?"

Patrick frowned at the phone. "That's a trick question, right?"

"Textbook answers, Patrick."

"The monster under the bed is real to the child."

"Exactly. Saying a monster isn't real, doesn't make it go away. It just makes the patient quit talking to you about it and the monster gets more powerful because no one believes it's really there but the child."

"I really hate this. Can we start playing with some new rules?" Patrick asked.

Kristen sighed. "No, we can't. That's the trap and everyone wants to fall into it at one time or another. Unfortunately, once you break the rules, the therapy is over. You lose, the patient loses and the monster keeps growing bigger and bigger. We can't take shortcuts."

"I'm feeling intellectually tired," Patrick told her. "Do you mind if I swear?"

"Yes, I do mind. I need help, Patrick and you're it. Think me through it. What's my next move?" Kristen asked.

Patrick took a deep breath. "Since you don't want to break the rules, you only have one move left."

"Which is?"

"Trust the patient. Hope he finds his own minishrink. The world is full of little blue blankets."

"True." A very long pause. "Damn." The word was almost too soft to hear. Evidently, Kristen had put the phone on her chest, Patrick could hear her heart beating. She finally came back on the line. "If that's all we have left, then that's what we'll do," she told him firmly.

"But,"

"Call the Weather Bureau, Patrick, I'll be home tomorrow. There's nothing left for me to do here. If there's a bigger storm coming, I'd like to know about it." She hung up the line.

Patrick threw his pen across the room. "Fuck!"

Chapter 30

Prospero: Thy shape invisible retain thou still...

Charles Denning waited for Raymond Hayes in the lounge, he was sick to death of his assigned room. He was wearing his three piece suit and tie, ready to face whatever cameras would be waiting at the airport, ready to backup the ridiculous story that had been cooked up regarding his injuries.

Evidently, according to the press clippings, he was supposed to be the victim of a burglary and shoot out and his memory was less than clear on details because of his injuries. At least that much of the story had been true, his memory was less than perfect.

Until now. Now his memory was as clear as a bell.

It was better before the memory returned, of that he was certain. Oh, the video of Danny's execution was bad, but he had seen the still pictures from that video before. The execution was probably the easiest thing Danny went through after those monsters had abducted him. This time, however, it wasn't the pictures that haunted him, it was the voices. Unfortunately, he knew one of the voices. Fucking Bastard. He knew that voice very well. One of the killers had been President Arturo himself. His *friend*. The man he had been backing and championing for more than a decade. The very man he had helped put into power.

The man who had tortured and killed his son.

Did he wait until the conference at the UN to confront Arturo, or simply let the press know as soon as he had the opportunity? The shock value would be better at the conference, but if he told the media, he could avoid the conference altogether.

No. It would be better to see the look on Arturo's face, the panic, the realization that he was unmasked. The bastard, pretending to be his friend, the psychopathic animal who was part of Danny's torture and execution.

For almost twenty years he had worked on the upcoming peace treaty. It was over. Everything was over. No matter what he did, the South American Block would be destroyed. Dreams of fools. Something he had worked most of his entire career to create and he would be the one to destroy it. And he would destroy it. It would be worth it, just to see the look on the Bastard's face when he denounced him to the world.

Danny deserved nothing less.

Charles put the press clippings into his briefcase, snapping the lid shut. He needed out of this job. He needed to find something that was honest, something Danny would agree with, something that would make Danny proud. Maybe Kristen was right, he should take up teaching.

Kristen Michaels. Poor Kristen. Going blind, having to wear those ugly glasses. He had heard that she was badly injured, been attacked somewhere off the grounds. That also made him furious. The bastards always chose the most innocent ones as their victims. A blind slip of a girl who only wanted to help people. He had tried to get more information about her, but very little was forthcoming. Evidently, she was still critical, he couldn't see her. He had sent her flowers, but it wasn't enough. Kristen had done so much for Danny. Danny had cared about her so much. He should have called her after Danny died, his aide had simply sent her a note, he probably hadn't even signed it. She shouldn't have had to find out about it through an impersonal note from an aide. Kristen was a good person, a good therapist. A caring, beautiful woman.

Charles smiled to himself. Imagine telling her about Chipper. He had never told anyone about that, not even his wife. Not even Danny. Hell, until she had brought up that little fairy of hers, even he hadn't remembered Chipper. Even now, the memory was fading again.

Remember the nice dreams. Balance the reality. It was probably for the best that he couldn't talk to Kristen about his 'friend' Arturo, it was better that she only hear about his good dreams, not that nightmare.

Certainly not the betrayal of President Arturo, the bastard.

He looked at his watch. An hour and ten minutes left before Raymond came to get him, assuming the man was on time. He had to figure out his strategy, how he was going to handle the press, before Raymond got there. Whatever he decided, he would have to discuss it with Raymond, the man hated surprises and it was his job to set up the interviews.

At least the State Department would be happy. They never did like Arturo, they felt the man was not firmly in the back pocket of the U.S., he was more interested in following his own dreams for South America. A man of honor... and a killer. A child killer. Danny's killer. He felt the tears coming to his eyes, he pulled them back the way he was supposed to pull them back. He couldn't cry, he couldn't show emotion when he saw the press.

Charles looked around the room, trying to steady his thoughts. The lounge was almost completely deserted, not too many people were still 'lounging'. They had their own rooms, their own problems.

Off to one corner of the room, trying to look small, was a teenage girl. She was young, maybe thirteen, maybe older, oh, hell, who could tell nowadays? She was playing solitaire. Damn, she looked so young. What was she doing here? He wondered if that was the kid Kristen had come to the Institute to see. She was about the same age Danny had been when Kristen first saw him.

All any kid needed at that age was somebody to listen, Kristen had told him. Charles looked at the child again. Somebody to listen. Well, Kristen would listen, the girl would be fine. He hoped the child knew it, they worried about everything at that age, took on too many adult responsibilities. They grew up too fast. He hoped she went to Colorado.

Danny loved it there, loved the skiing. So had Kristen, as he recalled. Could she still ski with her eyes going?

Charles looked at his watch again, he still had almost an hour to kill before Raymond came. It would be nice if he could say goodbye to Kristen, he wanted her to know he was alright, he knew she was worried about him, he saw it in her face after the last session. Kristen always worried about everyone. God knew how she managed to keep herself together during therapy sessions, but she always did. He had a suspicion she probably cried herself to sleep a lot, listening to some of the horror stories therapists had to listen to.

Charles stood up and started pacing. He had to hold it together until the conference, until he confronted that bastard. Calm, Charles, balance the nightmares.

Without conscious thought, he walked over to the teenager. "Excuse me?"

Lindsay Cummings looked up at him, suspicion and a little loneliness showed in her eyes. "What?" her tone was belligerent, suspicious.

Charles almost expected it, it was usual in kids that age. He found himself smiling at the familiarity of it. Just like Danny used to be, before Kristen. "Do you happen to know Dr. Kristen Michaels?"

The suspicion on the girl's face deepened. "Why?"

"My name is Charles Denning," Charles told her. "Kristen Michaels is a friend, I heard she was hurt. I'm leaving soon and I can't get in to tell her 'goodbye' in person. I thought maybe, if you knew her, you could let her know."

The suspicion left the girl's eyes. "Yeah, I know her. You just want me to tell her goodbye for you?"

"That would be exceptionally kind of you, yes," Charles answered.

Lindsay frowned, then nodded. "Okay. Is she your shrink, too?"

Charles smiled. "No. She took care of my son a few years back. She was his shrink."

"He was screwed up too, huh?" Lindsay asked.

Charles smiled. "He got better, she did a good job."

"Yeah? What's he do now?"

"He was killed in Columbia a year ago," Charles answered heavily.

"Oh. Bummer," Lindsay told him with the callousness of youth.

"Yes," Charles nodded. "So, you'll give Dr. Michaels my message?"

"Sure, no sweat," Lindsay shrugged, "I'm going to be seeing her anyway."

"Thanks," Charles nodded and started walking back to the sofa.

Lindsay watched him walk away and felt kind of sorry for the old guy. "Hey, Mister!"

Charles turned and looked at her. "Yes?"

Lindsay bit her lower lip. "I'm sick of solitaire. Wanna play some gin?"

Charles looked at his watch, he still had forty-five minutes before he left. He looked again at the lonely expression on the kid's face. "Yes. I would very much like to play gin." He walked back over to the corner table and sat down across from her.

"So, you're into politics, too?" Lindsay asked him, dealing the cards. Lindsay hated politics, but the guy looked so sad. Men always liked it when you pretended to be interested in what they did. She already knew the answer, everybody in this nuthouse was into politics.

"Yes," Charles answered, picking up his cards.

"I hate politics," Lindsay told him. "They all lie. I don't believe anything I see or hear. Everybody has some kind of secret agenda, you know? Even my dad." She finished sorting her cards. "You have eleven, you discard."

Charles threw a seven on the discard pile and watched the girl immediately pick it up. "Not everybody lies," he told her.

"Right. You running for office, too?"

Charles smiled. "No. I was appointed."

"Oh. That's different, then," Lindsay decided. "You don't have to lie to keep your job." She did know something about it and she knew how to sound grownup to adults, they were always surprised that she wasn't really a little kid who didn't understand.

"It is easier," Charles agreed. This was nice. He and Danny used to kill time by playing gin. He didn't even know Danny knew how to play gin until they went to Columbia. Danny talked more to him then, than any other time. Kids loved to talk, you just had to give them a chance. All they wanted was someone to listen to them.

By the third game, Lindsay had him on a blitz. "You a judge?" she asked. She was pretty sure judges were appointed, but that was the only thing she could think of. Or were judges elected? Damn. She hoped it wasn't a dumb question. She hated sounding dumb.

"I'm not that important," Charles smiled at her, "An Ambassador."

"That's cool," she wasn't exactly quite sure what an Ambassador did, but the guy seemed okay. He didn't make any mean comments, or anything. Probably a good Dad, he sure talked about his son like he was proud of him. Pretty sad the kid had to die, he sounded cool, too. Probably good looking. The Ambassador was old, but she bet he was good looking, when he was younger. Supreme court judges. That was it, they were appointed, she hadn't sounded dumb. "Gin," she said triumphantly for the fourth time.

By the time Raymond showed up, the kid had blitzed him repeatedly and had already reached more than the needed five hundred points to win. Nice little girl, Charles decided, loved to win like all kids and had a smile that would someday have every teenage boy knocking at her door.

Unfortunately, he also knew a lot more about Senator Cummings and his family than he needed to know. Thank God Kristen would have the girl in therapy.

Charles stood as Raymond entered the room and shook Lindsay's hand to say goodbye. Even though kids pretended to think it was stupid, he knew that grownup courtesies were important to them when dealing with adults. They liked being treated like equals. "You'll remember to say goodbye to Dr. Michaels for me?"

"Sure, no problem," Lindsay assured him. She shook his hand the way she had been taught. Firmly, like an adult, the way her Mom had taught her. "It was nice beating you, Ambassador," she grinned happily, "next time we'll play for money."

Charles smiled back. "I'll practice," he told her with a wink.

Chapter 31

Ariel: Just as you left them – all prisoners…

Politics.

Matthew Jeffers watched the limousine carrying Charles Denning away from the institute with relief. He hated politics and he loved politics, it was the only adult game worth playing.

The chess pieces were in place. Denning would blow, right in front of the cameras. Hopefully at the Conference with international media, but even local coverage would finish the Sudeste Block, permanently. It was now out of his hands. It didn't matter where it happened, just so long as it happened. He was covered, Neil Davidson was covered, Denning was released 'under protest'.

Whatever happened would not be blamed on the Institute. They would go on, unscathed.

Unfortunate, really. In many ways he liked Charles Denning, but the man was not a team player. Charles Denning was an idealist. He couldn't be blackmailed, he couldn't be bought, he wouldn't arbitrarily change his politics to suit current policy. No self-preservation, that man. Why the current administration had kept him in office he would never understand. If they had simply replaced him, none of this would have been necessary.

With Denning gone, at least Kristen was safe. Damn, he'd screwed that up. Thank God Neil had found her in time. Manipulation, fine, murder, however, was not part of the program. He'd have somebody's head for that one. Patriotism. National Security, bullshit. She was an innocent child. If they had simply told him they wanted her out that badly, he would have sent her home and she would have left without protest. The girl hadn't done anything wrong, just tried to help a patient.

That little issue he would resolve on Monday. Heads would roll, he still knew where all the bodies were buried. No one would ever touch Kristen Michaels again. He loved her like his own, he would protect her with his life and destroy anyone who got in his way.

The irony was, after his public meltdown, Denning would be back and Kristen would have been the best possible therapist for his real recovery. More importantly, she would have been working with Neil. Water and oil those two, but she honestly loved the man and he could have helped her with her blindness. Kristen needed help, but she would never ask for it. Now that idea was shot to hell, along with everything else.

Matthew shook his head. Damnit, he wanted her here. He wanted her close. He wanted to help her. He owed her so much.

Matthew Jeffers looked at his watch. Denning should be at the airport by now, surrounded by the media, questions about the burglary and shooting in his home, questions about the upcoming peace talks with President Arturo. A lot of stress for a man holding a dark secret.

Hopefully Hayes could keep Denning calm enough until the actual conference. Everything would be much more effective with an international audience.

Chapter 32

Prospero: Let us not burden our remembrances with a heaviness that's gone...

Saturday morning, Neil walked around the grounds of the Institute with Kristen. He held her arm tightly, not quite sure what to say to her, not sure what he could say to her. As usual when in doubt, he fell on a professional conversation. "Dr. Parker thinks you should stay another day," he told her. "So do I."

"I need to get home, Neil, I have my own patients. I'm also training a new assistant, he's just a kid himself. God knows what he's teaching my classes."

"You need more rest," he tried. "You're barely convalescent." He stroked her hair lightly. "Stay with me for awhile, baby. A month, a year," he turned, lifted her chin and looked into her eyes, "for the rest of my life."

Kristen turned and looked at him. "It's easier saying goodbye to you when we're fighting," she smiled.

Neil sighed lightly. "That's because we always assume that we have to get back together to either finish it, or make up. I just can't think of a damned thing to fight about with you, this time."

"Really? Hmm." Kristen thought about it. "Well, you know I still believe that Chipper is real, not some schizoid figment of Charles' childhood psyche. And, you know I'm right, you're just too arrogant to believe that anyone can have an opinion that isn't based on your precious 'reality' therapy. Also, Jory is a real leprechaun and he has full control over the lights everywhere I go."

"Oh, get over it, Kristi! Do you know how stupid that sounds? A child's invention of an imaginary friend is a simple need for attention based on psychiatric issues! A good tool, nothing more!"

"Invisible, not imaginary," she told him, eyes flashing.

"Imaginary. Learn to live with it. I love you, you impossible brat!"

"You're absolutely wrong and you know it. I love you too, you arrogant realistic bastard!" she glared at him.

"Good," Neil laughed, put his arm around her waist and kissed her gently. "That felt better," he told her, resting his forehead against hers.

"Yes, it did," Kristen agreed. "We are impossible together, aren't we?"

Neil sighed. "Not always." They started walking back to the Institute holding hands. "So now you go back to your District Attorney in Claren," he said with resignation.

"And you'll go back to Denise, or someone equally bright and

183

beautiful," Kristen returned. "Nice, wonderful people. Comfortable people." She smiled at him. "If we were wonderful people, we'd introduce them to each other."

"Except we're too damned selfish to give up our safety nets," Neil answered.

"I know." Kristen bit her lip. "Neil, were we ever 'lovers'?"

"Denise," Neil gave a humorless laugh. "I had a bit of trouble with that question myself when she asked me, that's why I laid it on you." He looked at her. "What was your first response to the question? The one you didn't give her?"

Kristen looked embarrassed. "I wanted to say, 'hell no, he's not my lover, he's my husband!'." She shook her head. "Barely caught myself, to tell the truth." She smiled, still embarrassed. "Family insanity, probably. Even after mom died, Pop still thought of himself as married, not widowed."

Neil squeezed her hand. "I know." *("What is your relationship to the patient?" I'm her husband...").* "I think we both need reality therapy."

"Never touch the stuff," Kristen changed the subject. "Any news about Charles?"

"No, and I admit I'm concerned. He made it through the media blitz at the airport, but he has that conference at the United Nations this afternoon. I don't know how he'll react," Neil told her, "he's been under a lot of stress, I don't think he's ready."

Kristen smiled at him. "He'll do great. You're a good psychiatrist, Neil, if anyone could have helped him, it was you."

Neil looked at her in surprise. "You're showing a lot of confidence."

Kristen touched his arm gently. "Trust your patient, Neil, he'll do fine. He's a very intelligent man and he's a good man. He's strong. He'll get through this. He'll find his center."

"'Left alone, the majority of the populace will find their own solutions to life's difficult problems, their own cure for mental illness'." He quoted. "You still giving that lecture? You still think we are only mirrors for our patients? Temporary blue blankets in their hour of need?"

Kristen grinned. "Of course."

Neil shook his head. "Kids, maybe, but adults are little more complex."

Kristen shrugged. "Are we? Do we outgrow our need for a hand to hold, a teddy bear to cuddle? Does the sub-conscious really have an age?"

"I don't know. Perhaps not. I hope you're right about Charles, but I doubt it. He'll be back." He felt like a heel. Denning was going to crash and burn, all according to plan. "I heard your little patient is coming around."

"Lindsay? She's a good kid, just needs someone to listen to her. We played cards this morning for almost an hour after Denise checked her leg. Boosted my spirits quite a bit, but I still think she cheats, I can't win a game off her."

"Still using a card game for temporary minishrink value," Neil laughed, "you never change." He lifted her hand and kissed the palm.

"Whatever works. Temporary or not, all minishrinks have value, you take what you can get," Kristen smiled.

Neil hesitated. "I want to ask you a question. I know you don't like to talk to me about it, but I really want to know. Actually, I think I *need* to know."

"I'll tell you anything you want to know Neil, if I know the answer, I'll give you the answer." she looked surprised that he would even ask.

Her response threw him off guard. He had never asked. Not really. He wanted her to discuss it, he wanted her to confide in him, break down in his arms and want him to help her, but he had never asked her a direct question involving it. His interest had taken on the role of professional, not personal. Now that he realized he could, he was almost hesitant to ask.

Kristen was watching him curiously. "What?"

Neil sighed. "When you were a little girl. After the... trauma. After you no longer had Goldie to hang onto, to help you escape."

"You mean after my therapist told me to get rid of her and I crashed and burned for real?"

"Yeah," Neil nodded. "What happened? How did you get over it all with her gone? Did you find yourself another minishrink?"

Kristen looked surprised. "Of course I did. I'm nothing if not predictable."

Neil looked at her. "Can you be a little more specific? What kind of minishrink?"

Kristen laughed. "Nothing spectacular, no new invisible playmates. A good old, run of the mill, category one minishrink."

"How 'run of the mill'?" Neil asked. "A pet? A teacher?"

Kristen shook her head. "No. There was a little boy in the clinic who had broken his arm ice skating. A great captive audience of one. I wasn't talking much then, I'd withdrawn pretty deeply, so we played cards."

"Cards," Neil repeated.

"Yup," she grinned. "War, I think, it was the only game he could handle with one arm in a cast and the only one we both knew aside from 'go fish'. After awhile, I talked to him."

"What did he do?"

"He listened."

"And?" Neil persisted.

Kristen sighed. "Well. I told him about the attack. His exact words were, 'ooh, that was a very bad man!'," she mimicked a child's voice. "I told him about the little girl who had died, he said 'ooh, I bet her mommy and daddy were awful sad' and then I told him how Uncle Wally died. That was the worst of it, I cried a lot. He said, 'oh, wow! He was a real hero! When I grow up, I'm going to be a hero, too'!" Kristen grinned at Neil. "I was getting absolutely *no* pity from the kid, not even with the tears, so I showed him the worst of my scars. I knew *that* would impress him. I wanted him to feel sorry for me. All the adults who saw them cringed and looked horrified."

"And was he horrified?" Neil asked gently. "Did he feel sorry for you?"

Kristen shook her head. "Hell, no. He was a *boy*, only seven. He thought the scars were 'really cool'." She laughed.

"Ah, "Neil smiled.

"You've gotta love kids, Neil. They're callous little shits, but no matter what happens, they can always put everything in its proper perspective. It took time, but things got easier after that."

Proper perspective. After the physical pain was gone, that's all anyone ever really needed, a healthy perspective. It was so simple for Kristen and so complex for everyone else. Neil felt an overwhelming need to laugh and cry at the same time. Instead, he felt his heart flip over. "What happened to the little boy?"

"He grew up. Like all little boys do."

"Do you still see him?"

"Occasionally. He's the District Attorney of Claren, Colorado."

Chapter 33

Prospero: Now does my project gather to a head...

The conference room of the United Nations General Assembly was crowded with media, foreign Ambassadors of twelve members of the Sudeste Block, eight representatives of the UN Security Council, Ambassador Charles Denning of the United States and assorted aides. The obligatory speeches had been made, final comments were now being offered by each Ambassador. The treaty would finally be signed, unless there were some last minute changes, additions, deletions, objections.

Charles Denning stood to make his final comments. He studied the faces at the assembly and nodded seriously. He looked directly at President Arturo. His *friend*. "Before we move to sign this treaty, I'd like to make a few personal comments."

The perfect Ambassador's aide, Raymond Hayes immediately put the prepared speech in front of Charles Denning and sat back, trying not to smirk. Finally, the moment of reckoning. It had been over a year in the making. The first try was the kidnapping and death of Ambassador Denning's son, which should have immediately forced him to quit. Somehow the man had overcome that obstacle, God knew how. Then several military coups that should have ousted President Arturo, but failed, finally the tape implicating President Arturo in the Denning boy's death.

Everyday politics paid for by a very private slush fund. If the Sudeste Block was allowed to remain in power, billions of U.S. dollars would be available for domestic affairs, this administration could not allow the economic scrutiny. More importantly, peace did not buy reelections, only the threat and fear of war and terrorism kept the right administration in power.

Raymond looked expectantly at the media personnel and the cameras in the room, wondering who would be the first to react to the horrific accusations made against President Arturo by Ambassador Denning. As Ambassador's aide, his role would be easy. First the immediate withdrawal of the Ambassador, ("pending a more detailed statement soon,") then the promise of a full investigation, ("the Ambassador cannot make any official comment at this time.") During the investigation the Sudeste Block matter would be "pending", ("other more immediate issues must take precedent,") and "we hope to visit this worthy idea in the future."

After the next election, no one would remember or care.

It was all a neat package, tied up with a fancy bow. Because Charles Denning would have failed to have the matter investigated before he made a public, official, "international" accusation, his services would no longer be "good for the image of the country". A new Ambassador of the correct political party would be assigned to South America. "We regretfully accept the resignation of Ambassador Charles Denning." Blame it on the other political party, more votes, more power in the House.

Raymond looked at Charles Denning expectantly and waited for the verbal bomb to explode. The silence of the assembly and media witnesses heightened his anticipation.

It was going to be very, very sweet.

Charles Denning finally spoke. "First, I would like to apologize for my recent illness and the fact that it has delayed this conference today. I would also like to thank all of you for waiting and allowing me the opportunity to be part of this historic event." He paused for several long heartbeats. "As the Ambassador to South America representing the United States," he finally continued, "I make the motion that we ratify this treaty, in Toto, with no changes, no additions, no deletions." He smiled handsomely at President Arturo.

"I second the motion," President Arturo immediately replied in perfect English, returning the smile with a nod of appreciation.

No one noticed the look of pure horror on Raymond Hayes face.

The motion was carried unanimously.

The UN Security Council representative from the U.S. Contingent of the Disengagement Observation Force quickly left to make an emergency call to the Weather Bureau, the Security Council's more clandestine group of 'worldwide storm observers'. It had taken them five long years to get someone from their unit into PSR, but Matthew Jeffers and the corrupt administration he represented would finally be stopped.

For now at least, the international playing field would once again be even. No public sanctions against the United States would be forthcoming.

Well done, Prospero.

Ambassador Denning sat down, sinking heavily against his chair. Thankfully, his temporary insanity had left. Somewhere between the Institute and the conference, Ambassador Charles Denning had decided to keep his suspicions about President Arturo to himself, until he could get the CIA to check out the facts, find out who had sent the tape and why it had been removed from his home. That should have been his first course of action, he was a fool to ever consider anything else.

("They all lie. I don't believe anything I see or hear.")

Kids were so bright, he'd forgotten how bright they were. They could see through dishonesty in a second. He must have made a mistake about the voice he had heard on the video. His memory had been playing tricks on him, or, more probably, someone else was. He'd been in this game for most of his life, he should have known better. Anonymous letters and videos were always subject to suspicion and for a moment he had actually taken it at face value. President Arturo was a good man, it couldn't have been his voice. He'd trust his own instincts, his own memories, and not destroy what he had built.

Nice little girl, Lindsay Cummings, he was damned glad he had taken the time to meet her, to play a few friendly games of cards with her.

It was unfortunate that no one would ever know that a young and lonely teenage child had single-handedly prevented an international disaster.

Danny would be proud of him today.

.

Epilogue

Ariel: On the sixth hour, at which time, my lord, you said our work should cease.
Prospero: I did say so, when first I raised the tempest...

Dr. Kristen Michaels sat on the edge of the desk in the middle of the lecture hall. She wore blue jeans and a soft, beige cashmere 'v' neck sweater, her pale brown hair was in a short ponytail. Her eyes were covered with opaque, rose colored glasses.

"Hi!" she announced clearly.

There were a few scattered responses.

"Hey, folks, I'm the one sitting up here all alone, your position is much more secure, your response should be much stronger. As a child psychologist, you will be required to sing silly songs at the top of your voice, make funny faces and pretend to be cowboys or Indians. Loosen up! Shall we try again?" She smiled cheerfully. "Hi!" She turned her head to one side and held a hand to her ear.

"Hi!" the group responded more enthusiastically.

"Thanks." Kristen took a deep breath. "Believe it or not, this is the right classroom for Child Psychology Two, I am Dr. Kristen Michaels, you have not wandered into the wrong building. I am a practicing Child Psychologist here in Claren; I am thirty-seven years old, I am not married, I have no children. I am five foot two inches tall, I weigh one hundred and five pounds in the winter, ninety-nine in the summer and I wear these glasses, not for comic effect, but because they match my outfit... and I happen to be blind."

There were a few murmurs of surprise in the audience.

"Those are my physical and social statistics, my psychological abnormalities are a bit harder to grasp...

Dr. Neil Davidson quietly left the hall, walking toward the exit. He didn't need the lecture, he knew it by heart. The beautiful woman who was not his wife and would always be the wife of his heart was fine, still predictable, still innocent to the intrigues and deceptions around her. Still and always his only link to fantasy.

His plane back to reality would leave before she ever knew he was here.

End.

A dose of International Reality...

All Members of the United Nations (of which the United States is a permanent Member State) agree to accept and carry out the decisions of the United Nations Security Council. The Council alone has the power to make decisions, which the Member States are *obligated* under the Charter to carry out.

The Purposes of the Security Council are:
*to preserve world peace and security;
*to encourage nations to be just in their actions toward each other;
*to help nations cooperate in trying to solve their problems;
*to serve as an agency through which nations can work toward these goals.

The functions and powers of the Security Council are:
*to maintain international peace and security in accordance with the principles and purposes of the United Nations;
*to investigate any dispute or situation which might lead to international friction;
*to recommend methods of adjusting such disputes or the terms of settlement;
*to formulate plans for the establishment of a system to regulate armaments;
*to determine the existence of a threat to the peace or act of aggression and to recommend what action should be taken;
*to call on Members to apply economic sanctions and other measures not involving the use of force to prevent or stop aggression;
*to take military action against an aggressor;
*to recommend the admission of new Members;
*to exercise the trusteeship functions of the United Nations in "strategic areas";
*to recommend to the General Assembly the appointment of the Secretary-General and, together with the Assembly, to elect the Judges of the International Court of Justice.

As to the existence of the "Weather Bureau" within the UN Security Council, it is your classic category three Minishrink. You can decide for yourself if it is 'real', 'imaginary'...
...or simply 'invisible'.

lwd

Made in the USA
Lexington, KY
14 May 2016